Private Spies

A Jesse Morgan Mystery

PJ Nunn

For information, contact Tidal Wave Publishing, P.O. Box , Waxahachie TX 75165

Cover design by Michael Canales
Formatting by Polgarus Studio

OTHER BOOKS BY PJ NUNN

Angel Killer: A Shari Markham Mystery

Praise for Angel Killer:

"Dr Shari Markham demonstrates skills Charlie Fox would be proud of in this tense hunt for a deranged serial killer. Crackles with romantic suspense."
— Zoe Sharp, author of *Die Easy* and the Charlie Fox Thriller series

ANGEL KILLER by PJ Nunn had me riveted. As a Forensic Psychologist, I tend to be critical of such characters, but Ms. Nunn's lead character Forensic Psychologist Shari Markham hits the mark! I was immediately hooked when a child's body is found and Shari begins the "magic" of a Forensic Psychologist. More bodies add to the suspense and a love interest adds to a realistic feel. I was right there with Shari, as PJ weaved her words into a thriller. Captivating! Delightful! A+
— Dr. Cynthia Lea Clark, Psy.D., Ph.D., MHt. CHS-IV Forensic Psychopathologist, Actress, Writer

Tense and enthralling, *ANGEL KILLER* is a first-rate story of nail-biting suspense and unpredictable mystery. From page one it grips the reader and never lets go. Bring on more of Shari Markham, Dallas PD profiler. She's a winner!
— Joanne Pence, author of the Angie Amalfi mysteries

For anyone that loves a well written and thoroughly developed murder mystery, I recommend PJ Nunn's *Angel Killer*. This book is dark and not for the faint of heart. It deals with a serial killer murdering the most innocent people in our society — our children. But don't despair, the protagonist Shari Markham is on the case!
— Michael E. Witzgall, Law Enforcement Consultant, Charlie-Mike Enterprises

To my Mom and Dad, who always made sure I was there when the Bookmobile rolled onto our street. I love you!

ACKNOWLEDGMENTS

From the time I was small, I was taught that if I could say it and believe it, I could do it. Like so many children of my era before technology took over our lives, I grew up in worlds of make believe and imagination, worlds created with my siblings and friends. My parents taught me to love reading; my Grandma Ford taught me to transition my pretending into becoming. I'm ever so grateful for that. And of course there have been countless others who made deposits of wisdom and knowledge into my life until I ended up surrounded by friends who were, like I am, writers.

There are far too many of you to mention, but in particular as this book goes to print, I have to thank Earl Staggs, Jan Christensen, Pat Reid, Charlene Truxler, my clients, and so many others who daily remind me what a joy it is to be part of the widespread mystery writer's community. I love coming to work with you every day.

Then there's Mike Witzgall, my partner in crime. He's endured endless phone calls, text messages and emails while I try to make sure I don't write anything that will make a cop throw the book against the wall. I promise if I messed something up it was my doing, not Mike's.

And of course I have to thank my family, especially my husband David and my two sons who are still at home, Dave Jr. and Caleb. Thank you so much for keeping things going around the household while I spent countless hours after work on the computer. I couldn't have done this without any of you. Thank you all.

CHAPTER ONE

Did you ever walk into the bathroom late at night and have a sudden urge to jerk back the shower curtain? Don't do it. Run. Giving in to those sudden urges can be a real mistake. Trust me.

Wait. You don't know me yet. Let me start at the beginning. Ever have one of those days where nothing goes the way it should and you spend more time explaining and apologizing than you do getting things right? I've been having one of those years. Mom says I'm having a mid-life crisis. I say thirty-four is way too young for that but according to Mom I did everything early. Never mind that she was referring to things like dropping out of college, getting married, getting divorced. Those kinds of things. I'll never admit it out loud, but I'm beginning to wonder if maybe she's right.

In the last month, I've buried my partner and best friend, inherited the business from him (much to Mom's dismay), and figured out that I don't know beans about running a private investigation agency. See, I've been different from birth. My older sister Caroline was Mom's little princess. Dad figured the next delivery would be his bouncing baby boy but he got me instead. Mom let him know there'd be no baby number three, so he did the only thing he could do. He passed his wealth of male knowledge on to me. While my sister took ballet lessons, I was down the street at the karate school. When Caroline and Mom hit the malls, Dad and I hit the baseball, football and basketball games. Mom drew the line at the World Wrestling Federation. We had to watch that on television at home.

So it really shouldn't have surprised anybody that Caroline grew up with a circle of frilly friends who practiced makeup and hairstyle techniques at sleepovers while I caught crawdads in the creek with Joey Catronio. Seemed perfectly natural to me. But all good things come to an end and Joey and I had to grow up. At least in theory.

Being the obedient children that we were, we headed off to college. I think that's where our parents' plans really started to go awry. Joey figured out he'd never make it into medical school if he couldn't pass chemistry and I figured out I didn't like college at all. So Joey changed his major to computer science and I quit and did the next expected thing. I got my MRS degree. I figured I'd already disappointed both of my parents. Mom wanted me to be a doctor or lawyer or at least something important. Dad kept hoping I'd buy a ranch and revive the old West. I didn't think I was likely to do either, but maybe marriage was something I could do right. At least it was respectable and my husband was a banker. That's good, right?

Unfortunately, he wasn't all that respectable after all. Two years after the wedding at the ripe old age of twenty-two, I decided to surprise him at the office and take him to lunch. I surprised him all right. His secretary, too. Silly me. When she wasn't at her desk, I just barged right in to his office. He was all comfortable, rocked back in that big leather chair. Too bad he hit her in the face with his knee when the chair hit the floor. Talk about being caught with your pants down. Probably dropped something under his desk and, like a dutiful secretary, she was picking it up. Right.

Always ready to do the wifely thing, I hurried over to help him zip his pants. He probably didn't realize his fly was open. Damned if I didn't screw up again, though. How was I supposed to know you have to tuck Mr. Wiggly back in the jockeys before you zip up? I can still hear that strange yowling noise he made almost fourteen years later. Still see Lucy's face, too. Man, was she surprised. Or maybe she was just annoyed about the huge hole in her pantyhose when she got up off the floor. I swear I don't know how that letter opener got close enough to do that much damage. Maybe if she wore dresses long enough to cover her ass that sort of thing wouldn't happen.

In the meantime, Joey graduated from college and started his own business. Private Spies. Catchy name, huh? A classic computer geek, he'd found his niche. Amazingly enough, he did pretty good business. With a huge web site he updated almost every day, he advertised world wide that he could find anybody, anywhere, if the price was right. And most of the time, he could. Some people, my mother included, thought it was a shady business, but it was legal. Mostly.

When Joey invited me to join him, I knew I'd found my dream job. I could sit in front of my computer all day. I could wear jeans and cowboy boots. I could set my own hours. Besides all that, I got business cards with my name on them. Never got those working at Wal-Mart. That was five years ago, and I've been there ever since. I even have my own parking space at the office. How cool is that? It has my name on it. Jesse Morgan. It's really Jesse Morgan Jackson, but I don't talk about that last part much. My parents are strange, naming me Jesse when they knew what their last name was.

Now that Joey has passed, parking in the space beside his every day was still unsettling, even though the building super removed his name for me. I'd offered the space to Bernice, our secretary, receptionist and jack-of-all-trades but she wouldn't have it. Honestly, after Joey died, I'd thought about selling out. Thought about it hard. Then I figured, it's all I have left of Joey and he loved it. Besides, what was I supposed to do? Go back to work at Wal-Mart? I inherited my dad's poker face. What I didn't know, I could bluff my way out of.

Determined to make it work, I crossed the room to flip on my computer. It seemed odd in there with no lights and no Bernice. Her desk sits right in front of the door with an assortment of chairs scattered around a big coffee table. Not that we had many walk in clients, but you never know. Mine and Joey's occupied opposite corners in the back.

I settled into the chair behind my desk and started sorting and stacking piles, making a clear space to work, then picked the stacks off Joey's desk and spent the rest of the afternoon making new ones. Things for Bernice to file, people to call, cases to close, bills to pay, invoices to send. When the phone rang, interrupting my intense concentration, I nearly jumped out of my skin.

"Private Spies, this is Jesse," I mumbled, cradling the phone with my shoulder while I searched for a place to set the latest stack.

"Joseph Catronio, please," a curt woman's voice snapped me back to the present.

"He's not in. Can I help you with something?"

Silence. "When do you expect him? I'd really rather talk to him personally. He's the owner, right?"

Thinking.

"Ma'am, Mr. Catronio passed away. I'm the owner now." It sounded even more weird when I said it out loud than it did inside my head.

"Oh. Well…"

"I'd be glad to help you with whatever you need," I tried to sound encouraging, looking at the stack of bills that was considerably taller than the stack of invoices waiting to mail.

The woman sighed - loud, like her annoyance would change anything. "I guess I don't really have a choice. The other firm that was recommended won't take my case unless I drive down there and meet them in person. I can't do that."

"Yes ma'am," I agreed, although I'm not sure why. To keep her talking I suppose.

"I need you to find my ex-husband," she offered. "He's there. In Dallas somewhere."

"All right," I wrestled a client form out from under one of the piles and cleared a spot to write on. "First, I'll need your name…"

"Beverly Gafford," she cut me off.

"… and address."

"What do you need that for?" her strident tones were already getting on my nerves.

"Standard procedure, Mrs. Gafford. I need it for billing, and I may need it for tracing your ex. That *is* what you want me to do, right?" Two could play the snotty game.

She recited her address and phone number faster than I could write.

"Thank you," I said after I made her repeat it a second time. "Now tell me about the man you want me to find." I slid my pencil behind my ear and rocked back in my chair, ready for her to launch into the everything-the-loser-ever-did-wrong speech.

"His name is Lawrence James Gafford," she said in clipped tones I'd heard a million times before.

I waited. "And?"

"And what?"

"Do you have an idea where I might look for him?"

Usually, these women start with the first date scenario and I have to stop them from a blow by blow that could take hours. This was new and different.

"Well if I knew that I wouldn't need you, would I?"

I was beginning to wonder if I really needed this woman's money.

"All I have is the name Lawrence Gafford," I reasoned. "I promise, when I start searching I'll come up with several of those. You were married to him; there must be something else you can tell me. What about his social security number?"

"Let me check," I heard her put down the phone. When she picked it up again, she read the number back to me.

"Okay, that'll help. Is there anything else you'd like me to know?"

"He kidnapped my daughter," she said simply.

"What?" This was a new twist.

"He had weekend visitation last week and never brought her back," she acted like I should have already known that. Worse, I've been more emotional when I lost my keys.

"Did you call the police?" This was definitely more than I was ready to handle.

"Uh! Of course I called the police! They can't do anything if he's crossed state lines."

I knew that seemed wrong, but she sounded like she knew what she was talking about.

"Mrs. Gafford, tell me more about your daughter's disappearance and why you think he brought her to Dallas." My mind was reeling with the possibilities. Usually, we're looking for deadbeat dads who didn't pay child support or missing heirs for some attorney trying to close out an estate. My standard script didn't fit this one.

"There isn't much to tell," she snapped. So much for the grieving mother scenario. She sounded more like the ex-wife from hell. "He had visitation last weekend and was supposed to bring her back here by 6:00 on Sunday. He didn't bring her back and he's checked out of the motel. I can only assume he's taken her to Texas."

"Why is that?" I began to accept the possibility that I'd stepped into the Twilight Zone, or at least Candid Camera.

"Why is what?"

I swallowed a groan. "Why do you assume he brought her here?" I spoke slowly in case she was having a brain cramp.

"Because that's where he lives," she said. "I told you that."

"All right," I conceded. "Do you know what kind of work he does?"

"I don't know shit about him anymore, and I like it that way!" I could imagine her stomping her foot and getting ready for a tantrum. "Now, are you going to find him or not?"

"Fine. I'll see what I can do," I told her, ready to forget the whole thing but the checkbook balance wouldn't let me. "Do you have a fax, Mrs. Gafford?"

"Ye-es, why?"

"I need you to fax me a picture of your daughter, along with her date of birth and social, and one of your ex if you still have one," I explained.

Loud sigh. "Oh, all right. Is that all?"

I bit my tongue, reminding myself that grief does strange things to people, then made arrangements to fax her a contract and told her where to send the retainer. Without another word, Beverly Gafford hung up.

Thoroughly disgusted with the whole idea, I decided to head home and get a fresh start in the morning. It was after five and there wasn't much I could do until I got her fax anyway. Maybe instead, she'd call the FBI or something. Nothing is easy.

A few minutes later, I pulled up in front of a two-bedroom frame house with weeds where there should have been grass, some kind of tweedy looking material that might have been carpet in another life, and furniture that looked more like yard sale rejects retrieved before trash pickup at the curb. Home, sweet home.

At least it was only five minutes from the office. I traded my semi-professional jeans and sweater for sweats and socks, pointedly ignoring the hinges that needed fixing on the bathroom door. Why is it there's always something broken?

"A man, that's what you need," I slipped into my Mom's voice to ease the silence. I'd gotten behind in my nagging exercises. See, I figured out a long time ago, if I keep up the nagging when I'm away from home, it doesn't seem so overwhelming when I finally visit. That's what I tell myself anyway. It's better than thinking I'm turning into her as I get older.

Padding back into the kitchen in stocking feet, I sidestepped Elvis, my fat, gray cat, and armed myself for hunting. Unfortunately, the cockroach I killed on the counter wasn't going to feed either of us, so I kept up the search until I located a can of tuna and a lone Hostess cupcake. Elvis chose tuna.

"I don't need a man," I told Elvis, who really didn't care. "What I need is a *wife*." Someone to cook and clean and do the grocery shopping. I despise grocery shopping. Maybe then we'd have something to eat besides tuna and a stale cupcake. Reluctantly, I picked up the phone and called Mr. Jim's to order a supreme pizza. As an afterthought, I tacked on a salad and diet Pepsi. They'd cancel out the calories in the pizza.

"It's coming," I told Elvis, who perched on the arm of the sofa and glared at me. "It's not like you're starving or anything." Under all the fluff, he was more solidly packed than the can of tuna he'd just finished off. Aside from his attitude, he was good company. Probably the only male I know who was safe enough to sleep with these days. Not that I'm opposed to the idea in theory. It's just that my luck with men was in a little slump and I was waiting for the upswing.

CHAPTER TWO

I hate mornings. Unfortunately, if I sleep through them like I like to do, I miss half the day. Time is money, or so I've heard. After a quick shower, I tugged on a sweater and a pair of jeans, promised Elvis I wouldn't come home without food, and headed out. An unlocked door and the smell of fresh brewed coffee greeted me at the office.

"Bernice!" I smiled for the first time in awhile. "I didn't expect you back until next week."

"I knew you'd need me," she smiled up at me from her desk, looking more like a weirded out fairy godmother than any receptionist I've seen.

At fifty something, her hair was more white than brown and she wore it in a variation of a beehive that I thought went out in the sixties. Bright blue eye shadow covered her eyelids like finger paint no matter what color of garish flowered muumuu she wore on her ample frame. I never did hear where Joey found her, but she was a whiz around the office.

"You're right about that," I said, retrieving the stacks I'd sorted from my desk. "Bills to pay, invoices to send, and stuff to file," I said, setting each one down on her desk in turn.

"Oh, girl, looks like you've been busy!" she clucked.

"Not busy enough," I groaned, sinking into my chair and glancing over at the piles still covering Joey's desk. He might have known right where everything was, but to me, it just looked like a mess. "I've got a new case, though, so I guess those will have to wait another day or two."

"No worries," Bernice said cheerfully. "I'll have it sorted out in no time. I know his system."

She'd get no arguments from me. I have enough trouble with my own mess. The sound of Bernice rustling around and muttering to herself was oddly comforting and I got right to work on the Gafford case.

"Look at this," I told Bernice, less than an hour later.

The picture Beverly Gafford faxed of her ex husband was grainy at best, but it still didn't look anything like the driver's license photo I picked off the Internet. Joey had us set up to get into all kinds of databases. Some of them, I was pretty sure we weren't supposed to get into, but sometimes it's better not to ask too many questions.

"Does that look like the same guy to you?" I handed the printout to her.

Bernice held the two photos in chubby hands an arm's length away from her bifocals.

"No," she said, shaking her head. "Not at all. You sure this is the right guy?"

I shrugged. "Same social, same name."

"Guess it's a really bad picture," she said, putting them back on my desk. "You know those DPS pictures are a plot from hell."

She nodded her head with her lips clenched in a tight line. Bernice thought everything was a plot from hell.

"Maybe," I said.

But I didn't think it was just a bad picture. Something seemed hokey about the whole thing.

"I'm going to see if I can find this guy in person," I told her, pulling my purse out of the bottom drawer.

Ordinarily, that was a luxury I didn't have, working on the Internet, but since he was supposedly here in Dallas I could do some actual investigating. That was a perk that didn't come up often. Most of the time, I just did all my searching online and Joey had done the rest. I missed him.

Expecting to find a little house similar to my own, I was surprised when the address led me to the Frost Farms section of DeSoto. Where the really rich who don't want to live in north Dallas live. Ranches and mansions with circular driveways and pools and stables and maids and limos. I heard one house actually has its own bowling alley. Not that I'd ever been inside one, but I could tell immediately that my whole house and yard would have fit easily in the garage.

My poor little Taurus probably felt like an unwanted stepchild. Hard to be inconspicuous in a Ford around there. Hard to see anything parked on the street, too. The house number was on the mailbox but the driveway was so long I had to rescue a surveillance bag out of the trunk and use binoculars. Joey liked to have all the right equipment, even if we hardly ever used it. Man, I missed him!

I didn't have to wait long to see someone; people came and went like it was moving day only they weren't carrying anything. Unfortunately, none of them even remotely resembled either of the men I was looking for, or the little girl, either. I was about ready to give up when a man came out of the stables and caught my attention. Even with the binoculars, it was hard to tell, so I took a chance and got out of the car. I needed to stretch my legs anyway. PIs do way too much sitting.

I had to hurry to cross the grass in time to catch him before he reached his truck, so I didn't really have time to think of anything clever to say.

"Excuse me!" I called when I got close enough for him to hear me.

When he stopped and turned, I knew it was the same face that Beverly Gafford had faxed to me. He wasn't very big, maybe five foot ten, a hundred and sixty pounds, but he had the wavy brown hair and the deep creases in his face that come from hours in the sun. Lawrence Gafford number one. The one that matched the picture that didn't match the name. Maybe I wasn't ready to be the boss yet. None of this made sense.

"Are you Lawrence Gafford?" I asked, trying not to breathe as hard as an obscene phone caller.

A scowl replaced the smile he'd been wearing. "Who wants to know?"

I pulled a card out of my pocket and handed it to him. "Jesse Morgan, Private Spies."

"I got nothing to say to you," he snarled and pitched my card on the ground, then turned and continued to his truck.

"Look," I chased after him, "I don't want to cause a problem, I just need to know…"

He couldn't hear me because he was driving away. Great.

Bernice was already gone when I got back to the office, but the place looked wonderful. Like she said, she had Joey's desk all cleaned off and what there was left for me was neatly stacked in my inbox. At least that was one thing I didn't have to worry about.

Frustrated, I pulled the two pictures out of a file folder she'd labeled "Gafford" and looked at them again. Now that I'd seen him face to face, there was no way the driver's license picture matched the man. Of course, the driver's license was expired and the picture was years old. But if the driver's license picture and address were Lawrence Gafford, who was the guy Beverly called Gafford and why was he at the same address? If she was married to him, she ought to get the name right.

On a hunch, I checked the address without a name on the Internet and found yet another man – a Marcus Brant. His picture didn't match either one. Hm. I printed the info for posterity and was still staring at it when the front door opened and a huge man filled the doorway, silhouetted in the setting sun. I had a flashback of Nicolas Cage saving the day in *ConAir*, but it passed. Too bad.

"Can I help you?"

"Jesse?" he asked, coming inside and closing the door behind him.

"Ye-es," I said. "Do I know you?"

No way I'd ever seen this man before. I wouldn't forget those muscles, or the long dark hair and incredibly blue eyes. He looked like the cover of a romance novel.

"Byron Montgomery," he crossed the room in three long strides and extended a hand.

I stared at it for a second, then looked back up at him.

"Jesse Morgan," I tried to smile, shaking his hand. "Have a seat." I suspected he would anyway, but it was polite to say.

"We finally meet," he said, sinking into a chair across from my desk.

I waited, wondering if I'd missed something.

"Have we done some work for you?" I asked when I couldn't stand it anymore. Nothing about this guy was remotely familiar, although I'd like it to be.

"No, I'm here to do some work for you," he smiled broadly like we were sharing an inside joke.

"I'm sorry, Mr. Montgom…"

"Byron," he interrupted, correcting me.

"Byron," I conceded. As if I'd forget that name. "I haven't the faintest idea why you're here."

"Joe didn't tell you?" He looked genuinely surprised.

"Tell me what?"

"He hired me to come work here. I was out of the country when I heard he died so this is the soonest I could get here."

My head reeled like I'd been punched. Was this guy for real? Would Joey really have hired someone without telling me? Of course he would. My heart sank. He was always nagging me about little things, then forgetting to tell me the big ones. Like oops I forgot to tell you your sister's in labor and they want you to come, or oops, I forgot to tell you they'll turn off the electricity if you don't get the payment in by five and it's four fifty now.

"He didn't tell you," Byron read my mind. "Well…what do we do now?"

"Uhhhh," I just stared at him, trying desperately to catch one of the random thoughts that swirled through my brain. "I don't know. I haven't had time to sort things out…I don't know how much money's in the bank or what we owe, or even what cases Joey was still trying to close."

"Good, then you need help," he smiled.

I guess I didn't look too sure.

"Let's start at the beginning," he suggested. "I knew Joe in college. For the last fifteen years I've been a police officer in Houston, but I got a bum knee and retired. Joe suggested I go for the PI license and help him build this business and I finally agreed."

"How long ago did you work for the police?" I asked, looking him over carefully.

"I just left a month ago," he said.

I ran through a mental list of all the police officers I knew and none of them resembled him even a little.

"You grew all that hair in a month?" If I thought for a minute that a hairdresser could sculpt those curls and waves on my own head, I'd have given up a month of cupcakes.

He laughed. "Hardly. I was undercover. Vice and narcotics."

"Vice," I repeated, doing another mental list. Homicide, Crimes against Persons, Narcotics, hmmmmmm. Vice. "So you have your license?"

"Just got it," he smiled again. "And, I've rented a house up here and my furniture is on the way."

Thanks, Joey. "I don't suppose he already drew up a contract for you?" I asked, not sure if I'd be glad either way.

"All done."

"Well, then I guess I should welcome you aboard," I didn't know what else to say.

"I'll grow on you," he nodded, sensing my uncertainty. "If I don't, then you can fire me."

Right.

I tossed and turned all night. My whole world was whirling like an amusement park ride and I couldn't get off. Or even find a place to land! When I finally admitted that I was awake and might as well go to work, I arrived at the office to find Byron had settled himself comfortably into Joey's desk. Bernice fell in love with him. He calls me the boss, but we both know the truth – I own the place, but he's the one who's in charge. What makes it worse is that I kind of like him. And he sure knows a heck of a lot more about this business than I do.

Byron had sorted through Joey's files and tied up everything he had pending. He'd even brought some new business with him. While he was busy with that, Lawrence Gafford continued to elude me. Every path I took came to a dead end. When I called Beverly Gafford to tell her I found the guy in the picture but his name didn't match, she told me to forget it – she didn't need me anymore. How's that for class? I was fired and didn't even know it.

But something wasn't right and I couldn't rest until I knew what it was, just to be sure I didn't screw something up. If the guy in the photo she sent wouldn't talk to me, maybe someone else would. On impulse, I decided to drive out to Frost Farms one more time before I filed it away.

I slowed the car as the Brant house loomed up ahead and pulled off to the side of the road. There was very little traffic out there and nothing moved but the horses in the pasture. Once I was satisfied that Gafford's truck wasn't in the lot beside the stables, I ventured out and up the long walk to the front door of the house, picture in hand. I knew I couldn't park in the driveway near the house if I wanted my car to remain incognito. When a gust of wind blew my hair in my face, I was grateful we were still enjoying Indian Summer before the pre-winter Texas temperature shifts from 80 to 40 and back again set in.

I knocked sharply when I reached the door and made sure I was smiling properly when a young woman in a maid's uniform answered the door. I started the spiel I'd been rehearsing.

"Good morning! My name is Jesse Morgan and I'm a private investigator." That always gets a reaction – good, bad, or indifferent. Hers was wide-eyed surprise. "Could I ask you a few questions?"

Her dark eyes darted around the doorway, looking for answers, or maybe escape. "I… don't know…what is this about?"

"Nothing to be alarmed about," I assured her with another smile. "Do you know this man?" I showed her the photo that was clearly recognizable despite the lines where it had been folded. That's the good thing about computer printouts.

I saw the recognition in her face before she answered. "Why? Has he done something wrong?"

Time to win her over.

"Listen," I leaned forward like we were sharing secrets, "I'm really not supposed to talk about the cases I'm working on, but it's not like you think. For instance," I let my voice drop to a conspiratorial whisper, "I work for an attorney who hired me to locate a missing heir for an old lady who died in New Jersey…she left ten thousand dollars in her will…" I let my voice fade off, hoping she'd draw the wrong conclusion without an outright lie on my part. I really do work for an attorney like that sometimes; it just had nothing to do with this guy.

"Wow," she said, taking the bait. "That's pretty cool."

I nodded and smiled, waiting. She was probably thinking of ways to hook up with him in case he was about to get rich.

"I just need to talk to him," I said finally. "Do you know him?"

"Well…yeah," she still didn't seem too sure. "That looks like Gary Greaves, our stable manager."

"No kidding?" I acted surprised. "How long has he worked here?"

"Oh, I don't know," she still seemed nervous, glancing over her shoulder now and then. "Not long, about three or four months I think."

"Great! Do you think he's out there right now?" I knew he wasn't, but I didn't want her to know that.

"I don't know," she said, closing the door a little, obviously ready to end this conversation.

"Well, thanks anyway. You've been a big help," I smiled at her. "Hey, listen, maybe it would be better if you didn't mention that we talked. I'd like to surprise him, you know?"

"Sure," she disappeared behind the door and it closed with a thud.

I strolled casually over to the stables and looked inside the big doors, thinking maybe I'd get a chance to look around the office, but there were several people in there and I didn't have a plan for that, so I ducked out quick. Gary Greaves, I thought, walking back to my car. What now?

I tossed a few ideas around on the drive back to the office. Fortunately, it wasn't far, but I still didn't have a clue what I should do with this.

"Morning!" Bernice chirped when I walked in the door.

"Morning, Bernice," I dumped my purse on my desk and headed straight for the coffee.

I don't know how people make it through the morning without coffee and the cup I had at home was already worn out from my efforts.

"Don't I get a good morning?" Byron swiveled around to face me as I sat down at my desk.

"Morning," I offered lamely.

"What's wrong?"

"It's morning for starters," I said, looking at the overflow in my inbox.

"Mornings are great!" he smiled.

I rolled my eyes. No wonder I didn't want to be here in the mornings. Two cheerful morning people. I was outnumbered.

"You having a problem with a case?"

"Oh, I don't know," I said, responding to the concern in his voice. He really was too nice not to like. "Actually, I'm off the case, but it bugs me."

"That Gafford thing?" he rocked back in his chair like he had all the time in the world to talk to me.

"Yeah. I went back out there this morning and got a name to go with the face," I admitted. "None of it fits."

"Tell me what you've got," he prompted.

I shook my head. "Nothing really new. I just don't understand how I can get a picture and a name and social, then I run it and find the name and social attached to a whole other guy. I follow up the address, but no Lawrence Gafford. Then I find the guy from the first picture at the second guy's supposed address. What kind of coincidence is that?"

"Unlikely," he agreed, nodding.

"Exactly. Meaning it's not a coincidence. And besides that, what kind of mother would drop the case so fast if her daughter was missing?"

He looked like he was thinking about it for a minute, then asked, "Did you check with the Tulsa PD?"

"No," I said. Oops. I knew I missed something.

"Why don't we?" he picked up the phone.

Better him than me, I suppose. I booted up my computer and stared at his back while he talked softly on the phone. It only took a couple of minutes – just long enough for me to wonder how broad those shoulders really were.

"No case," he turned to me after he hung up the phone.

"What do you mean, they found her?" Stay on target, Jesse.

"I mean there was never a report filed saying she was missing," he said.

"Well, now that really doesn't make sense. She told me she needed me because the police weren't able to do anything since he left the state with the girl."

"Do you believe everything you hear? That's not true," he said. "They'd keep looking alright and probably call in the Feds since it crossed state lines. She never reported it."

"Something's hokey about the whole thing," I frowned.

"Yep," he agreed, turning back to his computer. "Did she pay you?"

I nodded. "You think I should drop it?"

He got that thinking look again. "Probably. Maybe she just made up the story about her daughter because she thought it would make you work faster. In any case, you've got paying clients who want you working and she's not one of them anymore."

"You're right," I said with a sigh.

So much for the big time. I should be grateful for work even if it's the boring variety, but inside there was a little part of me that was tired of the feeling that my jigsaw puzzle was missing a few key pieces.

CHAPTER THREE

The rest of the day was relatively uneventful. Until time to shop for groceries, anyway. I stopped at Tom Thumb just a few blocks from my house, but I had very little enthusiasm for the whole ordeal. As usual, I hit the frozen foods, then veered to the cat food aisle and picked up some goodies for Elvis. Honestly, he eats better than I do most days. I grabbed a bag of litter and headed for the checkout, tossing a few extras in the buggy along the way. Necessities, you know, like cookies and Pepsi.

When I headed back to the car, I stopped, surprised to see a man who looked vaguely familiar peering in the back window.

"Hey!" I yelled, quickening my pace.

No matter. He was long gone by the time I got there. What was up with that? DeSoto was a suburb. No peekers allowed. I dumped the bags in the back seat and took off for home, breathing a sigh of relief when Elvis met me at the door. Twice, in that short distance, I thought maybe someone was following me. Probably I watch too much television.

Once I got changed, I fed Elvis and stared at my selection of TV dinners. Why is it that I can go to the store and buy bags of stuff, then go home and not want any of it? I was pondering the situation when the phone rang.

"Hello."

"Jesse," Byron's voice was warm and smooth. "Whatcha doing?"

"Not much," I said, wondering what prompted him to call. "What's up?"

"I have a dilemma," he said. "I've got a gift certificate to a new restaurant in Dallas and I need someone to go with me but I don't know anyone around here."

"Restaurant?" Perk.

"Yeah. A place called Fago de Chao's in north Dallas. It's supposed to be great, but I really hate to eat alone. You game?"

My eyes swept over the assortment in my freezer. "Tonight?"

"Right now."

"Yeah."

It wasn't a date, anyway. Just call it a business dinner.

"Great! I'll pick you up in half an hour," his voice was smiling. "Don't dress."

Yeah, right. He hadn't seen these sweats.

Reluctantly, I traded them for a sweater and a pair of khaki slacks, then headed for the bathroom to touch up my makeup and run a brush through my hair. I'm not very creative that way. I'm more of the wash and wear variety. Fortunately, my hair was thick and full with just a hint of curl on the ends. Low maintenance. It was also more auburn than mousy brown thanks to L'Oreal. Preventive maintenance. No graymeister was sneaking up on me unannounced.

My eyes vacillate between blue and gray for some reason I've never been sure of, and I always wear brown eye shadow. Unlike Bernice's neon blue, brown goes with everything. Mascara and a little bronze blusher and I'm ready to go. If I'm outside enough, I don't even need the blusher. Quick and easy. I wouldn't win a beauty contest, but I don't scare small children either. My sister is always giving me cosmetic gift sets for birthdays and things, but I rarely open them. The closest I come to lipstick is clear gloss, and that's more to prevent chapped lips than anything else. Dad was right. I should have been a boy.

I was peeking out the front curtain when Byron pulled into the drive and I met him there. Housekeeping is not my specialty and I wasn't sure he knew me well enough to see it.

"My car or yours?" he asked, climbing out of his Cobra. Forest green with a camel interior and convertible top. Shiny and fast. Man. On a cop's salary? I better watch this guy.

"Are you kidding?" I asked.

I love my Taurus. It's even called Mocha like my favorite coffee. But a Mustang Cobra would have been my choice if I could have afforded payments twice as high.

"I love your car."

"Let's do it, then." He smiled and opened the door for me. Who said chivalry was dead?

Fago de Chao's was crowded, even on a Tuesday night, and it was a long wait, but a glance at the enormous salad bar on the way to the table made it worthwhile.

"Nice place, huh?" he asked, looking very relaxed in his open collar black shirt and jeans. Dangerous to a woman who hadn't had a date in a year or so. Forget that. From the looks he was getting, he was dangerous to a girl who was still in the middle of her last date.

"Different," I nodded, looking around.

The tables were close together, but not so close they prevented the gauchos with balloon pants from slipping between them and slicing off strips of steak cooked to perfection over an open fire. It was a festive atmosphere, filled with the aroma of hot, spiced meat and the laughter of young and old alike, punctuated by the tinkling of wine glasses and silver on china.

On guard at first, Byron's warm smile and smooth voice charmed me into letting my walls down as dinner progressed. By the time I'd eaten all I could hold, I was putty in his hands.

"Tell me about yourself, Jesse Morgan," he smiled, lounging back in his chair.

"Tell you what?" I countered, knowing I couldn't tell him that all I wanted was to unbutton my pants right then.

"What makes Jesse tick? Or should I say Jessica?"

"No. Jesse with an e," I explained for the millionth time.

"Not short for anything?" he cocked an eyebrow in surprise.

I wrinkled my nose. "Short for Jesse James."

"No shit?" he laughed. He has a nice laugh. "Well, at least Morgan is a nice name."

I shook my head. "Earp."

"Huh?" He probably thought it was reflux from dinner.

"Morgan Earp, Wyatt's brother," I explained. "I'm the second daughter and my Dad really wanted a boy." See? I was spilling my guts.

"I see," he chuckled. "It suits you."

"Oh great," I laughed with him. "I look like a cowboy to you?"

His eyes narrowed and I stifled a shiver. "Hardly. I guess he didn't have much choice with the Morgan part, though. No middle name, or are you afraid to tell?"

"Morgan is my middle name. Jackson is my last name." I waited.

This time, he laughed right out loud, drawing glances from the couple sitting at the next table. "Jesse Jackson. Now *that's* a good one!"

I shrugged, wishing I could shrink a little. "He wasn't famous back when I was born, I don't think."

He managed to stuff the laughter back into a wicked grin. "No matter. Jesse Morgan it is."

"You should talk, Byron." Like nobody ever said anything about *that* name. "Or should I just call you 'Lord'?" A girl can only take so much.

"Not if you know what's good for you," he warned with a smile. "My mother was a hopeless romantic and my dad was gone before I came along so there was no one to talk her out of it."

17

"Well, we're quite a pair then, aren't we?" I smiled.

A man who was all man, with a frilly name and better hair and eyelashes than most women I knew, and a woman who's a tomboy named after two Wild West heroes of questionable and violent nature.

"I like to think so," he smiled back and I suddenly wondered where this evening would lead. "Come on, let's get out of here before we're tempted to eat any more."

The ride home was even better than the meal, with the car top down and the cool breeze in my hair, I could look up and imagine the star filled sky reaching all the way to Alaska and beyond. When we finally pulled into the drive, he turned off the car and looked over at me. "I had a lovely time with you, Jesse."

"It's early," I glanced nervously at my watch. "Why don't you come in for awhile?" It might be risky, but I was so tired of being alone.

He looked as though he was considering it for a moment, then said, "Deal."

He followed me inside, and I pointed him to the refrigerator for a beer then ducked into the back for a quick trip to the bathroom, grabbing a few misplaced items of clothing along the way. If I hurried, I'd probably get away with trading my slacks for a pair of sweats with a stretchy waistband. But it was not to be.

I have two bathrooms in my house. One in the hall that nobody ever uses and one off my bedroom that I use all the time. It has a nice window and a view of the backyard. Maybe I should have noticed that the curtain was askew, but, not being very domestic and with my mind on what to do with Byron next, I didn't. I did notice a distinct odor, but I assumed it came from Elvis paying me back for leaving him alone all evening. Cats do that.

After I washed my hands and ran a brush through my hair, then checked my teeth in the mirror to be sure some little something wasn't stuck there and Byron was just too nice to say so, I gave in to the urge and peeked behind the curtain. What I saw literally knocked me on my butt in the bathroom floor and it was at least a year before I could make a sound come out of my mouth.

When it did, it didn't sound much like "Byron, come quick, there's a dead guy in my bathtub!" It sounded more like "AAAAAAAhh hhhhhhhhhhhh!!"

I did the backwards crab walk thing until my back bumped against the door, never once taking my eyes off the bloody hand resting along the side of my tub.

I tried again. "MmmmmmmAAAAAAhhhhhhhhh!!" Still no words. It must have worked, though, because a minute later I heard Byron on the other side of the door.

"Jesse?"

Oh thank God! Once I heard a real word, my own came back.

"Byron! There's a dead guy in my bathtub!"

I felt the door bump against my back and scooted forward just far enough to let him open it and come in.

"There's a ....holy shit!"

I guess he saw it.

"Byron. There's a dead guy in my bathtub," I said again, like he didn't hear me the first time.

I watched, horrified, as he stepped over me and walked over to the tub and looked down. He seems bigger in a small room. Carefully, like I might break the spell, I scooted around the door and camped just outside. I could see, but I didn't want to be that close.

"He's dead, alright," he said, turning back to me.

Brilliant.

"Who is he?"

Like I knew. I looked at him dumbfounded.

"Jesse?"

"What?" He meant for me to answer that question?

"Did you get a look at his face?"

I slipped through some sort of time warp and everything was in slow motion.

"Face?" I think I had a rare form of parrot disease.

"Jesse," he sounded like he was speaking to a small child. "Come look at his face."

"No," I said. That was easy.

He sighed loudly. "You have to look. There's a dead guy in your bathtub."

A little slow, but he finally got it.

"No. I don't want to look." I wasn't sure of a lot of things, but I was sure of that.

"Just a quick look," he took a step toward me, then another.

All of a sudden, his hands were around my shoulders and he lifted me off the floor like I was no bigger than Elvis. There was no point in resisting, so I let him lead me back to the tub, but my eyes were squinted tightly shut.

"Look," he thundered.

I figured I could either look or stand there forever so I peeked out of one eye until the guy's face came into focus.

"Oh, man." Close the eyes again.

"You know him?" Byron's voice came from somewhere near my ear.

I nodded, eyes still closed. See no evil. "It's Gary Greaves."

"The guy from the Gafford case?" he sounded incredulous.

I nodded again. This time, I followed him willingly out of the room and sat down on the couch while he phoned the police.

"They'll be right here," he said, sitting down and sliding a strong arm behind me on the couch. Not exactly the way I'd hoped the evening would end.

"Where's Elvis?" I asked, sitting up straight and looking frantically around the room.

Byron was too nice to say it, but I know he thought I'd lost my mind.

"Jesse, sit back and try to relax," he said with a look of concern on his face.

"No, I can't find Elvis," I said, crouching on the floor to look under things.

"Elvis is dead," he said flatly.

My head jerked up in shock before I realized he didn't know who Elvis was. "Elvis is my cat." Good to know he can't read minds.

"Oh," he breathed a sigh of relief. "Your cat. He's probably hiding. Don't go back in the bathroom until the police get here," he called as I headed down the hall.

As if. Like I suspected, I found Elvis glaring at me from under my bed. He came out reluctantly when I crawled halfway under, but the look in his eyes told me I'd not soon forget the trauma I put him through.

"Elvis, huh?" Byron said as I sat down beside him again, cradling the furry gray bundle in my arms. "You don't strike me as the type."

"Cole," I said, stroking Elvis more for my comfort than his.

"Huh?"

"Elvis Cole," I explained. "World's Greatest Detective."

Byron still had that maybe-I-better-call-for-professional-help look.

"He's a detective in a book," I explained.

"Ah," he said, nodding. So much for a romantic evening.

"Maybe now is a good time for a beer," I suggested.

"Why don't we wait until the cops get here?" he said.

"Why? It's not like I'm drunk and imagined there's a dead guy in the bathtub," I said. "Hey! Maybe you better go check and see if he's still there!" Like he climbed out the window and it was all a bad joke.

Poor Byron. He was saved from answering by a sharp knock on the door.

I just sat on the couch with Elvis glaring at the strangers who'd invaded our home. Byron took charge, introducing himself to the officers and showing them around like he'd been here a hundred times. It took hours for them to get through. The homicide investigators grilled me three or four times, asking the same damn questions over and over, but they finally decided to call it a night somewhere around four in the morning.

"Ms. Morgan, we may need to talk to you again," Detective Ferguson warned me in an ominous voice.

I need to go to school and learn how to talk like that. I'd be a better PI.

"I'll tell you the same thing again," I answered with a shrug, tired of the whole thing. So tired, in fact, that I didn't even argue when the po-po declared my whole house a crime scene and Byron offered to let me stay at his house so I didn't have to wake my parents and explain this all to them. Yet.

CHAPTER FOUR

When I woke up to the smell of fresh brewed coffee instead of Elvis pawing at me, I wondered just for an instant, if it was a dream. The sound of a pan crashing to the floor in the other room jerked me out of bed like I was on the wrong end of a fast reel. Halfway down the hall, it dawned on me. This wasn't my house. That's why Byron was still here. I slunk back to my room before he saw me looking like something the cat dug up. That business of sexy bedroom hair is for the birds. One glance in the bathroom mirror proved my point.

Once I was sufficiently presentable, I ventured back out. Wouldn't you know, Byron looked as fresh as ever! Men. Course, in the light of morning, the house didn't look quite as fresh. In fact, it looked full of boxes with stuff hanging out. At least he's not perfect.

"Morning, sleepyhead," he smiled and sat a pan of scrambled eggs on the dining room table, already set with plates and flatware.

My plate had a steaming mug of coffee beside it and that was all I saw.

"Morning," I mumbled. Must have coffee.

"Sleep okay?" he asked, sitting down across the table from me.

"Mmph," I answered in morning talk, provoking another smile. What is it with these cheerful morning people? Maybe he had amnesia and forgot there was a dead guy in my bathtub last night.

"Eat something, you'll feel better," he said, dishing up my eggs and perching two slices of toast on the edge of my plate. He must know my mother. She thinks eating makes everything better.

Oddly enough, he was right. When I'd finished my plate and a second mug of coffee, I could actually talk and sound human.

"Thank you."

"You're welcome," he said, munching his toast. "I think we better get in to the office and do a little more research on this, don't you?" He ignored

22

my comment and I made a face when he wasn't looking. No fair getting to the coffee first. Mine hadn't had time to work yet.

"Heck, I don't know," I said. "You're the ex cop. Is that what we do?"

"Yeah." He nodded and got up to clear the table. "That's what we do."

I spent the morning trying to get the goods on Gary Greaves, but without a social, there wasn't much I could be sure about. Nothing matched. Convinced I'd done all I could, I turned my attention to other, more easily resolved cases. Byron was out most of the day, but when he came back, he looked like an ad for Soldiers of Fortune toting boxes that contained an arsenal.

"What is that?" I asked because Bernice was too polite. Or too scared.

"Protection," he said simply, plopping the box on his desk. When he sat it down, I saw that he was wearing a shoulder holster with a mean looking gun tucked inside.

"From *what?*"

"I take it you're not certified," he said.

"Not." My calm little world was spinning again. Maybe I'd start smoking again.

"Well, it's time you got that way," he said as if that was the answer to everything.

"Not," I said again. The way my luck was running, I'd shoot myself in no time.

"Look. I can't always be there for you. Or did you want me to move in?" a wry smile lit his face and his baby blues started to twinkle.

Bernice turned away and got very busy at her desk, but not before I saw her eyebrows disappear under her helmet bangs.

"You can't be serious," I said helplessly.

"Jesse," there goes the talking to a small child tone again. "You think that guy accidentally died in your bathtub on the way to somewhere else? Somebody put him there for a reason. They know you. They know where you live. And we don't know who they are or what they have against you."

"So?" It was all I could think of at the time. Bernice wasn't impressed.

It was his turn to roll the eyes. "At least come with me over to the range and let me show you how they work."

"We can go in your car?" I asked, wavering.

"My car," he agreed.

"Deal." I get a ride in the Mustang and I get to shoot a gun, something my Dad has tried to get me to do most of my life. Of course Dad's idea came with a holster and a revolver and I'm pretty sure there was going to be a horse involved somehow.

The shooting range was in Duncanville, just a few miles from the office, and just as intimidating as I thought it would be. Tough looking men who grunted more than they talked were the only ones there. At first I wondered why they didn't have day jobs, but then I noticed that customer service probably wasn't a high priority for any of them.

"They're all undercover cops, right?" I whispered to Byron as he ushered me inside.

"Ri-ight," he grinned. Smug-ass.

Surprisingly, the guy behind the desk knew who he was and greeted him with a big smile and a handshake.

"Chuck! You old dog, you! What brings you up here?" The man sent a pointed glance my way and I wrapped my arm around my waist in case my shirt suddenly flew off. I started to ask Byron who Chuck was but he poked me in the side with an elbow so all that came out was, "Unh."

"I'm working up here now," he smiled broadly. "This is Jesse Morgan, my boss." I didn't look up fast enough, but I suspect there was a wink in there somewhere. "Jesse, this is John Cramer, an old friend."

"Nice to meet you," I lied politely. I usually run from characters that look less shady than this man. And what was that smell?

"She has her PI license, but no conceal and carry. Hell, she's not even certified," Byron added as we followed John through a side door.

John turned back and looked at me like I was some kind of alien life form. Rude. "Brave man, trying to teach a b-dame to shoot." John shook his head.

Oh brother.

Once John crawled back in his hole, I stood on tiptoe and whispered in Byron's ear, "Chuck?"

"Long story. I'll tell you later."

Byron spread an assortment of things on the table inside our little cubby and started pointing. I pretended to listen earnestly, but in spite of my namesake, I'm not fluent in gunspeak . I must not have been pretending very well because he stopped, mid-lecture.

"Here," he pulled a pair of leather earmuffs off a hook on the wall and placed them on my head, then did the same for himself. "You don't care about all that. This," he picked up one of the guns, "is a Glock, 9 millimeter. It's what most cops use these days." He picked up a small, rectangular box and slid it up in the handle until I heard a click. "That's your magazine, your clip."

I stared at him.

"Bullets," he finally figured out he'd lost me again. Not that I didn't know what a bullet was. Just because I was pretty sure I didn't want to do this. "Now. You see this little ridge?" he pointed to a spot on the barrel.

I remembered that word.

"You use that to aim." He demonstrated the technique pointing it at a man-sized target that was way on the other end of the room. "Now you try." He handed it to me.

I didn't dare drop it since it was loaded. We might both be shot. Gingerly, I took it from him with two fingers, then let it nestle in my hand. It didn't feel half bad, not nearly as heavy as it looked. In fact, it would make my Daddy proud. I looked up at Byron in surprise and he stifled a grin. Damn. How does he know these things? I'm in serious trouble if he knows what I'll like better than I do.

"Look down there," he pointed to the target man. "Can you see where to aim?"

I nodded. I sure hoped I was right, but it's pretty easy to tell which end of the gun points where.

Byron stepped up behind me and slid an arm around my shoulder, placing his hand on mine and adjusting my aim. I could really learn to like this part.

"Here's the trigger," he put my finger on it and held his hand around my wrist. "You'll probably want to hold it with both hands, it's going to kick."

"Kick?"

He nodded but didn't elaborate any further. "Ready?"

I put my other hand up and grasped it with stiff arms like I saw Renee Russo do in Lethal Weapon.

"Good. Now pull the trigger."

It took a moment, but I did what he asked. Actually, I couldn't think of many things I'd refuse him when he stood so close and whispered in my ear. Kick? How about knock me smooth on my butt if he wasn't standing behind me?

"Whoa! I thought it was supposed to hurt the other guy!" Even with the ear muffs, the sound was ringing in my ears.

Byron laughed. "Do it again."

"No." Fool me once.

"Yes," he insisted. I frowned. Did I sense a pattern forming here?

This time, I took aim, then closed my eyes and braced myself before I pulled the trigger. It wasn't so bad and I actually hit target man on the leg. Never mind that I was aiming for the bullseye on his chest.

"Hey! I got it right!"

"Indeed," he smiled broadly. "One more time."

I took three more shots, getting a little closer to the bullseye each time.

"You know," I handed it back to him, "it's not as bad as I thought it would be."

"See?" he smiled indulgently. I hate when I'm wrong.

I watched him hit the target every stinking time, then had to try again. Before I knew it, almost two hours had passed and I was actually laughing out loud with the exhilaration of the experience. What a trip!

"You done good, kiddo." He beamed at me as we walked back to the car. "Best first time I've ever seen."

"Really?" I smiled, proud in spite of myself.

"No shit. Good thing, too. I've already submitted the paperwork for your conceal and carry license."

Before I could stop myself, I'd punched him in the arm. "Oops," I gasped and rubbed my fist with my other hand. He seemed nice enough, but let's face it. He was six-two, two twenty pounds of trouble. No small fry here. Time to think about tae kwon do again.

"That'll cost you," he warned, but his smile was sweet.

It was three days before I got the call that it was ok to go home. Ever the gentleman, Byron helped load my things back into my car and even carried Elvis in his kennel so I wouldn't have to. I started thinking he might really be one of those nice guys you hear about until I wondered if he was just that glad to get rid of me. Seemed more likely.

"You want to come in for awhile?" I asked when we carried the last of my stuff in the house. I thought I'd be glad to be home, but it was starting to seem a little scary in there, dead guy memories and all.

"You want me to?" he asked, eyes narrowing and one eyebrow cocked.

Well, duh. "I asked, didn't I?"

"That you did. I'll remind you of that. I'm not much on TV dinners, though."

God, he looked hot sitting there in that Mustang with his wrist draped over the wheel.

"What?" Pay attention, Jesse.

"I'll go get some food. Chinese?" he grinned again. Oh man. Did he know where my mind was wandering?

"Suit yourself." I tried to be cool and failed miserably. He was laughing when he drove away.

The fresh, clean scent of Pine Sol greeted me at the front door and Elvis wouldn't look me in the eye when I let him out of his kennel. Once he'd taken his perch on the window sill, he took time to glare at me before he drifted off to sleep. Great.

"Some detective you are," I mumbled at him on my way to my room. "Maybe I should have got a big dog and named him Pike." I appreciated the humor, even if Elvis didn't. My bathroom was cleaner than it had probably ever been and it felt almost like trespassing. Whoever the police and Byron sent over was worth their fee in spades. They'd even replaced the shower curtain and all of the fingerprint powder was gone.

I reached instinctively for the sweats I keep hanging on a bathroom hook, then drew my hand back. Byron was on the way. What to wear? When in doubt, choose jeans and a sweater. That's my rule.

With Hall and Oates on the CD player to drown out the "there's a dead guy in the bathtub" chant that haunted me, and Elvis watching from a new perch on the back of the couch, I tidied up the front of the house and started some iced tea. Beer just doesn't go with Chinese and I don't know about wine. Except that Manischevitz Blackberry is socially incorrect.

When Byron arrived with the food, I was ready with plates and utensils on the table. It wouldn't be as elegant as last night's dinner, but it sure beat eating TV dinners alone. Mom would be proud.

We spent the first half hour divvying up the spoils. Broccoli beef and chicken, sweet and sour pork, General Tsao's chicken – extra spicy, all the best foods that make a person cry and sweat.

"How many people did you hope to feed, anyway?" I asked around a mouthful of house rice.

We'd been eating awhile now and there was still food all over the table, not to mention a few shrimp under the table for Elvis. He wouldn't eat it until he'd had time to pretend he'd hunted it down and caught it himself.

"I didn't know what you liked," he answered, shoving his plate back and stretching.

"All of it," I smiled. Good thing, too. I'd have leftovers for a week. "Want a beer now?" I asked when he got up and shuffled over to the couch.

"Beer would be good," he agreed, lowering himself into the cushions like he planned to stay awhile. I got a couple of bottles of Coors out of the refrigerator and joined him on the couch, handing him one when he reached for it. I was suddenly unsure where to sit. Maybe he didn't want me right next to him on the couch, but the only chair in the room was way on the other side. I opted for the couch, but not too close and tried to act casual. I am so not good at this.

"So what does a big, tough cop like you do for fun, anyway?" I asked, studying him. When we weren't in the office, he seemed more relaxed, not so distant.

"Fun?" He shot me a glance from the corner of his eye. "Leap tall buildings in a single bound."

"Right. Come on," I nudged the knee he had propped up on the couch between us. "The other night you kept talking about me. Tell me about you."

"You saw my resume," he teased.

"You know what I mean," I pretended to pout.

He rolled his eyes so I gave that up but I still stared him down.

"Tit for tat," he said smugly.

I waited, hoping any second I'd know what he just said. Didn't happen. "What does that mean?" See? I'm no good at these games.

"It means, whenever I answer a question for you, you have to answer one for me."

"Eww. Like truth or dare or something?" That might not be the best idea.

"Sorta. You game?" Why did that twinkle in his eye bother me?

"Why not," I agreed. Like he ever heard me when I said 'no,' anyway. I could always make something up if I had to.

"Okay. For fun… I like to ride big Harleys and go deep sea fishing. How 'bout you?"

The look on his face begged me to argue with that, but there was no point. It was easy to picture him astride a Hog, wind blowing the hair back as his thighs hugged the machine roaring down the road. All too easy. Or maybe with biceps bulging while he reeled in a monster from the deep with ocean spray plastering his shirt…Whoa, Jesse! I shook my head and tried to remember how I got there.

"Well?" he prompted, jerking me back to reality.

"Mmmmm I like to rent a cabin in the woods of Minnesota and go fishing all day, then curl up with a good book by a fire at night."

If I'm not on the back of a Harley or deep sea fishing, that is.

"Really?" he looked surprised. "You've done that?"

"Not exactly," I admitted. "We used to go there on vacation every summer when I was growing up, but I haven't been back since I've been grown."

"You should do that, then. Sounds like a good time," he smiled for real, this time. No joking.

"My turn?" I asked. Turnabout's fair play.

He nodded.

"Who's Chuck?"

Byron laughed out loud. "I thought you'd forget."

I started to say "an elephant never forgets." Thank God I caught myself in time! I shook my head.

"Long story short, some of the guys in Houston…"

"Cops?"

He nodded. "… didn't much like my name."

"Byron?"

"Byron. So they decided I should replace Chuck Norris on Walker, Texas Ranger and then the name just kinda stuck."

I waited for a punch line or something that didn't come. "Guess you had to be there," I said when I figured out that was the whole story.

"Guess so," he chuckled. "You know what I'm thinking?"

Man, what I wouldn't give for that. I shook my head, suddenly aware of the silence.

"I'm thinking I better go before one of us does something we'll regret." He stretched his long legs and got up, not waiting for an answer.

Regrets, I've had a few, but then again... My mind's weird that way. I followed him to the door where he hastily kissed my cheek and said, "See you tomorrow."

I'm not sure how long I stood staring at the door, but I frowned when I realized that's what I was doing.

"Men are nothing but trouble," I told Elvis who was lurking under the couch.

CHAPTER FIVE

An empty bed isn't usually something I complain about. In fact, I rather enjoy it. No one to smog the covers. No elbows intruding on my ribs or feet that always managed to find their way to my side. It was such a relief to have my ex-husband gone that I decided the empty bed was a good thing and, even though it probably wasn't so great several years later, I still liked to think that it was.

Imagine my surprise when I went to bed last night and closed my eyes only to see visions of Byron. The same overactive imagination that kept me in time-out in grade school paraded one scenario after another across my mind, narrated by my mother and my sister listing all the reasons why I'd probably be everlastingly single. I don't wear enough makeup. I dress too mannish. I talk too much. I don't talk enough. I say all the wrong things. I eat fried chicken with my fingers. And all the while, I was in that dazed place between asleep and awake until I was justifiably afraid to go either way. If I fell asleep, I'd be at my mother's mercy. But if I woke up, I'd see all the things she'd been talking about in living color. Needless to say, I didn't feel too rested when the alarm went off and it was all Byron's fault.

I'd spent the morning running every possible errand I could think of, doing my best to delay an appearance at the office as long as I could. If Byron thought I was ready to make a move on him last night, he was probably right, but he didn't have to be so smug about it. He wants to play hard to get? I'll show him hard to get. Who needs him, anyway?

I was so pissed about the whole thing, I couldn't even drive without running up over the curb. No one can ever live up to Elvis Cole anyway. Hey! I jerked the wheel and turned right at the next corner. Bookstore time. When reality bites, I dive into the fictional world of Elvis Cole, the World's Greatest Detective. There was a new one out I hadn't had time to buy yet. Now was the time. I glanced up in my rearview mirror before changing lanes and noticed a small, blue Subaru truck I'd seen before. Nah. It had to be a coincidence.

But when I emerged from the bookstore with a couple of Robert Crais novels in hand, I saw it again. Squinting against the sun, I tried to look casual and still scope the guy out but all I could make out was a shadow behind the wheel. I didn't want to jump to a hasty conclusion. After all, this was DeSoto. Small town. There were lots of cars I'd seen before. They'd probably seen me before, too. I turned off Beltline onto Hampton Road and headed back to the office. If I got lucky, Byron would be gone to lunch by now.

Happily cursing his smug self in my mind, I got in the right lane and made a turn on Wintergreen when it hit me like a ton of bricks! That Subaru was the truck Gary Greaves got in when he wouldn't talk to me that day! And Gary Greaves was dead. What the heck does that mean? I stepped on the brakes purely out of reflex, although if anyone ever says I can't drive and think at the same time I'll deny it.

The next thing I heard was the sound of squealing brakes right behind me. I shut my eyes tight and braced myself, but nothing happened. Releasing a death grip on the steering wheel, I looked up and saw the Subaru snug up against the rear end of my car with an angry looking man in my rearview mirror.

All right, that's it! I threw the car in park and jerked open the door. The traffic light was red and there wasn't another car in sight. I had time.

"What do you think you're doing following me around town?" I shouted, marching toward the truck.

In Texas, mid-day sun is fierce, even in October, but it was no match for the time bomb ticking inside of me. The rejection I felt when things didn't go right last night had festered and I was furious with myself for caring, but now I had another target. An unsuspecting guy in a little blue truck. If I had any sense, I'd have backed up when he got out and started toward me, but my coffee was all worn off and I hadn't seen a piece of chocolate all day.

"We need to have a little talk," the man muttered and kept walking, getting taller by the second. I think he's been to the same scary school as Detective Ferguson. He had the growl down pat. His shadow reached me before he did, towering a good six inches taller and maybe fifty pounds heavier than I am. I made up for that in mad.

"We sure do," I stood as tall as I could, grateful for the two-inch heels on my cowboy boots. "I work hard for my money and this is the first new car I've ever had in my whole life!"

I waved toward the spot where his bumper sat a mere inch or so from mine.

"If you don't get off my tail, I'm gonna jam on my brakes and let you rear end it real good. Then you can buy me a new one!" I emphasized my point by jabbing him in the chest with a well-placed finger.

I'm pretty sure that's not what he expected me to say because his face went blank for a moment, then he reached out and grabbed me by the arm. I'm not crazy about being grabbed, but I think it was the wicked laugh that ticked me off.

"Let me go!" I yelled, stomping down hard on his foot with the heel of my boot.

He let go with a shout, then grabbed at my arm again, wrestling me toward the truck.

"Unpfh!" I bounced off the side of the truck while he held fast to my left wrist and tried to open the truck door with his other hand.

Taking a deep breath, I rammed the palm of my right hand up his nose, then toppled over as he lost balance and fell to the ground with a thud. Works pretty good, I congratulated myself, dusting my jeans as I climbed off of him and got back on my feet. He'd let go of me to grab his nose. Big tough guy went down like the water balloons I used to throw off the roof. Well, not quite. He didn't splat.

"Don't follow me anymore or you'll be sorry!" I barked at his prone form, then turned around to go back to my car.

I was almost there before I realized that an audience had gathered from the nearby parking lot at Solar Combines. Byron emerged from a group near the right fender of my car with an indescribable look on his face.

"What are you doing here?" I snapped, still crazed from adrenaline, and a little embarrassed that I'd made a spectacle of myself. Great. A squad car too, I noticed, looking past Byron's shoulder.

"I was on my way to lunch," he said, eyes wide. Shock, no doubt. "What happened?"

I looked over at the guy stirring around on the ground, blood leaking out between the fingers that covered his face. The police officer told me to stand still and went over to help him.

"The creep kept following me, almost rear-ended me," I explained. "I got out when the light was red and told him to stop."

"Jesse," Byron seemed to be having trouble processing.

"What?" It seemed plain enough to me. "You got a cigarette?" I asked a guy standing by the curb who handed me one without a word. "Thanks. Got a light?"

"You don't smoke," Byron looked disgusted now.

The little old man who'd handed me the Marlboro was ready with a lighter, so I joined him with Byron following behind.

The uniform stood beside the Subaru guy, talking and pointing at me. I saw him shake his head.

"I told you you don't smoke," Byron said when I started coughing.

"Bite me, Byron," I was in no mood.

"Could I see your license, please?" the uniform walked over to me as the Subaru guy got in his truck.

"Hey! Is he leaving?" I asked, ignoring his request.

"He's not pressing charges," Officer Holt told me. I read his name on his shirt.

"Unh! *He's* not pressing charges? You're letting him go?" A travesty, that's what it was.

Byron put a hand on my arm like he was afraid I'd hit this guy too. I do have some restraint.

"Your license, please," the uniform insisted. Where's Cordell Walker when you need him?

With an exaggerated sigh, I walked over and reached through the open door of the car for my purse.

"Here," I handed it to him, making sure he knew just how annoyed I was by the whole thing. "I didn't do anything wrong!"

"Why don't you tell me what happened?" Holt used his practiced, patronizing tone as he handed the license back to me.

"The guy's been following me all over town, then he almost rammed into my car. Look at that car," I pointed to my beloved Taurus. "Not a scratch in three years! Now this guy's gonna ruin that? I can't afford to buy a new car!"

"Yes ma'am," Holt said, looking helplessly over my shoulder at Byron.

"All I did was get out of my car and tell the guy to stop following me! Is it my fault he got out and grabbed me on the arm? I'd have never touched him if he didn't grab me! He should have kept his nose out of my way and his hands to himself, that's what he should have done."

"All right, calm down," Holt said, looking around for reinforcement, no doubt.

"Is that what he told you?" Byron asked the officer, ignoring me completely.

"Pretty close," Holt said, turning back to us. "Although he said he wasn't following her." This time, his eyes zeroed in on me, examining me carefully.

"Like hell he wasn't!" I snapped. "Look at me! I was defending myself and my property. You don't think I pick guys at random on the street and just punch them out for fun, do you?" Maybe he did. Maybe I should.

"Hey! I know you!" Another uniform joined us. Barker, his name tag said. "You're the lady with the dead guy in your tub!"

I rolled my eyes. One crisis at a time, please.

Holt's head snapped up like he'd been jerked on a string. "Dead guy?" he asked.

"Yeah, you know – the dead guy in the bathtub. It was at her house." Barker cocked his head my way, then both men looked me over carefully.

I shrugged. "I didn't do it."

"Maybe I better take you in," Holt said, shoving his notepad in his shirt pocket.

"Look, Holt," Byron stepped up now. "We're private investigators. I came from the Houston PD. If you'll check with Detective Ferguson, he'll explain it all to you."

"Well, there are no warrants out," he wavered.

"Our office is just down the street here," Byron pointed that way. "I'm sure you can call and we'll come in if we need to."

I've gotta give him credit, he can be charming when he needs to be so I kept my mouth shut.

Taking a cue from Barker, Holt nodded. "All right. But ma'am, next time you think someone's following you, it's probably best not to get out of your car."

Best for who? Byron pinched my arm. "Yes, officer."

"Can you drive back to the office?" Byron asked when they left us alone.

"There's nothing wrong with me. Of course I can drive." I jerked my arm out of his hand. What was with him, anyway?

"I'll meet you there," was all he said.

I was tempted to get in the car and just keep going, but I didn't.

"Hi," I barked at Bernice when I reached the office.

"What's wrong with you?" she looked up in surprise.

"Him," I pointed at the door, knowing he'd burst through there any second.

I was right and Bernice was smart enough to leave it alone. To my amazement, he sauntered in like he'd been for a walk in the park and sat down at his desk. Oh sure. He's the calm, cool voice of reason and I'm the ditzy broad with PMS. I wiggled around in my chair and stared at my monitor while the computer booted up.

When she thought it was safe, Bernice shuffled over to my desk with a stack of messages and a note. "I thought you might want that," she pointed to a newspaper clip on top.

"Thanks," I mumbled, wishing we had separate offices. "Oh no!"

It was a funeral announcement for Gary Greaves. My watch told me I was too late for the funeral, but if I hurried, I might just make the graveside service. I looked down at the black jeans and sweater I had on. Black is for funerals, right? My olive green blazer was still hanging on the coat tree where I left it last week. It would have to do.

"Where you going?" Byron asked when I grabbed my jacket and headed for the door.

Would it be too rude not to answer? There's no way I didn't hear him in this tiny room.

"Gary Greaves' funeral." I couldn't hear his answer because the door slammed behind me.

I made it to the car before he hit the door.

"What?" I groaned, turning to face him with my hands on my hips.

"I'm going with you," he said. Sternly.

I guess he was. I unlocked the door so he could get in. At least he was armed, just in case.

"Don't get in my way," I mumbled.

"What's eating you, anyway?" he asked soberly once we were on the freeway.

"I'm fine," I lied, looking at him with my most convincing expression. It must have worked; he didn't say anything else.

The service was being held at Laureland, an old cemetery in Oak Cliff. Not the best part of Dallas, but I heard it was nice once. Fortunately, today, it was close, too. Just a ten-minute drive up I-35 and Laureland Exit loomed up ahead. Midday traffic was mild and I turned into the cemetery gates with little interference. A green tent and a handful of cars and trucks marked the location and I parked my car just down the hill.

"What are we doing here?" Byron asked when we got out of the car, following me up the path.

The canvas was really only a tent shaped awning that blocked the sun but it was plenty big enough to hold the folks who came to offer their goodbyes. Not a real popular guy, Greaves. Instead of joining them in that intimate space, I lingered beside a large tree near the road.

"The guy that was following me was driving the truck Gary Greaves got in the first time I saw him," I admitted. He was my partner after all.

"Why didn't you tell me that before now?" he hissed, keeping his voice low.

Sigh. "It didn't come up."

He gave me disbelief.

"I didn't think of it until I saw the truck again today." I scanned the group, but it was hard to see anything from the back. Not like I could go around behind the casket or anything so I could see their faces. They'd have to get up to leave sometime. Then I could look around.

"Jesse, we need to talk," he said, leaning beside me.

"The last guy who told me that hit the pavement," I said without taking my eyes off the group.

"Yeah, well I'm not him."

The tone in his voice compelled me to look up. He was right. I nodded. I could picture myself mad enough to try it, but somehow, I couldn't visualize him going down. Better not try it.

When I looked back toward the tent, the crowd was dispersing. I say crowd. Maybe twenty people. The maid was there. A couple of guys with their companions. The guy with the bloody nose wasn't there. And that looked like – it was – Marcus Brant! There was a woman beside him and a little girl.

"Aw, man!" I took off for my car at a dead run with Byron close behind. Reaching through the window, I grabbed the folder stuffed in the pocket of the door and wrestled out a computer printout of Melinda Gafford, holding it up for him to see. "It's her!"

"Who?" he asked. "That little girl is with…"

I was already running back up the hill.

"Excuse me!" I stopped the woman who'd just put the girl in the back seat of an Expedition. Texas has fancy trucks. Marcus Brant was nowhere in sight.

"Yes?" she offered a soft smile, suitable for the occasion.

"Are you Mrs. Brant, by chance?" I asked, trying to speak pleasantly without gasping for breath.

"Yes, I am. I don't believe I know you," she said with a question in her voice.

"No, ma'am. I'm Jesse Morgan and I'm a private investigator." Hastily, I fished a card out of my pocket and handed it to her.

"Oh, dear! That's where they found Gary," her voice trailed off and she looked confused. Emily Post never covered this particular issue.

"Yes, ma'am," I nodded. No need to finish that sentence. "Is this your child?" I nodded at the girl in the back seat.

An interesting look crossed Mrs. Brant's face just for a second before the plastic mask snapped back in place. "Why do you ask?"

Popular question, that one.

I took the photo from Byron's hand and showed it to her. This time, I recognized the look. It was panic and it didn't go away.

"I was hired to find this child. Her name is Melinda Gafford." It was only partially a fib.

"Her *name* is Charlotte Brant and I don't have anything else to say to you!" She jerked open the door and slid inside before I could think of anything else. I believe she'd have run over my feet in her hurry to leave if I hadn't moved.

Byron bent over and picked up the picture from the ground where she'd dropped it. "Interesting."

"Yeah."

On the way back to the office, I pulled off the freeway and into the parking lot of El Chico's. My head was spinning and my stomach was rumbling. Byron followed me inside. I guess he didn't want to wait in the car. I didn't even try to talk until I had a basket of chips and salsa and a Marguerita in my hand.

"Was it really her?" I asked him, wondering if I was hallucinating, wanting so badly for something to make sense.

"Yep," he said. "It was. What do you make of that?"

I shook my head. Don't know. "You're the expert. What do you think?"

"I think," he spoke slowly and deliberately, "we better figure something out before someone else gets hurt."

"Even if we're not getting paid?" I asked, munching chips like I was starving.

"You're sure that was the same truck?" he asked.

I nodded.

"Well, then, we can run the plates on the truck and see where that goes," he offered.

"Did you get the plates?"

"No, but I can get the number from the PD. And then, I think you better start back-tracing the lady who started all this."

"Beverly Gafford?"

He nodded, moving aside when the waitress delivered our plates.

"When all else fails, go back to the beginning and see where you took a wrong turn."

I thought about it while I ate my chicken fajitas. Food mellows me. He was right, I needed to stay objective.

"I'm glad you're here," I admitted, finally.

"It's not what I expected, but I think I am too."

That's probably the most honest thing he'd ever said to me. Maybe I'd been too hasty earlier.

"Ya think?" I grinned at him. "Then you must be crazier than you look."

He laughed at that and I felt a lot better. I really missed Joey. He was great help when I had computer trouble, but if I was going to find dead guys in my bathtub, Byron was definitely the better choice.

CHAPTER SIX

I'm sure there's something to be said for time alone, I'm just not sure it's worth much. Over the next few days, I had time to wash my hair. Time to watch old reruns on Nick at Nite. Time for Elvis, not that he cared. But after three straight days of computer work that led me down one bunny trail after another, and three straight nights of TV dinners, I was ready not to be alone.

Byron was very helpful in the office. Polite. Disgustingly so. After our lunch the other day, I thought things would be better, and I suppose they were, compared to me being mad as hell and ready to punch him out and die. But he was acting different, distant, like he was afraid to get too close to me or he might catch something. Desperate times call for desperate measures.

My car goes on autopilot once I take a turn on Pleasant Run and head for home. Actually, so does my brain. It doesn't pay to think too much. If I did, I wouldn't be headed for home. Don't get me wrong. My parents are good people. They didn't lock me in the basement or beat me up every weekend. They just occupy a reality that exists on a different plane.

Mom and Dad still live in the same house out on Joe Wilson Road, somewhere in the unclaimed vicinity that connects Duncanville, DeSoto, and Cedar Hill. All three suburbs have grown to the point where they run right into Dallas, but their neighborhood is oddly unchanged. The houses are still old, the paint still peels, the trees are still enormous, blanketing out the sky in some spots. Joey's parents still live two streets over. The only real difference is that most of the owners are getting so old they just leave the Christmas lights out all year.

Home, I sighed, getting out of the car. I had to park on the street because my Dad's driveway is full of boat. He never uses it anymore, but don't tell him he should sell it. That's the only thing that makes him loud anymore. I thought maybe he'd enjoy Joe Pool Lake just down the road a ways, but since they didn't build it until the 70s, to him it's not a real lake.

"Jesse!"

How does my mother get to the door before I'm halfway up the sidewalk? Must be watching from the kitchen window again. The title "Private Spies" is far better suited to Mom than to me.

"Hi Mom," I put on my happy-to-see-you-Mom face. Why is it the feeling of desperation that drives me to go home goes away immediately upon arrival?

"You'll stay for dinner, right? Oh," her face fell.

My mother carries a thinner picture of me in her imagination than what she sees in real life.

"I have pot roast and potatoes and gravy." She looked me up and down the way only a mother can do, no doubt wondering if temporary anorexia would be a bad thing. "Well, that's all right. We can go light on the potatoes." She nodded and smiled. Thank God that's settled.

"Need any help?" I followed her into the kitchen and stepped back in time twenty years. Same avocado green appliances. Same yellow wallpaper with little vegetables all over it. Some things never change but there's a certain comfort in sameness. Besides, it never smells this good at my house.

"No, no, it's better if I do this," she smiled again.

Silly me. I forgot I can't do anything right. Wouldn't want to ruin dinner on my first visit home in two months.

"Why don't you go in the den and talk to your Dad?" she suggested, protecting the oven from me as I passed by.

Why don't I? I wandered down the hall and around the corner into the remodeled garage. God forbid Dad should ever prop his feet in the living room.

"Hi Dad," I offered, assuming he was in the recliner behind that wall of newspaper.

"Mmph," he grunted, then pulled the paper down far enough for me to see his eyes. "Jessemmmm."

There's no M on the end of my name. I don't know why he always does that, but he has as far back as I can remember.

"How you doing?" It was a script I knew by heart after all these years.

"Unh," he grunted again. Tim the Tool man should be paying him royalties. "And you?"

"Good, Dad," I smiled at the newspaper.

Maybe I really should get therapy. I sat on the couch staring at the blank screen of his huge TV and wondering what possessed me to come here in the first place. At least if I waited until my sister was here I'd have someone to talk to.

"Dad?"

"Hmm?"

"There was a dead guy in my bathtub last week." That should get his attention.

"That's...," his head jerked up before he said "nice, dear." "What?"

Wow. Complete, undivided attention.

"There was a dead guy in my bathtub last week," I repeated it slowly.

"What'd you do that for?" He lowered the paper so he could examine me carefully through narrowed eyes.

"No, Dad," I closed my eyes and shook my head.

My parents aren't really crazy. Just...I don't know what they are.

"I didn't do it. Some guy came in my house and put a dead guy in my bathtub." Man, it sounds worse when you try to explain it out loud.

"I don't understand," he looked at me intently and I looked back.

He's older. Most of his hair is gone and his thick glasses ride a huge beak of a nose. Thank God none of us inherited that feature. Aside from that, he's pretty scrawny. Wiry, he calls it. I think I'm bigger than he is now and, contrary to Mom's opinion, I'm not that big. He's shrinking.

"It's no big deal, Dad. I don't know why I even said that," I smiled a limp little smile. It was enough.

"Well, if you're sure," he said, going back to his paper.

I got up and went back to the kitchen just as Mom called for us.

"Sit there, in your usual place," she pointed to a chair on the end of the table. Even though my sister and I moved out years ago, she insists on eating at the big dining room table that seats six. She was at the head, I'm sure that's significant somehow, and Dad sat beside her. She'd already made me a plate, light on the potatoes and gravy. Probably measured it. "So how are you doing?"

"I'm fine, Mom," I smiled.

When I thought about it, I realized it was true. All things are relative. After all, I could still be living here.

Mom launched into a grocery list of grandkids and family happenings while we ate. True to form, she whisked our plates away as soon as we lifted the last forkful, then eyed me carefully before cutting a sliver of apple pie. It would be rude not to offer me any and my Mom would never do anything rude. One of the things I like best about these visits is that I hardly have to talk. She chattered away for an hour and a half, filling my mind with all the accomplishments of my sister and her husband and their children and the neighbors and anything else I might be remotely interested in. When she started in on the neighbor's Chihuahua, I knew the time had come. I broke out the goodbye script, gave them both the traditional kiss on the cheek, and walked slowly to my car. No running. She'd watch out the window until my lights disappeared into the night.

Whew, don't I feel better now? Honestly, I do. It's reassuring to know that some things never change, and for the last two hours, I didn't have to think about Byron or wrestle with the non-case that occupied most of my waking hours. Not a bad trade, all things considered.

When I got home, I found a neatly wrapped package on my porch and my heart skipped a beat. Byron decided to make up and left me a gift! How's that for conclusion jumping? I'm not obsessing. I scurried inside and sat the box on the table, searching the kitchen for a knife to cut through the tape.

"Look, Elvis," I said when he joined me there, sniffing and licking his lips. That should have been a clue for the master detective. "Look, it's a................ ewwwwww. Oh my God! It's a..."

I dropped the knife on the floor and jumped away from the table, leaving Elvis. Unfortunately, he wasn't nearly as repulsed as I was. He thought I'd brought a treat for dinner.

"Elvis!" I reached out and grabbed him. Stupid cat! He thought it was food. My "gift" was a dead duck, complete with feathers and a noose around its wobbly neck. Staring at it and making low, moaning noises didn't make it go away. Neither did closing my eyes real tight then opening them again. When Elvis finally scratched my arm trying to get back to his treasure, I knew it was time to act.

"No!" I told him sternly, snatching the box up and running down the hall. "There!" I tossed it in the hall bathroom and slammed the door while he watched, glaring at me from the floor. "Tough!"

A dead duck. A dead guy in my bathtub and now, a dead duck on my porch. This was getting incredibly monotonous. Beer would be good. Lots of beer.

Mechanically, I walked into the kitchen and opened a bottle, sucking a nice long drink that only choked me a little. Then I picked up the phone. Once, when I thought maybe Byron and I would...you know... I programmed him into my speed dial. I was glad right then. Even more glad when he answered the phone since his voice drowned out the strange quacking sound I kept hearing in my mind.

"Byron?" My voice sounded like my mother's, an octave too high and syrupy. Not my normal voice. "Could you come over here for just a minute?"

"Jesse? Is that you?" Guess my voice sounded funny to him too.

"Byron?" I tried again, but my voice still had that strange, octave above normal sound that only dead things in my house can produce. At least so far. "Could you come over..."

"Jesse! What's wrong?" Damn, he sounds so normal. Why can't I do that?

"There's a dead duck in my bathroom and Elvis wants to eat it," I said, clearing my throat and coming back into the semi-normal range.

"What?" he thundered. "Jesse, you mean somebody came in the window again?"

"Oh, man! Hold on!"

I dropped the phone where I stood and ran for the bathroom. Mine, this time. I never thought to check. Throwing open the door, I stared first at the window, then skulked in and pulled back the shower curtain, just a little bit. Enough to see there was nothing dead there.

When I got back to the phone I heard him yelling.

"No," I panted. "Not in the window." I knew the package was on the front porch, but one can never be too sure.

"Jesse, dammit, would you please tell me what's going on?"

I smiled. It's the first time I'd ever heard him out of control like that. I liked it. It's not just me.

"Okay. I went to my mother's for dinner," I started.

"No, not that!" he yelled again.

"Byron, don't yell at me," I reasoned, grateful my smug expression wouldn't show over the phone. "When I came home there was a box on my porch. It had a dead duck in it. A feathery one. With a noose."

I glanced down the hall toward the bathroom door, just in case.

Silence.

"I'll be right there. Don't touch anything." He hung up.

"Okay," I said to no one. Like I was going to play with it. I touched my beer.

When he got there, he barged right in and found me sitting on the couch, beer in hand. Guess I forgot to lock the door.

"Why isn't this door locked?"

Figures. I shrugged.

"Where is it?" He seemed calmer now, but his eyes looked a little buzzed, darting around.

"The duck?"

He gave me the "get serious" look.

I was serious. I thought he meant beer. He looked like he could use one.

"In the hall bathroom so Elvis can't eat it," I explained.

Byron moves pretty fast sometimes.

"Do you have to put it on the table?" I asked when he brought it in and plopped it down right where I opened it. He used a towel to carry it, probably so he wouldn't get fingerprints on it. I should've thought of that, huh?

"Got a better idea?"

"Not right off hand, no."

He looked at me like I'd done something.

"Hey, don't look at me like that!" I felt some of the earlier anger creep back in.

Byron turned and carried his phone into the kitchen. I heard the refrigerator door open, but couldn't hear what he said.

"They'll be right here," he snapped, coming out of the kitchen with a beer in hand and shoving his phone in his pocket.

"Who?"

"The cops, who do you think?" he sank down beside me on the couch.

"Well, hey. Do I know how to throw a party, or what?"

"This is not good, you know that," he said, ignoring my weak attempt at humor.

I laughed. "No?"

He didn't see the humor in that, either.

"Maybe you shouldn't stay here," he said, obviously not talking to me.

Just in case, I said, "I'm not going anywhere if that's what you're thinking."

The only where I had was my parents and I couldn't risk that. I couldn't even escape her in my own bed. What if I morphed into a clone of my mom overnight?

"Jesse," uh oh. Mr. Persuasive. "This is getting way out of hand."

"Oka-ay," I shrugged. "Exactly what might I have done differently so I didn't cause all this?"

He sighed loudly. "I never said you caused all this."

"It does just keep coming back here, though, doesn't it? Did you get any dead things at your house yet?"

Our conversation was interrupted by a loud knock at the door. Byron glared at me as he opened it and Officer Barker stood there, grinning. "What is it this time?"

Byron still wasn't laughing. He picked up the box and shoved it at Barker. "This was on her porch when she came home tonight."

"No shit," Barker said, peering into the box.

Must be a good phrase for situations like this. I made a mental note to read my thesaurus before bed.

"Who's it from?" he looked at me.

I laughed again. "Gee, who *could* it be from? Maybe the guy in the Subaru?"

Barker lost his sense of humor then. "Why do you say that? What do you know about that guy?"

I sighed. "I don't know that guy. But it didn't come from my mother. She'd have plucked it and cooked it. It didn't come from him," I nodded at Byron, who glared at me from the end of the couch, "and I'm assuming it didn't come from you, did it?"

"Maybe you two better tell me everything you know," Barker sat the box down and took a seat in my only single chair.

Everything I know. Surely that's an overgeneralization.

Byron raised his hands. "Look. We don't really know anything. We got a case to look for a guy named Lawrence Gafford. But the picture the ex wife sent didn't match what we found on the driver's license. When we traced the address, we found Gary Greaves, who was the man in the picture she'd told us was Gafford."

Barker already looked confused, so I kept quiet.

"Right after we figured that out, he turned up here. Dead."

"In the bathtub," Barker added. As if I'd forget.

"And I thought someone was following me," I chimed in, "and then I remembered that the Subaru was the same truck I saw Gary Greaves get into."

"Before he was dead," Barker nodded. Duh.

"Then I came home and found the duck."

Both men sat silent like statues, looking at me, then at each other, and I had a sudden, almost uncontrollable urge to giggle. I hate giggling. I managed to bite my lips and hold it down to a small smile, but I didn't know how long that would last. It must have been the beer. I set my beer on the table beside the couch.

"All right," Barker said, getting to his feet and picking up the box, still wearing gloves he put on after he arrived. "I'll take this in and we'll see if we can get any prints or anything. I suppose you've both handled it."

"Byron used a towel, but I touched it," I offered. "And my cat," I added, making his eyebrows shoot up. "He thought it was for him," I explained. "He didn't touch the duck though. I put it in the bathroom. He just sniffed the box."

"Yeah." Poor Barker. "I'll be in touch."

I got up to let him out, then fetched another beer from the refrigerator. "Want one?" I called to Byron.

He did.

I opened them both, then joined him on the couch again. "Well, that was festive, wasn't it?"

"You beat everything, you know that?" It sounded like a joke, but his eyes were dead serious.

"What?" I was tired and confused and scared and it probably wasn't the best time, but there you go.

Guess he knew it wasn't a good time, because he got up, shaking his head. "You all right to stay here by yourself?"

"I'm not by myself," I answered, lifting my chin, "Elvis is still here."

"Okay," he said, moving toward the door. "Call me if you need me."

Right.

CHAPTER SEVEN

"That's another one!" I chirped, shoving myself away from the desk after pressing the send button on my computer keyboard.

"Happily ever after?" Bernice asked, looking up from a stack of bills.

"Of the best variety," I said, strolling over to the mini-frig to rescue a Pepsi. "She wanted to find her college sweetheart since her hubby died last year. Only took me a day to find him, but it took her another month to get up the nerve to call him. Turns out he's widowed too and she just sent me an email to tell me they had their first date last night and it was a smashing success, to use her words."

I wandered over and looked out the front blinds, basking in the afterglow of a case solved. I figured I better take it wherever I could get it.

"Ain't love grand," Bernice said, her mind already on other things.

"I wouldn't know," I told the blinds. "Bernice?" I turned her way, "is there anything wrong with me?" Her eyebrows disappeared again.

"Wrong with you? Like what?"

"Do I look funny or something?" I didn't think so, but it never hurts to check these things out.

Bernice's eyes rolled around and she snorted. Bernice does that. "I should look like you!"

Good point.

"What you worried about?" she asked in a tone that was a close to motherly as she'd likely ever get.

"I don't know," I sighed, going back to my desk. "Sometimes I just wonder. I meet a lot of men. How come I never seem to click with any of them?"

"I've seen plenty of sparks flying around here lately," she offered in a tone that sounded suspiciously like "I know something I won't tell."

"Oh, yeah, right. I said 'click' not clash."

She sent me a smile that matched the tone. "We'll see."

It had been three days since the dead duck incident and Byron had spent more hours out of the office than in. I hardly knew the guy, so I can't really say I missed him. But I did.

The pile of open folders on my desk had dwindled down to just a couple. If Byron wasn't going to promote the business, maybe I better. With a serious lack of enthusiasm, I signed back on to the Internet and sat staring at the screen, waiting for it to load, when the front door opened and Barker walked in.

"Can I help you?" Bernice asked.

"I'm here to see Miss Morgan," he smiled, first at her, then at me.

Grinning cops look suspicious. Bernice gave him the once over, then looked over her shoulder at me and winked. Guess he passed her test.

"Hey, Barker! Take a load off," I waved at the chair beside my desk.

With his hat in hand, he crossed the room in three strides and sat down. He was kinda cute, now that I think of it. You know, dark hair, dark eyes, sharp jaw, tight buns. All the important elements. I didn't realize I was staring until he shifted uncomfortably in his seat.

"Tell me, Barker, how do you guys keep from smelling bad when you're outside in the heat all day?"

Bernice made a whooping noise she tried to pass off as a cough, then shot a warning glare at me from behind him. I did it again, didn't I? Sometimes my thoughts just jump out of my mouth before I can stop them.

Barker looked at me, wide eyed, and said, "Uh."

"Never mind," I shrugged and tried to pretend like I hadn't said it. "So what brings you by?"

"Well," he cocked his head to one side and looked suddenly shy. "A couple of things."

Now Bernice was playing charades behind his back, making faces and waving her arms. Very distracting.

"Did you get some news about the duck?" I asked before Bernice drowned us out with flapping noises.

"Oh yeah," he shifted into cop mode. "Got the report back this morning, but they didn't find any prints on it but yours." He looked over at the other desk like he might find Byron there. "On the box," he added.

Like I thought he meant the duck.

"Well, that's not good," I said, frowning.

"No, but it's kinda what I expected," he said. "You don't have any idea who might have sent it?"

I shook my head then Bernice caught my eye. She was making kissee faces. "Barker," I stood up, choking back a cheesy grin. "Let's go get some lunch, want to?"

Bernice smiled and sat down like her job was done.

"Sure," Barker smiled too. Probably not for the same reason.

I was on a roll.

"You're not married or anything, are you?" Bernice asked as he walked past her desk to the door.

"No, ma'am," he looked shocked.

"Just checking," she mumbled after I gave her one of those 'watch it!' looks.

"I'll drive," Barker said outside when I walked toward my car.

"Okay," I shrugged. Wonder why he didn't want to ride with me? "Can I play with the siren?" I grinned to let him know I was kidding.

He seemed relieved.

Cheddar's isn't far from the office so we went there. As usual around lunchtime, it was crowded, but when the hostess saw him, she got us a table right away. That uniform business might not be a bad idea. I tucked it away to think about later.

"What's your front name, Barker?" I asked after we were seated.

"Jeff," he said, adjusting his holster so he didn't sit on it.

"Jeff," I nodded. "Nice name." Jeff and Jesse. No. "What's your middle name?"

A lot of people raise their eyebrows when they talk to me. He did, too.

"Jeffrey Alvin Barker," he said, shrugging. I know. The things our parents do.

"Barker's not a bad name," I smiled. "You can call me Jesse, you know."

He smiled. "So, I was wondering, Jesse. Are you… seeing anyone?"

No wonder he looked so nervous. Hard question.

"No," I shook my head emphatically. "I'm not." Don't be too eager.

"Hmmm," he said, suddenly incredibly interested in his menu. "I thought maybe you and your partner…"

"No!" Oops. Too loud. "I mean, no. We're just friends." Hardly that, but it seemed like the right thing to say.

When the waitress came to take our order, she spent a lot more time looking at Barker than at me. It made me think. Maybe Prince Charming drives a squad car these days.

"I keep a bottle of cologne in the glove box," Barker told me when the waitress was gone.

"Huh?"

"Your question earlier," he grinned.

After that, everything seemed to relax. He didn't even laugh when the cherry tomato shot out of my salad and onto the floor. Well, not out loud.

We were like old friends, laughing and talking, by the time we got back to the office. I stood in the parking lot, waving as he drove off in his squad car.

"Well?" Bernice asked the instant I walked through the door.

I smiled.

"Ooohhh!" She jumped up and started clapping her hands together.

"We're going to the Crystal Palace tonight," I admitted, nodding my head.

Is that cool, or what? The Crystal Palace is a steak house and country dance club. The south side's version of elegant dining and night life. All the real fancy places are on the north side of town.

"Oh!" she made a clicking noise with her tongue and waved a hand at me. "Then you've gotta go shopping, girlfriend!"

"Shopping? What's wrong with what I have?" I despise shopping.

"No, no, no! New beau, new clothes! It's a rule!"

"Who's got a new beau?" Byron snuck in the door behind me.

"Jesse does," Bernice brought out her sing song voice.

"Oh really?" There go the eyebrows again. He sauntered casually over to his desk and perched on the corner. "Who might that be?"

"Auhhhhh, it's no big deal," I tried to shrug it off, walking a wide berth around his swinging legs on the way to my chair. "Barker's taking me to the Crystal Palace tonight, that's all."

"Hmmmm," was all he said.

I turned to my computer, determined to lose myself in there so I wouldn't feel uncomfortable. Since he didn't try to stop me, I guess I didn't need to worry.

"Hey! Look at this!" I said, half an hour later.

"Whatcha got?" he asked without looking up.

"Beverly Gafford's dead," I swiveled my chair around so I could look at him.

"Dead?" he stopped what he was doing and looked up at me.

"Yeah," I scanned the rest of the email while he got up and walked my way. "Worse, she's been dead for six years." I looked up at him, perching on my desk now.

"Shit. Then who the hell hired you?" he asked.

"Guess that's the next question. I don't know." I tried to think but my head was fuzzed.

"Where'd you get that?" he nodded at the screen.

"County Courthouse in Sapulpa, Oklahoma," I answered. "When I tried to trace the address, I came across an old forwarding order and followed it there. The clerk couldn't find the records at first, now she sent me this," I pointed at the screen.

Byron leaned over so he could scan the text. "Death certificate. That pretty much settles it, doesn't it?"

I sighed and leaned back in my chair. "Somebody who's not Beverly Gafford hired me to find a guy who's not Lawrence Gafford, but in reality was Gary Greaves, who turned up dead in my bathtub."

"Don't forget – she also wanted you to find her daughter Melinda Gafford who turned out to be Charlotte Brant," he said.

"Wait a minute!" my chair crashed to the floor. "Bernice! Her credit card cleared, right?"

Even I get an occasional burst of inspiration. Blind squirrels and all that.

"No, dearie," Bernice shook her head. "We got a money order from FedEx."

I sighed. So much for inspiration.

"No, that's still good," Byron said, reading my mind again. "You still have the envelope?" he turned to Bernice.

"Yes, sir," she got up and shuffled over to the file cabinet, extracting the FedEx envelope from the file. Bernice is a whiz. I'd have thrown it away. But did she have to call him sir?

Byron took it from her and sat back down at his desk, tapping away on the keyboard immediately.

"What can you do?" I couldn't help asking.

"Track the sender, of course," he said, typing furiously.

Of course. I sat back down at my desk, but couldn't seem to concentrate on anything. Three o'clock, my watch said.

"I think I'll call it a day," I said, gathering my papers and stacking them in the in box.

Byron looked up at me. "Have a good time tonight," he said seriously.

"Yeah," I smiled. Why didn't I feel like smiling?

Unfortunately, I figured it out on the way home. That made me feel even worse. Barker wasn't Byron! Damn. How could I be so hung up on a guy with a name like Byron? I argued with myself about it all through my shower. Even yelled at myself about it while I was blow drying my hair. It got so bad, Elvis left the room. I hate when he does that. It's harder to convince myself I'm not talking to myself.

"There you are, you traitor," I told Elvis, who came out of hiding once he heard the can opener and jumped up on the kitchen counter, waiting impatiently. "You've been no help at all."

I indulged in a beer since it was obvious I'd never drive Barker anywhere and sat down on the couch, dressed and ready half an hour before he was due to pick me up. In an effort to feel festive, I'd wrestled a slinky black top out of the back of my closet. Caroline bought it for me for my birthday once. Honestly, it didn't look half bad once I put it on. It was some kind of slippery material that stretched and the low neckline made it look like I even had cleavage. Growing up with a sister who wore 34Ds was no picnic for a 36B. Life can be harsh.

Anyway, the blouse had tiny threads of metallic colors, all kinds. Blue, red, gold, purple. They twinkled in the light. I tucked it into my best pair of black jeans, complete with a fancy belt buckle, and topped it off with my red power blazer. My favorite snakeskin boots were great for dancing if you like that sort of thing. Hey. It's the best I can do on short notice.

With a sigh, I laid my head back against the wall. Elvis must have heard because he leapt down from the counter and curled up beside me on the couch. He hardly ever does that.

"There's only one thing wrong with Barker, Elvis," I stroked his head. "You know what that is? He's not Byron." Oh God. It sounds so much worse out loud. Elvis didn't care. He purred and licked his paws and smelled of fish. "Here goes nothing," I gave Elvis one last pat when there was a knock at the door.

Barker was even more handsome in a black suit with his boots on. The way a smile lit his face and his eyes lingered on my front, I guess I didn't look too bad, either.

"Ready?"

I smiled and nodded, locking the door behind me. Life's a dance, right?

I hadn't been to the Crystal Palace in a long, long time. I forgot how incredibly loud it is. A real party atmosphere. Barker wangled a corner table and we were seated right away. Country music played in the background, and the smell of sizzling sirloin filled the air. My mind wandered back to the evening at Fago de Chao's with Byron and dropped a funk on my mood. I did my damnedest to act charming and carefree anyway.

Things were going pretty well, I thought. We ate salad, then steaks and baked potatoes. Thank God my mother didn't see what I ate. Barker did most of the talking, telling me about his childhood in Brownsville and his college years at Sam Houston State. He's a really nice guy, Barker.

"What?" My mind wandered and I didn't hear what he said. I'm a lousy date. That's what's wrong with me. It's not how I look, it's how I am.

"You don't really want to be here, do you?" he said quietly with a kind of sad look on his face.

Ohhhhhhh, I felt like shit. "I'm sorry, Barker."

"What is it?" he watched me closely. "Your partner?"

I made a face and covered my eyes with one hand.

"I'm insane." I mumbled.

He laughed for the first time that night. "I don't think so, Jesse."

"What do you know?" I grumbled.

"I have three sisters," he smiled.

"Bummer," I said.

"Sometimes, yeah."

"What makes you think it's Byron?" I asked suddenly, wondering how I could be so obvious.

"That's easy," he said, relaxing back against his seat. "The way he looks at you."

"Huh?" I never expected that.

He rolled his eyes. "Don't tell me you haven't noticed."

I shrugged. Some detective I am.

"How come you're being so nice about this?" I asked when I dared look at him again.

"I don't want you mad at me like that guy in the Subaru," he joked.

As if.

I smiled. "Not likely."

He sighed. "I got married when I was barely twenty," he said. "I really didn't want to, but she tried so hard to make me happy." His eyes got a faraway look. "Worst six years of my life," he shook his head like it would scatter the memories. "I wouldn't wish that on anyone. I figure if it works, it works. If it don't, move on."

"Sounds good," I played with the ice left in my glass and wondered where that waitress wandered off to. "But what do you do...no," I caught my foot before it went all the way in my mouth that time.

"Go ahead," he urged.

"No," I shook my head.

"Jesse," he leaned over the table and talked softly. "Maybe you and I aren't destined to be Romeo and Juliet, but that doesn't mean we can't be friends, does it?"

"I don't want to do something rude," I said, squirming like a naughty schoolgirl.

"Hey! I collected a dead duck from your house. Surely you can talk to me about anything." His grin was persuasive.

"Okay," I leaned forward, too. "Why does it have to be so damn hard? I mean, you meet this guy and you start getting the feeling that he likes you. A lot. And you think you might like him that way, too. Then all of a sudden, he's like a million miles away. All polite and everything." I shut up. It sounded like a conversation I had in junior high.

"I don't know, but don't think it's any easier on this end," he grinned.

I thought about that for a minute. I could believe that if I tried hard.

"Hey, Barker?"

He waited.

"You wanna dance?"

"I thought you'd never ask," he teased and whisked me away to the dance floor.

A great dancer I'm not, but then again, neither was he. Still, it was a relief to just let go and have a good time. Not bad to know the feel of a man's arm around my waist again, either. It had definitely been too long.

When he deposited me on my front doorstep a couple of hours later, it was like stepping down off a magic carpet that had transported me briefly to a willowy, soft cloud where people were real, and truth was truth and happily ever after was only a cloud step away.

Looking up into his face in the not so romantic glow of my yellow bug light, I felt myself sinking into a pair of warm, gray eyes and wondering if those strong, full lips tasted as good as they looked. Maybe I wrote him off too soon. We're both grown, right?

"I really had a good time," he told me, speaking in a velvety soft voice that gave me a chill.

"Me too." Did I dare ask him in?

That question was answered by the crunch of gravel as Byron's Cobra pulled up beside my front curb.

"Unh!" I was flabbergasted. What could he possibly be doing here at midnight?

"I guess I better go," Barker said, winking at me and touching my cheek with one finger. No more magic tonight.

"I'll see you later," I tried to smile, but inside I was seething. I almost got it right and he had to show up at the worst possible moment!

I watched as Barker got in his car and pulled away while Byron got out, whistling, and headed across the grass.

"What are you doing here?" I'm sure my annoyance was evident.

"Did I come at a bad time?" he asked seriously, joining me on the porch.

Brother.

I put the key in the lock and he followed me inside. Elvis gave me a sleepy look with one eye, then it slowly closed again.

"So, are you going to tell me?" I waited until he sat down, then perched on the other end of the couch.

Getting off a magic carpet ride can be quite a let down. Shadows played across his eyes and for the first time since I met him, I saw a hint of uncertainty beneath the arrogant expression.

"I just had a funny feeling," he spoke slowly. "I didn't want to ignore it, then find out later that something was wrong. I'll just check the windows and go."

That took the wind out of my sails. I didn't know how to answer so I sat very still while he walked through the house. When he came back and walked to the front door, I followed him.

"I'm sorry I snapped at you."

"No problem," his eyes were fixed on a spot somewhere over my shoulder. He opened the door and started out, then turned back. "You ever wonder what might have happened if you and I met in another place and time?"

"Not really," I said, surprised. "Why? Have you?"

"No biggie," he grinned a little, shaking his head. Thinking. "We didn't meet under the best of circumstances, you have to admit."

True.

"Byron?" It popped out when he started to walk away.

"Yeah?"

"Did I ever say thanks?"

"Yeah. See you tomorrow." He almost smiled.

"Night."

I stood in the doorway and watched until I couldn't see the lights of his car anymore. When it seemed pretty certain he wasn't coming back, I fed Elvis then took a cold shower. Well, maybe lukewarm. It's the best I could do. They're grossly overrated anyway.

Dressed in my coziest sweats, I wandered back into the living room and plopped on the floor in front of the TV. Banjo Kazooie time. For a couple of months last year, I kept my nephews after school and bought a Nintendo 64 to help keep them entertained. If I couldn't sleep, and couldn't have a man in my bed, maybe I could at least help Banjo rescue his sister Tooty from the wicked witch Gruntilda. See? When you're single, you can party every night!

CHAPTER EIGHT

Some people think there is no winter in Dallas, but I think they're wrong. Sometimes winter comes and you just can't see it on the outside. Not the Frosty the Snowman, Santa Claus is coming, jingle bell kind of winter. I'm talking about trees with no leaves and rain so cold that when the wind blows it shoots through you like a thousand tiny needles, piercing to the soul and stealing the breath from your very life. The winter that comes with the knowledge that your best friend is dead and gone forever and you're destined to be alone, even in a crowd and that no matter what you do right, it's never enough to bring justice to an innocent victim. Sounds bad, huh? That's where I woke up. I never rescued Tooty, either.

Actually, it was mid-October, around seventy-five degrees, and most of the plants were still green. I couldn't explain the empty feeling inside. PMS? I never allowed that before. Why would I start now?

"Morning Bernice," I offered, grateful to see Byron's chair empty.

"Morning," she smiled.

"Yeah," I answered shortly. She got the hint. "Anything going on?" I shuffled the stacks on my desk, looking to see if there were any waiting messages.

"Quiet as church," she said. Just as well.

I spent about an hour sorting through emails and following up on a couple of advertising leads. One drawback to working so much on the Internet is that people will write and ask all sorts of weird questions, but they don't really want to hire us. Only one way to weed them out, though. Once I'd done what I could, I rocked back in my chair and stared at the screen. The Gafford thing really bugged me.

"How far to Tulsa?" I asked with sudden inspiration.

Bernice looked up, eyes wide. "About four or five hours, I think," she said. "Why?"

I shrugged, not meeting her eyes. "I don't know. I'm kinda in between things here. Maybe I'd find out more about this Gafford thing if I just drove up there." I watched to see how she'd react. It wasn't something I'd ever done before.

"It's your dime," she said. "You got a pretty good fee, though, with cancellation and all."

"Yeah," I agreed. "Maybe the drive would clear my head."

A knowing look crossed her face.

"Might be just the ticket." She nodded emphatically. "I say go."

"Good," I smiled. "Then I will."

An hour later I had my duffel bag in the back seat and my Taurus headed north on I-35 with the radio cranked up as loud as I could bear. Therapeutic, that's what it was.

Therapeutic my butt! After five hours in the car, I was numb. I lucked onto the Turner Turnpike in Oklahoma City and saw a sign heralding Sapulpa just as I got off the other end. I've never been so glad to see a Holiday Inn in all my life! No wonder Elvis Cole always flies.

It didn't take long to get checked in and I was on my way to the courthouse. Sapulpa was a little larger than I'd imagined, but finding the courthouse was a breeze. I parked my car in front of a stately, red, two-story building in the center of town. The square was surrounded on four sides with tiny shops and boutiques boasting antiques and Native American artifacts and the people that browsed the sidewalks echoed the theme. I wondered what it was like, living in small town America these days.

Entering the double doors atop a short flight of stairs, I was greeted by the musty, quaint smell of history. High ceilings and dark, tile floors caused my boots to announce my arrival, echoing through the empty halls. Feeling a little nervous in all that quiet, I stuck my head through the first open door.

"Hi!"

An elderly woman with a bonnet of blue tinted hair looked up from her work, giving her bifocals a shove up the bridge of her nose.

"Can I help you?" she asked pleasantly.

"Yes, ma'am," I smiled, hanging around the doorframe. "I'm looking for Candace Hastings in records."

"Oh," she nodded, "you'll find her upstairs, third door on the left."

"Thank you," I smiled again.

That was easy. I followed the hall around a corner and took the first stairwell I saw. High school. That's what it reminded me of. Third door on the left. Sure enough. Records. I started to knock, but thought better of it and turned the knob quietly.

"Hi." A studious looking young woman was dividing a handful of papers into three piles on her desk.

"Hi," she looked up and waited, all blonde hair and dimples.

"Are you Candace?" I asked, venturing inside.

"Yes. Can I help you?"

I took a seat across from the desk and leaned forward. "Candace, I'm Jesse Morgan. I talked to you on the phone the other day."

"Right," her face registered surprise. "I didn't know you were coming. Aren't you from Dallas?"

"Yeah. I just thought I better come check some things out for myself." Jesse Morgan, private eye.

Candace set her stack down and got up from the desk. "Your life just sounds *so interesting!*" she enthused, opening a file cabinet and pulling out a sheet of paper. I reached for it, but she went past me to the copy machine by the front wall.

"Well," I drew my hand back, nodding, "it has its moments."

"I'm sure!" she gushed, sitting back down and handing the paper to me at last. "I keep telling myself I'll quit this boring job and get a real life, but you know how that is!"

"I sure do," I commiserated, scanning the death certificate in my hand. Not much to go on.

"Does that give you what you need?" Candace asked.

"What I need? No," I laughed, getting up. "But it's better than a kick in the head!"

"Can you tell me what it is you're looking for?" she leaned forward like she was telling a secret, or maybe wishing I would.

I considered it for a moment. Should I accept help from a girl probably ten years younger than myself? Yes.

"A lady calling herself Beverly Gafford hired me to do some work for her. Said she was from Tulsa and gave me a social security number. Turns out, the guy she wanted me to find wasn't who she said he was, and now," I waved the paper in the air, "it seems she wasn't either."

"Oohh, I love stuff like this! Who do you think she was?" she wiggled with excitement.

I smiled at her enthusiasm, feeling older by the minute. "That's what I'm here to find out. Got any ideas?"

"Well you know," she lowered her conspiratorial tone even more, "I have access to all sorts of things. I don't see what it would hurt if I dug around a little. Do you? I mean, she's dead now, she can hardly sue me."

My turn to say 'ooh'. I shrugged. "You know better than I do what might get you in trouble."

She looked thoughtful for a moment then grabbed a stack of post it notes from the corner of her desk. "Where can I reach you?"

I had the hotel number on the tip of my tongue. "I'm in room 215 but here's my cell number." I handed her a crumpled card from the pocket of my jeans. "Just leave a message if I don't pick up, okay?"

"Cool," she said.

Cool, indeed. "Talk to you later!" I was already out the door when I remembered I didn't know where I was going. Sticking my head back around the door jamb, I asked, "Where's the hospital from here?"

By the time it got dark, I was armed with all sorts of things to write on my list. I debated calling room service, just for the heck of it, but I suspected being alone in that little room might get old before the night was done and opted for the restaurant instead.

It was beautifully appointed, overlooking an indoor pool. Great for atmosphere, not that anyone was using it. The restaurant was surprisingly full, though, and had a marvelous all you can eat buffet and salad bar. Beats the heck out of cupcakes and tuna. I doodled on my notepad between plates, then, when I started to feel conspicuous, headed back to my room.

Maybe it was beginner's luck, but I had two previous addresses for Beverly Gafford, a birth certificate for Melinda Gafford, and an address for a Bonnie Dean, Beverly's sister. Not bad. I sat down at my laptop long enough to fire off a few inquiries on the new information, then shut it down and headed for the shower, determined to get an early start in the morning. If tomorrow was half as productive as today, I'd be headed home. Or maybe I'd just take a few days' vacation. I'd earned it, right?

I fell asleep feeling pretty proud of my solitary efforts, but when I woke to ominous gray clouds, I should have taken a hint. Guess some things are just too obvious. After a quick breakfast and a few cups of coffee to start me up, I braced myself and forged out into a mist that was really drizzle holding still. By the time I got to my car, my hair was already sticking to my face and the little puffs of smoke that came out of my mouth got bigger with each step.

Pulling my jacket tightly around me, I slid behind the wheel and turned on the heater, shivering as I waited for it to warm up. The windows immediately fogged up and the wipers didn't clear it like I thought they would so I had to sit awhile longer with the defroster on high. Great day to be driving all around in a town I've never seen before. For a moment, I considered heading back inside, but talked myself out of it. If the mail people can do it, so can I.

When I could see through a spot on my windshield, I eased the car out onto the road with my GPS loaded on my cell phone on the console beside me. The first address wasn't far, but it was a house. I parked in front and hurried to the door, only to be met by a harried looking young woman in a robe with a baby on her hip.

"Ma'am," I said when she cracked open the door, "I'm looking for Beverly Gafford and I understand this was her last known address." It occurred to me as I stood shivering in the cold that I should have thought this plan through. Gafford was dead and this woman looked at me like I was crazy.

"Never heard of her," she said, closing the door.

"Ma'am," I tried to stop her, "just tell me – did you buy this house or do you rent it?"

She sighed and let go of the door long enough to pull the baby's chubby fist out of her hair. "We bought it five years ago."

"Which realtor?" I called at the closing door.

"Century 21," I heard, just before the sound of a deadbolt sliding in place.

Hurrying back to my car, I realized that you never get the answer the first place you go and wondered if it still works if you skip the first one and go right to the second. Oh well. Too late now.

I'd passed a Century 21 office on the way, so I knew right where it was. The first thing I noticed inside the door was the smell of coffee. Fresh brewed. A tall, blond man in a linen jacket jumped up from his desk when he saw me and came at me, hand extended. Not much business on a morning like this, I guess.

"Good morning! Can I help you?" Is it just me, or did he really say "can I sell you a house"?

"You'd help me a lot if you gave me some coffee," I smiled, keeping my hands warm in the pockets of my jacket.

"Of course! Help yourself!"

He sashayed over to the coffee table. Another cheerful morning person. Too many of them loose, these days. By the time I joined him there, he already had it poured and I shook my head when he reached for the sugar.

"Black is fine, thanks," I assured him, grateful for the warmth in my hand.

"What can I do for you this lovely morning?" he asked with a smile, actually rubbing his hands together in anticipation.

"I need to talk to you about something," I adopted a confidential tone, aware of the two women at nearby desks watching us closely. Ready to swoop if he bombed out, no doubt.

"Of course," he nodded, still smiling. I followed him to his desk and sat down while he did likewise. Fishing a card out of my inside pocket, I wondered idly how you manage to keep them from getting bent as I handed it to him with a corner tucked under.

"I'm Jesse Morgan and I need to ask you a couple of questions," I smiled again, noticing that his smile faded almost immediately. "What was your name again?" I asked, pretty sure he never told me.

"Darryl," he nodded. "Darryl Jennings."

"Well, Darryl, here's the deal," I leaned forward over the desk like we were best buds and showed him a sheet of paper with Beverly Gafford's name and the address of the house. "I've tracked this lady to a house that was sold by your company and she's fallen off the face of the earth." It was only a little fib. "I wonder if you might have any records of when she lived there?"

"You say we sold the house?" he looked at me suspiciously then back at the paper in his hands.

"Right. About five years ago," I took a guess.

He looked at me for a minute, then turned to his computer and punched in the address. "Okay-y," he said, nodding at the screen.

"You found it?" I smiled my most winning smile. "Great!"

The look on his face said "not great". "I can't give you any of this information, it's confidential."

I chewed on my lip for a second. "I know," I leaned forward again, making a note to practice my flirting skills when I had a chance, "I have another address. What if I show that to you and you can tell me if you recognize it? That's not cheating. You can't give me something I already have, right?"

A tiny smile tugged at the corner of his mouth. A real one this time. "We could try that," he finally agreed.

I pulled another piece of paper out of my pocket and unfolded it, handing it to him. He looked at it, then at his screen. When his eyes slid back over to me, I knew. "That's it, isn't it?"

"That might be the forwarding address we have on file," he hedged, starting to enjoy the game.

"Darryl, you're a sweetie," I got to my feet and he followed me to the door.

"You're from Dallas?" he asked, examining my card and stepping outside with me.

"Yep," I said, tucking my papers back in my pocket before I braved the wet again.

"How long will you be in town?" he asked a little too casually.

"Not long, I hope," I looked up at the sky but couldn't find it. "From the looks of things, another day or two anyway."

"I don't suppose you'd like to go out for dinner or anything," he said.

"Ah, gee, Darryl, I…" I thought about it. Eating alone last night was no fun. How bad could he be, working at Century 21 in Sapulpa? "You know," I smiled, "I just might."

"Great!" he smiled again. "What time is good for you?"

Did I say might? I wrinkled my nose. "I have no idea what time I'll be done with this. Why don't we say eightish? I'm at the Holiday Inn. I'll meet you in the bar."

"I'll look forward to it," he said.

Interesting. At least it gave me something to think about while I drove around in the rain. The next address, when I finally found it, was an apartment. It wasn't easy to find, either, even in this town that didn't have many, because it had been sold and had a new name. I felt pretty proud of my detecting skills in finally locating it until I realized that it was under new management and nobody had the records from six years ago. Nobody. Dead end.

I decided to go back to the hotel for lunch and a change of clothes and was excited to get a call from Candace. I offered to drop by, but she was itching to get out and said she'd join me for lunch. When I saw her enter the restaurant, she was bristling with excitement.

"Guess what?" she said the moment she slid into the booth.

"What?"

"I got some really good stuff," she enthused, pulling papers out of a portfolio.

"Well, I'm glad one of us did," I said wryly, not sure of her definition of good stuff, but willing to take a chance.

"You didn't find anything?" she looked up in surprise.

"Nada," I shook my head. Unless you count Darryl, but it was a little premature for that.

"Look!" she laid a couple of pages on the table in front of me. "This is her work history for two years before she died!" You'd have thought she struck oil. I half expected her to pull pom poms out of her purse and lead a cheer.

"Wow," I said, not quite as excited as she was. What good would this do me? The woman was dead.

"Yeah," she agreed. "Just think! Some of the people she worked with probably know all about her!"

"Yeah!" I said with a little more enthusiasm. Why didn't I think of that? "Wonder if any of them are still there?"

Candace looked as though she might burst. "I hope you don't mind I did this," she said. Uh oh. "I called over there and said I worked for you. This lady is still there!" She pointed at a name triumphantly.

"Wow! Candace, that's great!" The goose that laid the golden egg. Or at least brass.

"I did good, right?" she beamed.

"You did good," I smiled. "Thanks."

I bought her lunch and listened to her incessant chatter while my mind worked on the possibilities to come. When it was time to go, I promised to call her tomorrow and let her know how things went.

I found my way to the insurance agency where Beverly Gafford once worked, and met with Juanita Moffatt who was only too glad to talk with me, but I didn't come away with much of any use. Unless you count that she was convinced Lawrence Gafford was having an affair with his bombshell blonde secretary and urged Beverly to unload him repeatedly. Still, she'd given me some names I could run through the computer. Who knows? Maybe one of them would pan out.

Even though it was only four, I headed back to the hotel to regroup. The drizzle that turned to light rain in the late morning was now a steady downpour and it was cold. A good hot shower and maybe a drink would warm me and I could sit in my room and watch a movie or something until time to meet Darryl. It seemed like a good plan.

CHAPTER NINE

Drips left tiny trails in the condensation that coated the windows in my room when I emerged from the shower. I'd opened the curtains, hoping for a hint of daylight, but there was none. Only gray. I towel dried my hair, then pulled on a pair of jeans. Silly me. I hadn't come prepared for Oklahoma night life. Or maybe I had.

Comfortably situated at the table with notes and papers spread all around my laptop, I jumped when the hotel phone rang. In my haste to answer, I bounced off the table, fell onto the bed and knocked the receiver on the floor trying to reach for the phone.

Pulling it up by the curly cord, I said, "Hello?"

Dial tone. Great. I called the front desk to see if there was a message, but there wasn't.

Thinking maybe Darryl would decide to come early, I padded back into the bathroom and finished drying my hair, then put on a touch of makeup and pulled my warmest sweater over my head. This, I told myself looking in the mirror, is as good as it gets tonight. Wandering back to the table, I glanced at my watch. Seven o'clock. Should I make another list, or just head down to the bar early? Bar. Definitely the bar, I decided, picking up my purse and extracting the pepper spray. Better to have it in my pocket.

I turned off the light, shut down my computer and was heading for the door when I heard a knock. Odd, it sounded far away. Opening the door, I peered out into the hall, but there was no one there. I hadn't given my room number to anyone but Candace, anyway. There it was again. I stopped, holding completely still, and listened. It was coming from the adjoining door on the side wall. Weird.

Walking over as quietly as I could, I waited and it came again. Sliding my hand in my pocket for good measure, I said, "Who is it?"

"It's me. Open the door, Jesse," a muffled voice crept through the wall.

If I didn't know better, I'd swear it was Byron.

I didn't know better.

"What are you doing here?" I asked, opening the door just a crack.

"Open the door!" he insisted.

I did, but I didn't like it. The first thing I noticed was his hair and I stared at it intently. Nobody's hair should look that good for no good reason. The thought crossed my mind that I should touch it and make sure it was real, but I resisted. Even naturally wavy hair should be frizzed in this humidity. How does he do that?

"What are you doing here?" I asked a second time, trying to avoid the blue eyes so I could stay annoyed.

"I came to make sure you didn't get into trouble! What do you think I'm doing here?"

Like I was the one annoying him.

"Why didn't you tell me you were coming here?" he barked.

"Why would you think I need a babysitter? I'm a professional, grown person, aren't I?" I put my hand on my hip and gave him my most offended, wounded expression.

"Oh, gee, I don't know, Jesse," he gave me sarcastic. "Maybe that I've known you for a month and in that time you've found a dead guy in your bathtub, cold-cocked a stranger on the street who was trying to drag you into his truck, and then found a dead duck with a noose around its neck on your front porch."

I couldn't think of a good answer to that. "Besides that." There, that's telling him.

He wandered over and looked out the window. "Do we have to fight about this?" he turned back to me. "I'm here now, why don't we just go get some dinner and talk about what you're doing here?"

Dinner. "I have a date, that's why," I said smugly. "Don't wait up for me!"

He gave me one of those Jesse-I-can't-believe-how-you-treat-me looks so I hurried out the door before my huff turned into a feel-guilty-because-he's-right thing. It's not his fault that I'm totally infatuated by him. Or is it? Sigh.

The bar outside the restaurant was cozy and warm. I perched on the nearest bar stool and ordered a Coors on tap, my drink of choice largely because I don't know wine. I really like good ones and really hate bad ones and don't know the difference until I taste it and then it's too late because it costs too much not to drink it anyway even if it tastes bad.

I tried hard to walk through the case in my mind, hoping to keep Byron out of it, but I was failing miserably. I must be cursed. I sipped at my beer, not wanting to imbibe too much before dinner and hoped that Darryl would show up a little early. Deep in thought, I never noticed someone standing directly behind me until I heard the voice say, "Buy you a drink?"

"Are you following me?" I asked, looking over my shoulder straight into Byron's eyes.

"Why did you tell me you had a date?" I spied a grin tugging at the corners of his mouth. Smug-ass.

"Because I do. Why are you following me?"

"Invisible man?" he teased, sitting down on the stool beside me.

"He's not here yet, if you must know." Cursed.

"Sure he is," he smiled. "I'm him."

"My mother sent you, didn't she?" Oops. I didn't mean to say it out loud.

"Huh?"

"There he is," I said with relief, seeing Darryl over Byron's shoulder. "Over here, Darryl." I waved, noting that Darryl looked much more attractive without the Century 21 blazer. So much better, if you tossed in about fifteen or twenty years, he'd look like Harrison Ford in the dark. I can't think of a better place for Harrison than in the dark, if you had to pick just one.

Sliding off the stool and ignoring Byron's pointed stare, I walked over to meet Darryl and smiled up at him, batting my eyes.

"Are you ready, or did you want to have a drink first?" he looked a little confused, but glad to see me.

I glanced back at Byron who was now pointedly ignoring me.

"Let's go," I said. "I'm famished, aren't you?"

"Let me go get the car for you," he said at the door.

I didn't argue, peering out into the pouring rain that had clouds of steam rising from the hoods of recently driven cars. I turned to take a quick peek at the entrance of the bar, half suspecting to see Byron creeping out on tiptoe. Too many Pink Panther movies. I didn't see Byron, but I did see a man who looked oddly familiar. When my eyes met his, just for an instant, he immediately looked away and changed course, disappearing behind a potted palm. To each his own.

Darryl pulled up a minute later in a sleek, white Lincoln Towncar. He must be good at this real estate stuff. I settled into the cushy seat, grateful to see he had the seat divider down and even more grateful that he was driving in this mess.

"You like Mexican?" he asked as we got underway.

"Love it," I said.

When I saw the car and the suit he was wearing, I was afraid he'd take me to some posh place where I'd spend the evening uncomfortable because I brought no suitable clothes.

"I didn't expect to be going out while I was here," I offered an explanation so he wouldn't think I was totally without class. "All I brought was jeans and sweaters."

"No problem," he said. "I'd have changed too, but I had a late appointment."

I'm sure he was lying, but it was a nice gesture. In spite of the weather, or maybe because of it, traffic flowed smoothly and the accompanying "shhhhhhhhh" sound of the tires running in water made me sleepy. The elevator music playing on his CD didn't help, but soon we arrived at a huge, pink, hacienda-looking building with the name Casa Bonita scrawled across the front in neon lights.

"I just love this place," he said, getting out of the car and coming around to open my door. "I hope you like it. I don't take clients here; they expect something a little fancier."

I don't know what that was supposed to mean, but the atmosphere inside was festive. Little rooms with different themes separated by stucco walls. We passed through what looked like an outside patio with stars painted on a black ceiling and went into a room that was some cozy kind of cave with a little waterfall in the corner. Everything was casual and all the staff wore theme costumes. The food was wonderful and all-you-can-eat if you raised a tiny flag. Good deal.

Darryl told me a little about himself, how he'd married, divorced, married again, divorced again. Bleak.

"Seems the only thing I'm really good at is selling houses," he shrugged, raising the flag for another beer and a basket of sopapillas.

"I'm sure that's not true," I said, feeling a little sorry for him. He seemed like a nice enough guy to me, but hey. So did my ex and he was no prize.

"What about you? You seem like you've got it all together," he quizzed, probably anxious not to talk about himself anymore.

"I do okay," I smiled a secret smile, amazed at how easy it is to look like you've got it all together when you know you don't. "I was married once too, a long time ago. Caught him with his secretary on her knees. It wasn't good."

His eyes widened a little and I wondered if that's where his ex found him. "Think you'll ever do it again?"

"No," I shook my head. "I stay away from him." What kind of question was that?

"No," he laughed. "I meant get married."

Oh. Duh. Must be the beer. "I don't know. Maybe. No rush, though. I have a cat."

Now he looked confused, but he was too polite to say anything. "Private investigating. That sounds pretty exciting."

I laughed. "It does, doesn't it? It's not. Mostly it's boring, but the pay's good and I can work when I want."

"I've always thought I might be interested in something like that, but I doubt if I ever quit real estate. Unless the market crashes. Then I might call you."

I laughed again. Right. Everybody wants to be James Bond. We finished our meal talking about nothing and I waited for him by the front door while he got the car since it was raining again. On impulse, I went back inside to the cashier to pick up a couple of mints and surprised the same guy I'd seen at the Holiday Inn right before he darted into the men's room. Strange.

I was still pondering the thought when I slipped into the front seat of the Lincoln. "Do me a favor, would you? Pull back out into the parking lot and park where I can see the front door."

"What is it?" he whispered like anyone could hear us from inside the car.

It was contagious, though, so I whispered back, "I don't know for sure. I just want to see something."

I kept my eyes glued to the entrance while he pulled down the first lane of cars and parked, leaving the engine idling. Sure enough, the same man came out a moment later and stood, scanning the parking lot before moving on to his car.

"Okay," I said, trying to get a look at the car. "Pull out slow and let's see if this guy follows us."

"Gotcha," he nodded, but it sounded like "oh boy!"

We'd no sooner pulled out on the freeway than I spotted the car, three cars back and one lane over.

"Is he back there?" Darryl asked, glancing in his rear view mirror so often I worried about crashing.

"Yes, but keep your eyes on the road," I warned. "I'll watch."

"Who is it?"

"Beats me," I shrugged, turning sideways in the seat so I could glance out the back window periodically.

After that last "following" fiasco, I couldn't think of much I could do about it.

"This is exciting!" he said, whispering again. "Is it dangerous? You have a gun, right?"

I gave him my best I-can't-believe-you-asked-me-that look, mixed with a touch of concern. "I hope it's not dangerous, and no, I don't have a gun. With me, anyway." I wasn't about to tell him that Byron wouldn't let me have it yet.

It wasn't far to the hotel, and the guy stayed right with us all the way.

"What do I do now?" Darryl asked, pulling into the parking lot.

"Well, I guess you should let me out at the door." I'd never, ever admit it, but I was glad to know Byron was inside.

"All right," he seemed a little disappointed, but he pulled up under the awning. "Not exactly how I hoped the night would end, but it's been fun."

"Yes, it has," I smiled, trying not to look relieved. He was handsome and all, but I was in no mood to play fight the octopus if that's what he meant. "Thanks, Darryl," I leaned over and gave him a quick peck on the cheek.

"Call me if you decide to stay a few days!" His voice followed me out of the car.

I waved.

Inside, I started for the elevators, then stopped, and turned back to the bar. No self-respecting detective would just go to bed now. I needed to wait and see if the guy followed me back inside. Was he really following me? Maybe Darryl is really part of the Mob and the guy was following him. Do they have a Mob in Oklahoma? Definitely time for another beer.

The bar was full, not surprising on a night like this. I stood near the entrance then grabbed the first small table that vacated near the door. If the guy did come looking I wanted to see him first. The waitress dropped off a beer and a basket with about five chips in it on her way to another table. At least I think she was on her way. Hopefully it wasn't something she picked up from another table. I shrank back into the corner and tried to disappear into the shadowy atmosphere of smoke and country music. They're big on that in Oklahoma.

I didn't wait long before the guy in question entered the bar. He hadn't seen me yet, so I examined him curiously through the plastic plants that separated the tables, not quite able to put my finger on where I'd seen him before. Tall and slightly heavy, he was dressed plainly in a gray suit with a white shirt and a tie at half-mast. Black wing tips covered his feet and his hair looked more dark than gray, although I suspected that was due in part to the rain. Boredom was his primary expression, sprinkled here and there with a hint of annoyance. Intriguing. If he was so bored, maybe he should find something else to do besides follow me all over creation. Makes sense, doesn't it? Unless someone was paying him to follow me. But why would anyone do that? Maybe I should just ask him.

I watched as he strolled among the tables, looking into the dark corners. He wanted to find me, bad. When he turned and locked eyes with me, I didn't turn away. I just waited to see what he'd do next. Interestingly enough, he started toward me, then stopped and took a seat at the bar.

"Back so soon?" a voice behind me broke my concentration.

"Your timing sucks, you know that?" I glared up at Byron, who smiled anyway and took a seat at my table.

"Does it, now? Lining up another date?"

I shot another glance at the gray guy sitting at the bar. Byron followed my glance. "That your next victim?"

"He's following me," I said. I wasn't really in the mood for sparring anymore.

Byron looked at me until I looked down at the condensation on my beer mug. "You're serious," his voice showed his surprise.

"Yep," I traced my initials on the mug with my finger. "He was here, then I saw him at the restaurant in Tulsa and he stayed about three cars behind us all the way back here. I was about to go ask him why when you got here."

"You were about to go ask him?"

"Yeah."

"Just like that?"

You'd think I said something foreign. "Yeah. You got a problem with that?"

"Yeah," he mocked me. "You ever stop to think that might not be smart?"

"What's he going to do to me in here?"

"Put a gun in your ribs and walk you outside would be my first guess," he said.

"Oh." I'd have thought of that if I hadn't been interrupted. I glanced back over at the bar and was surprised to find his seat vacant. "Guess it's too late now."

Byron turned around. "Where'd he go?"

I shrugged. "Must be another door. He didn't go past here."

He looked intently at me for a long time. Long enough to make me wish he'd stop. "Wonder what the hell you've stumbled into?"

"Stumbled? Did it ever occur to you that maybe I've done damn good work and I'm getting close to solving the whole thing?"

If he wasn't laughing so hard, he'd have seen the fire in my eyes.

"It's on you tonight." I got up from the table and stomped out of the bar without a glance back.

I made it upstairs and was putting the key in the door when he got out of the other elevator and came running.

"Hold on," he said, catching me just as the door opened. "I was just joking."

All the fight went out of me with a loud sigh and I turned to look up at him. Is there a "for better or worse" clause for partners? I stared at him for a long, long time.

"Would you like to come in and start over?" I asked, finally.

"I'd love to," he answered with a soft smile and followed me through the door.

"If you don't mind, I'd like to change my clothes," I shrugged out of my jacket and hung it up.

Feeling a little awkward, I grabbed my sweats and ducked into the bathroom to change. And to settle the butterflies in my stomach. That took longer than changing. When I ventured out, the scent of fresh brewed coffee drew me to the dresser like a magnet, but the sight of Byron pulling his shirt off over his head through the open adjoining room door stirred the butterflies up again. When he came back in, wearing a tight T-shirt and a holey pair of jeans, I was safely situated at the table with my papers spread out around me. Right at home, he poured himself a cup of coffee and sat down on the couch across the table from me.

"All right, Sherlock, tell me what you've got."

I glanced up quickly to see if he was kidding again, but his expression was open, even curious.

"What I've got? I'd rather tell you what I've done," I said, shuffling papers. I'd done a lot. I just didn't have much to show for it.

"As you wish," he nodded, almost smiling.

"I thought maybe I'd get more coming here in person. So I went to the courthouse and got copies," I rifled my stacks and retrieved them, then handed them over. "Then, the clerk helped me find a couple of addresses for Beverly Gafford, and I got one on her sister too, but she lives out of town."

He looked over the copies then nodded some more.

"I went to the addresses. One of them led me to Century 21, which is where I met Darryl."

"Your date, I presume," he said.

I nodded. "He confirmed the other address as her forwarding address but it was an apartment that's been bought and sold and they don't have the records anymore."

"Okay-y," he said like he was waiting for more.

"That's pretty much it," I shrugged.

"Really?"

Like I should have done a lot more in a day and a half.

"It takes a lot of time to drive all over looking for stuff," I said, on the defense again.

"No, it's good. Really," he waved at me. "It does take a lot of time."

"Oh! I almost forgot! I went to the insurance company where Beverly used to work and talked to someone, but she didn't remember much that was helpful."

He perked up at that. "Did she give you any names?"

"Yep. I've got tracers out on them already," I nodded, feeling a little less incompetent. "But, you know what bugs me?"

"What?"

"All this is looking for someone we know is dead. How can we be sure it'll lead us to the one that called me?"

"Well. I look at it this way," he said, settling back into the couch again. "There has to be some link – she didn't pick the names out of the sky. She also told you she was missing her daughter. The Gafford's have a daughter about the same age."

"That's true," I said, my mind suddenly whirling in another direction. Without even thinking I got up and went to join him on the other end of the couch. "The daughter is where I should be focusing, not the mom."

When I looked over at him again, he was smiling.

"What?" I asked, feeling a little embarrassed. "How long did it take you to get good at this stuff, anyway?"

"You think I'm good at it?" he asked, cocky.

I hated to say that. "You think of things I don't think of," I admitted grudgingly.

"Jesse," he had that voice again, "I just took a retirement from the force earlier this year. I was a cop a long time."

I looked at him closely. He must be older than he looks.

"I'm forty-one," he said, reading my mind again. "And I say we shelve all this and get a fresh start in the morning," he tossed the copies back on the table.

I sat back and waited, watching him size me up. Doing the same. He was handsome any damn time, but sitting here in low light, late at night, with his hair slightly mussed and sleepy eyes, it was almost unbearable.

"I have an idea," he said, reaching over and taking my hand. "Why don't you walk me to the door?"

To the door? What now? Getting slowly to his feet and holding tight to my hand, he pulled me closer and I followed him to the door between the rooms. Without letting go of my hand, he used his other one to slide around the back of my neck under my hair and leaned over to kiss me soundly.

"I've wanted to do that for a long time," he told me, smiling softly while I still fought to stay on my feet. I'm sure my eyes were big as saucers and my mouth wouldn't quite close. But no words came out, either. He came back for seconds and I closed my eyes, savoring the sweet coffee taste of his lips, the faint, familiar scent of a cologne I couldn't name, and the sexy, scratchy feel of his whiskers against my skin. Heaven. When he pulled away, there was nothing I could do but lean against the broad expanse of chest, listening to the beat of his heart and loving the feel of those big, strong arms holding me close.

"Jesse," his voice whispered, ragged, as he stroked my hair, then tilted my head back to look at him. "I have never in all my years met a woman quite like you."

That's a good thing, I hope. I didn't trust myself to ask, though.

"I'll see you in the morning," he said with a wink and disappeared into his room leaving me standing, rooted to the spot.

There was no Elvis and no Banjo Kazooie, so I laid in bed for a long, long time before I finally fell asleep.

CHAPTER TEN

Morning came early, or night gave up too soon. With the little bit of sleep I got and the horrible way I felt when I woke up, it was hard to tell. I flipped the switch in the bathroom to shine enough light into the room so I could make coffee without blinding myself. That done, I wandered over to the curtains and pulled them back, but only darkness greeted me. The radio alarm said 6:03. No wonder. The coffee still had miles to go, so I braced myself, turned on the entry light, turned off the bathroom light and took a warm shower in semi-darkness. Less of a shock that way.

Feeling a little better when I stepped out, I hurried to dress so I wouldn't be caught off guard. In spite of the humidity, my hair turned out good. By last night it looked pretty limp. I gathered my clothes into a laundry bag and set them outside the door with a tag for laundry service, then made myself a cup of coffee and ignored the rumbling in my stomach. I usually don't eat breakfast and don't miss it. Maybe that's because I'm usually asleep.

The phone rang, invading the silence with an obnoxiously loud noise, and I dashed across the room to get it, expecting Byron and hoping he was ready to eat. But the voice on the other end wasn't Byron.

"Jesse Morgan?" came the growl.

"Who's this?"

"You want information about Gafford?" the voice asked roughly.

"Who IS this?" I demanded loudly, staring at the door between our rooms and wishing Byron would suddenly appear.

"There's a phone at the bus stop on the corner outside the hospital. Be there in fifteen minutes. Alone."

Dial tone.

Shit! What now? He said alone. But I knew alone wasn't good. I looked at my watch and grabbed my purse, shrugging into my jacket by the door. I hesitated for an instant, then went back to the adjoining door and eased it open. Byron hadn't locked his side but the room was dark. As I stepped tentatively inside the door I heard the shower running. No time to wait for that. I grabbed a notepad off my table and jotted a quick note then stuck it to my laptop screen with a Post-it and tilted it so Byron would see it when he came looking for me.

The sun was just creeping up over the horizon enough to tell that everything was still wet, but at least it wasn't raining. It was cold, though, and I took off for the hospital rubbing a clear spot in the windshield with my sleeve until the defroster kicked into high gear. Wishing I'd brought my mini-tapey, I hurried to the bus stop two minutes early by my watch and stood shivering, waiting.

"What?" I barked into the receiver when the phone rang a minute later.

"Jesse?" it was the same growling voice.

"You know damn well it's me, now who are you and what do you want?"

I was cold and scared and definitely rethinking the wisdom of not dragging Byron out of the shower.

"Go back the way you came only turn in at the cemetery. Follow that road around to the back. You'll see a big mausoleum there. Get out of your car and walk up to the front of the mausoleum. You'll find what you're looking for."

Another dial tone.

Well, hey. I wanted excitement. I wanted to get out of the office, right? I got in the car and drove back the way I came, easing off on the accelerator the closer I got. The few lights on the road cast grim shadows under the low branches of trees, compounded by my headlights that gave movement to the ghostly specters. Dark surrounded by trees in a graveyard isn't my favorite place to be, even in the daytime.

I reached in my pocket for my cell phone and groaned when I realized it was still on the charger at the hotel. I made a mental note to buy one of those cheap ones to keep in the glove box when I got home. No doubt Byron's calling me right now and here I am with no phone. I'm really not good at mornings. Shivering as much from fear as from cold, I got out of the car and started walking slowly toward the mausoleum, sticking close to the trees and ignoring the disgusting, sucking sound of my boots sinking in the mud. Since there were so many shadows, I preferred to be one of them.

It was farther than it looked from where I parked the car and my trepidation increased in direct proportion to the volume of my heartbeat. Moving around to the front of the huge marble structure, I spied a manila envelope lying on the grave marker in front of it. I paused long enough to take a quick look around and thought for a moment I saw lights from another car cruising slowly along the same road I came in on. Not good.

Crouching, I moved forward. When I got close enough, I abandoned caution and ran, diving for the envelope. I hadn't counted on the wet marble. My feet shot out from under me, dropping me to the ground with a thud at the exact moment a bullet whizzed over my head. At least I thought that's what it was. I sure wasn't going to hang around to find out. Clutching the envelope tightly, I ran full out back to the nearest tree. Another shot rang out, followed by a spray of gravel and the sound of a car racing away. Damn!

Using the trees for cover, I dashed from one to the next, wishing like hell I hadn't locked my car. When I reached the tree nearest the spot where I parked, I fished the keys out of my pocket and pushed the remote key-lock button, praying that the spewing gravel was the sound of my pursuer leaving. It wasn't.

I was almost to the car when another shot rang out, followed immediately by the ting of metal and the sound of Byron's voice.

"Jesse! Get on the ground!"

I have never been so glad to hear anything in my whole life. Byron crashed through the brush somewhere nearby, then another shot rang out, and another, followed by more spewing gravel and more tires spinning. Not waiting for instructions, I crawled as fast as I could for the other side of the car and that's where Byron found me about a hundred years later.

"Jesse, are you all right?" he asked, sinking to the ground beside me and enveloping me in his arms. The compassion in his voice coaxed a few stray tears from my eyes, but I was too pissed to cry.

"Define 'all right'," I demanded, trying desperately to wipe the mud off my jacket.

"You're not hit, are you?" he asked urgently, examining me closely in the coarse, gray light of dawn that crept over us.

"If you mean shot, no I'm not!" I barked, still shivering. "What the hell is going on here, anyway?"

"I don't know. Come on, we've gotta get out of here," he said, brushing the hair back from my face. "I'll drive. We'll come back for my car later."

He pried the keys out of my hand, got to his knees, then put his hand on the small of my back and urged me in the door. He was kind enough not to rebuke me for of the unbelievable mistakes I'd made this morning. I'm sure I'll hear it later.

"Well," I said, exhaling slowly and feeling some of the tension drain from my body. "That was festive."

Byron made a snorting sound. "Would you like to tell me what you were doing out here alone at the crack of dawn?"

"You were in the shower, what did you expect me to do?" I snapped.

"Get me out of the shower would be one idea," he said, shooting a sideways glance my way. "Was it worth it?" he nodded at the envelope I still held on my lap.

"Whoa!" In the process of running for my life, I'd forgotten all about it. I tore it open, then looked up at him in amazement. "There's nothing inside."

"There ya go," he said, turning the car in the parking lot of an IHOP. "Hungry, much?"

I nodded, speechless for the moment, and followed him inside.

"Lots of coffee," he told the waitress who seated us. When she left on her mission, he turned to me, deadly serious. "I think maybe we need to develop some ground rules, you and me."

"Ya think?" I tried to laugh and failed miserably. He was right. I knew better.

"We're either in this together or we're not," he said seriously. "I've had good partners and bad ones. When you've got a bad one, sooner or later, one of you gets dead."

I looked into his eyes, but didn't say anything. My chin was trembling. Going out there alone was a bad-partner thing to do. If he hadn't been there, I'd have been the dead one today.

"How'd you find me?" I asked when I was able.

"I came out of the bathroom about the same time I heard your door slam. When I saw the note I got downstairs and followed you."

"Good thing, huh?" I offered.

He answered with a frown. The waitress brought coffee and took our orders before he spoke again.

"Yeah, I'd say it was a good thing."

"Okay," I said. "You're the expert, you tell me."

"First, never, ever do that again," he said.

I nodded. Not a problem.

"Second, we've gotta get you armed," he said. I shrugged. "There's not much we can do about it here, but when we get home, you do an hour a day in the range until I know you're safe to carry. No arguments."

I nodded again.

"Oh," he pulled my phone from his pocket and tossed it at me. "And don't leave home without that." He waited but I didn't say anything. "Aside from that, you stick to me like a shadow and don't do anymore of this lone ranger shit. At least not until you know what you're doing."

I sighed and sank my chin into one hand. "Maybe I'm not cut out for this kind of work."

"Aw, c'mon," he said, nudging my hand with his, "you're doing something right."

"Why do you say that?" I asked dejectedly.

"Because somebody took a shot at you."

"Oh," I laughed, not that it was funny. "There's good news."

He smiled. "It is. It means you're close to finding something somebody doesn't want found."

"Well, hell! I wish they'd tell me what it is."

I moved to the side so the waitress could set my plate down, then we ate for a while in silence. Gradually, I got warmer and my stomach stopped rumbling and things didn't seem quite as bleak as they had an hour before.

"So, what other rules do you have?" I asked, pushing my plate away.

"Oh, I think those'll do for now," he shrugged. "If you can't get those right, the rest won't really matter. What about you?"

"I can live with that," I agreed.

"Don't you have any rules for me?" he asked.

I wasn't sure if he was kidding. "Not right this minute, but I'm sure I can think some up," I said.

"All right," he said, getting up. "Then let's go to work."

I wandered outside while he paid the check. Approaching the car, I saw a small, black splotch on the front fender and hurried over to investigate.

"Oh my God!" I yelled full blast, not believing what I saw.

"What?" Byron ran up behind me.

"They shot my car!" I turned to face him, so furious I could hardly speak. "Those idiots shot my car!"

"Those idiots were aiming for you," he said somberly.

"Yeah, well, they hit my car!"

"Jesse," he reasoned, "we can fix your car."

But my mind was already in gear as I stalked back to the other side. I knew I should be grateful they shot my car and not me, but it didn't feel that way.

"We better find those suckers," I muttered, half under my breath.

Byron shook his head and maneuvered my car through the early morning traffic and back to the hotel. I was still muttering about it when we entered my room, but the scent of coffee, still strong from when we left, lifted my spirits a little and I hurried to put on another pot.

I don't usually drink coffee all day. Too much makes my hands shaky. But, since there was so much gray outside I couldn't be sure the sun ever came up, I figured it was okay.

"What's your plan?" I asked Byron when he came back into the room with a clean, dry shirt on.

"Why don't you tell me?" he countered, pulling his damp curls behind his neck and fastening a rubber band around them. "You're the lucky detective. If I wasn't here, what would you do next?"

I stuck my tongue out when he wasn't looking then turned my attention back to the coffee maker. Too damn slow. Remembering my mother's instruction that a watched pot never boils, I ambled over to the couch and plopped down. Squinting up at him through narrowed eyes, I shivered at the memory of his kiss last night. Now was not the time to go there. When he sat down beside me, I popped back up like I'd been sprung and snatched my cup off the table.

"Well?" he prompted, interrupting my tortured thoughts.

"Well, what?" I snapped, hovering over the coffee pot.

"What would you do next?" He had that smug, all-knowing half grin on his face that made me want to slap him.

Focus. I need focus. "Hmmmm," I pretended to focus. What would I do? "I guess, maybe I'd ask around and see if I could get a bead on the guy that followed me last night," I looked over at him to see if I'd said the right thing. It was hard to tell. "Or, maybe I'd go back to the beginning and see about tracing the little girl." I waited like there was a brainstorm due any minute, but none came.

"That seems logical," he agreed, nodding. "Coffee's done."

In all the excitement of getting something right, I'd forgotten I was on coffee detail. Pouring a cup for both of us, I sat his on the table in front of him and perched on the farthest end of the couch.

I needn't have worried about it. He was busily sorting and stacking the reams of paper spread around my computer. I sipped my coffee and watched the master at work, then jumped when he looked up at me suddenly.

"How did you know to go to the hospital?" he asked.

"The guy on the phone," I said like he should know that.

His expression reminded me he didn't.

"The phone rang this morning and I thought it was you but it wasn't."

"Who was it?" I had his undivided attention now.

"Funny, I asked him that, but I guess he's shy," I rolled my eyes.

"I thought maybe you recognized the voice," he said, completely ignoring my sense of humor again. "What did he say?"

I thought about it for a moment. I'd heard a lot of things since that phone call. The sound of those bullets in the graveyard kind of erased some of the other things. "I don't know. Something about if I wanted information on Gafford I should go to the bus stop by the hospital in fifteen minutes and wait."

"Did the caller say your name?"

I frowned at him. How does he always think of everything? "Yeah. He did."

"You think it could have been your boyfriend from last night?"

"Darryl?" I asked in surprise. "No, I'd have recognized his voice."

"So the voice was clear," he said, "not muffled or disguised."

I thought again. "I wouldn't exactly say clear, it was a little muffled, but I don't think it was disguised. There was noise…"

"So maybe it was the guy in the gray suit. Let's get at it, then," he said, folding a few slips of paper and stuffing them in the pocket of his jeans.

CHAPTER ELEVEN

There's something entirely too intimate about being in a closed car for long periods with someone who smells as good as Byron. After spending the day chasing dead ends, we finally decided to head for home but the gray, dreary weather went with us, aggravating my gray, dreary mood. We stop at the rental car agency and made arrangements for them to pick up the car Byron rented then hit the highway. He wanted to drive and I wanted to sleep so I let him.

"Wanna talk about it?" he asked, keeping his eyes firmly fixed on the road ahead.

"Talk about what?" I mumbled, staring out the window as he drove swiftly down the highway.

He was the mindreader, not me. Besides, how could I talk to him about something I couldn't even get a handle on myself?

"You haven't said much about what happened this morning," he said barely loud enough for me to hear above the blare of golden oldies coming out of the radio speakers.

"I screwed up! Okay? I'm sorry! I said all there is to say," I told him, wishing like hell it was the truth.

In reality, I'd spent the day with grim possibilities circling my mind like vultures waiting for the wounded prey to die. For years, I'd called myself a private investigator. Even had the license to prove it. But, in reality, I was little more than a glorified snoop, searching through people's most private information on my computer and selling it for a price. Not much about that to make a mother proud. Hell, it didn't even make me proud.

And now, when I finally had the chance to work on a real case, nothing was going right and the bad guys were winning, whoever they were. All I had to show for it was a dead guy in my bathtub, a guy with a bloody nose on the street, a dead duck on my porch and a bullet hole in my car. The lousy retainer from Beverly not-Gafford would surely cover all of that, right?

To his credit, Byron seemed to sense my mood and didn't talk much all the way back to Dallas. By the time we arrived at the airport where he'd left his car, it was nearly midnight and I'd had it. With a quick goodbye, I dropped him off and headed for home, hoping Elvis and a warm waterbed would ease the chill I'd caught in the graveyard before dawn. But when I looked up into my rear view mirror, Byron was right behind me. I started to stop, but was just too tired to worry about it. When I pulled into the driveway and got out of my car, he pulled up just long enough to give me a wave and wait till I got the front door open. He might've waited a little longer to see if I ran back out again, but I didn't look to see.

"Bed, Elvis," I mumbled as I shook a can of tuna into his dish. "I'm going to bed."

True to the promise I'd made in Oklahoma, as soon as I'd finished sorting my emails, I collected my gun from Byron and headed for the range. Although I'd slept like the dead, something must have been going on in my brain because I woke with all my options laid neatly in a row. I had three choices. I could call it quits now and admit I'd wasted years of my life in pursuit of a career that was going nowhere; I could let Byron handle all the outside work and go back to my computer where it was safe; or I could bite the bullet and learn to be good.

Never one to take the easy road, I opted for the latter choice. If I was going to carry a PI license, I better buck up and be the best damn private eye I could be. I was only sure of one thing – I had plenty of room for improvement.

After almost two hours in the gun range, my hearing could stand a little help, too, but my aim was sure. When I took off the muffs and started packing up to go, I was surprised to find Byron standing behind me a few feet away, watching.

"I'm impressed," Byron said with a look I interpreted as grudging respect. "You handle it well."

"Thank you," I said, hoping my quick smile would soften the curt reply. "Are you going to let me keep it yet?"

I saw him thinking, weighing the options. "You think you're ready for that?"

"I don't know," I said, as honestly as I could. "I'm not ready to wear it, but I think I'd like to keep it handy."

He studied my face. Maybe his mind reader was on the fritz.

"That might not be a bad idea. Especially when you're home alone."

Great. That way he doesn't have to come save the day, right? I nodded and ducked my head so he wouldn't see in my eyes. Eyes tell things when they should stay quiet.

"Want some lunch before we go back?" he asked, ignoring my lack of response.

"No, I think I'll just head back to the office," I said, getting in the car. "I need to drum up some new business."

"Yes, ma'am," he didn't argue. "I've got a few errands to run. Try to stay out of trouble till I get back, okay?"

"Okay," I answered by rote, returning the smile as a matter of politeness.

Cradling the Glock in my hand, I watched as he pulled away, the tires spraying mud on his beautiful wheel wells and making that wet, swishy sound. When I got to the office, I was surprised to find the door locked and had to dig in my pockets for the key. Bernice had left a note on my desk to let me know she had a doctor's appointment and probably wouldn't be back this afternoon. Just as well, I thought, sitting down in front of my computer. Somehow, I had to get a grip on this mood.

I worked awhile in silence, posting ads on sites that traditionally got the best responses for Joey. When the silence got too thick, I roused myself long enough to get up and turn on the radio, then started a pot of coffee in hopes it would warm me and speed my metabolism a little. Unfortunately, Phil Collins was feeling a little blue, too, but his coping methods weren't helping me.

When I sank back into my chair, I turned to the Gafford file. It wasn't an active case and I'd spent too much time on it already, but it haunted me, like it was the epitome of my failure. Convincing myself that I'd done my duty in posting the ads and following up queries, I decided it wouldn't hurt to spend half an hour or so just tying up loose ends. After all, there was still Beverly's sister, Bonnie. We hadn't followed that lead at all. Of course, there wasn't much to follow. Just a name.

Spurred on by the coffee, or maybe the possibility of finally finding something that made sense, I returned to my favorite sites and soon had it narrowed down to two names and locations in Oklahoma. When I got to the point where I could go no further, I reached for the phone.

"Candace?" I asked, recognizing the bored voice on the other end. "It's Jesse. How are you?" It seemed like years since I'd last seen her.

"Hey! Ready to hire me away from this God-forsaken place?" her voice perked up.

I had to laugh. "Not exactly, but I could use some help again. You game?"

"Buy me lunch?" she countered.

"Next time I'm back in Oklahoma," I promised.

"Awwwww, you're already gone?"

"Fraid so," I told her, strangely cheered by the friendliness in her voice.

"Shoot!" County clerk swear word, I guess. "Whatcha need?" she asked with an exaggerated sigh. It didn't take long to give her the little information I had about Bonnie Dean, then I hung up the phone to wait.

I caught myself staring at the nearest window, imagining that the raindrops were tiny paratroopers colliding painfully with the ground, but, undeterred, picking themselves up and marching off in a chaotic pattern to the ultimate goal of their mission. Was that happening to me? Was I letting the minor collisions in this case take my focus from the ultimate goal?

With a sudden surge of resolution, I turned back to the folder lying on my desk. The decision was easy. Until another case demanded my undivided attention, I had to keep searching. By fate or happenstance, the Gafford case fell in my lap. Of necessity, it would stay there, at least until I no longer had strangers following me and dead things turning up in my home.

Since Candace was working on Bonnie, and we'd exhausted our leads on former acquaintances of Beverly Gafford and had no real luck with the little girl, I decided to go back to Lawrence Gafford's last known job and see if I could find an old friend who might want to chat. People don't usually just vanish. My mind clicked off possibilities. Witness protection? Maybe. The guy was an accountant. Do accountants in Oklahoma have any contact with gangsters? I think I decided earlier they don't even have gangsters in Oklahoma. But they do have crooked businessmen. Every state has those. My fingers clicked relentlessly over the keyboard, taking me to one source after another.

Deeply engrossed in scanning lists on the screen, I didn't even realize the phone was ringing at first.

"Private Spies," I said quickly, grabbing the receiver.

"Jesse," it was Candace. "Are you ready for this?" she sounded breathless.

"You bet!" I told her, giving her my full attention.

"I finally found her," she enthused, "and guess what else I found?"

I waited, sure it was a rhetorical question. "What?" I prompted, finally figuring out it wasn't.

"She was appointed guardian of the little girl when Beverly Gafford died."

"No kidding!" I sat straight up and grabbed for a pencil and piece of paper. "Details," I told her, writing as fast as I could while she filled me in. "Man, that's great," I said when I had it all down. "Fax me copies of everything you have, okay?"

"Sure," she purred, obviously pleased with herself. "What now?"

"Hmmm," I wondered the same thing. "Odd that she'd be named guardian, don't you think?" I thought out loud. "Can we get copies of wills?"

"Of course," she assured me, "but hers is filed in Tulsa, not here. I'd have to drive over and get it."

"All right, you're hired," I told her, knowing it was what she wanted anyway. "When can you go?"

"Hold on," she said, then her voice was replaced by canned music. "Okay," she came back on the line. "I'll go now, I just told my supervisor I'm getting a migraine."

"Candace!"

She giggled. "There's nothing going on here anyway. I'll fax it when I get there."

"Super," I said, thinking my detective work wasn't all bad. I found her, didn't I?

Inspired by her willingness to drive into Tulsa to get court records, I locked up the office and pointed my Taurus toward the Ellis county courthouse. Why hadn't I thought of it before? Because I'm new at this, I reminded myself, cranking up the CD player in my car to drown out the monotony of the rain. Oddly comforted by Stevie Wonder's rendition of Superstition, I traveled the twenty minutes without incident and hurried inside. It was already after four and they close at five.

Once the clerk pointed me in the right direction, I started with Marcus Brant and the property records for the Frost Farms address. No Gafford. Moving from one section to another as quickly as I could without fearing I'd missed something, I tried to be unobtrusive, but the gray haired clerk watched me like a hawk. No way she'd forget I was here and maybe work a little late.

"We close in five minutes," she warned when I looked up.

"Just one more thing, I'm almost done," I tried to sound confident. Actually, I've never seen so much paper in all my life. I moved on to the next year and hurried to the Bs. There! Finally! An adoption record. Pulling it gingerly from the files that pressed against it, I waved it like a trophy.

"Just need a copy of this one!" I smiled and hurried to the copy machine by the desk.

The woman glared her disapproval and reached for her coat. She was out of there. Ever the obedient little researcher, I carefully folded my copy and tucked it inside my jacket, then set the file on her desk in the appropriate basket.

"Thanks!" I called on my way out the door, wondering if she'd run me over in her hurry to get out.

I was so excited to have found something, I didn't even notice the rain as I ran to my car. I did notice the flat tire when I got there, though.

"Unh!" I stood and stared, then glanced around the parking lot. Only three other cars, and one of them belonged to the gloomy clerk who passed on her way and shook her head. Probably thinking if I'd left earlier this wouldn't have happened. Great.

Mumbling incoherently, I opened the trunk and dug the spare and jack out, grateful at least that it seemed intact. In the three years I'd owned the car, it never had a flat. The way my luck was running, the spare should have been flat too. Rebuking myself as I hauled it out on the ground, I tried to think "half full" instead of "half empty" and snorted when I remembered my roadside assistance service ran out when I hit 36,000 miles sometime last month. Timing is everything.

Fortunately, being the designated boy in the family meant I'd changed more than one tire and it really wouldn't have been so bad if it wasn't pouring down rain and getting darker by the minute. Apparently the county had their lights on a timer instead of a sun sensor, so the parking lot lights didn't know it was almost dark as night. I managed anyway, retrieving a blanket from the trunk and placing it over my seat before I finally slid my soaking wet self behind the wheel.

Almost six o'clock, the digital readout on my radio said. There's an hour well spent. Jerking the car in gear, I turned on my lights and cut across the lanes to the exit. As my headlights swept across a church parking lot, they passed over a small, blue truck parked on the street. Was that guy following me again? Seriously?

Damn! The street that bordered the courthouse was one way, so I made my way around the square, but by the time I passed the church, the truck was gone. Unh! If he had to follow me, he could at least have helped me change the tire. Or did he let the air out of my tire? The car slowed as I thought about that. I'd looked for a nail or something, but never saw a reason for the tire to be flat. At the next red light, I cracked open the window that was starting to fog up and turned up the CD player. When the changer started Clint Black singing about the rain, I turned it back off. Where's Bob Seger when you need him?

All the way home, I kept an eye on the rearview mirror, hoping to spot that little Subaru, but it was impossible to see in the dark, especially when I had to watch the front of the car, too. I was tempted to run by the office and check the fax, but my wet clothes begged to be changed and I gave in.

Elvis met me at the door, glowering at me with a low rumble.

"What's up?" I asked him, scooping him up.

It wasn't like him to be so vocal before I even got inside. He wriggled away, offended by the wet jacket, no doubt, and stood in the hall, waiting.

"Fine then," I told him, pulling my jacket off and hanging it on the hook.

I took time to turn on the lamps, then headed for my room, shedding clothes on the way. A hot shower would do a world of good. Then I'd worry about dinner. In my room, I closed the blinds and turned on the lamps, then turned on the radio to drown out the quiet.

"What?" I asked Elvis as he followed me into the bathroom.

"Naow!" he said, which was very strange. He usually doesn't speak until after he's fed.

"Not now, after my shower," I told him, assuming he was unusually hungry because I was a little late.

Picking up a comb to pull the tangles out of my wet hair, I glanced in the mirror and noticed my curtains were crooked. Freeze. Nah, that's ridiculous.

"Have you been playing in the window again?" I asked him, setting the comb down to straighten the curtains.

They're barely long enough to cover the window, so when they get kinked, I always worry someone will peep through the window when I'm showering. Not likely, I know, but it's a thing I have. Standing to the side to avoid the imaginary peeper, I reached up to straighten the kink, then took a closer look. The window wasn't all the way closed and I felt a little clenching in my chest. Weird. I never leave it unlocked. I slammed it down and locked it, then pulled the curtain down.

"That's not good, Elvis," I said, standing naked in the bathroom while he looked up at me from the doorway.

"Naow," he agreed.

"What happened while I was gone?" I didn't really expect him to answer, but it needed to be said.

I glanced over at the tub, almost expecting the curtain to be drawn, but it wasn't. It was just like I left it.

"Let's check one more time," I told him, grabbing my robe from the hook on the wall and slipping it on.

I walked slowly back through the house, checking my spare room and all the windows and doors. Everything locked up tight, nothing moved or missing. No dead things.

"See?" I told Elvis, walking back into my room. He was still sitting where I'd left him. "No worries."

Right. Feeling a lot less enthusiastic about a shower than I was a few minutes before, I hung the robe back up and went to turn on the water in the tub. That's when I saw them.

"AAAghhhh!" I yelled, jumping back and nearly stumbling over Elvis in my haste to leave the room.

"Naowwwww!" he echoed, running to a safe place under the bed. Shit!

I hurried to the side of the bed and picked up the phone, dialing Byron's number and praying he'd answer. He did.

"Now I'm really pissed!" I told him without preface.

"What?" he asked warily.

"There is a bouquet of dead roses in my bathtub!" I paced back in there to stare at them, feeling bolder with the phone in my hand.

"You're shitting me," he drawled.

"Oh I promise you I am not!" my voice started to rise an octave. "This is the most ridiculous thing I have ever heard of and I want you to come here and make it stop right now!"

He made some kind of noise that sounded suspiciously like a chuckle but I chose to ignore it. "I'll be right there."

I paced up and down the hall, looking in the bathroom periodically just to be sure they were still there. When he finally arrived, I met him at the front door.

"What took you so long?" I demanded.

"What happened to you? You look terrible," he breezed past me and headed down the hall.

"Well, I've had a lousy afternoon," I told him, following him down the hall in a huff. "See?" I stood behind him as he stared into the bathtub.

"How'd they get in here?" he asked seriously.

"Oh," I said. Why didn't I think of that? "The bathroom window."

"You sure?" he looked over at me.

"It was open," I admitted.

"And you were still going to take a shower?" he sounded incredulous.

"Well I didn't see anything odd until I looked in the bathtub!" Lame, I know, but it was all I had.

Byron shook his head and pushed past me, looking for the phone.

CHAPTER TWELVE

When I finally emerged from the shower in the hall bathroom, Byron and Elvis were in the living room, munching on pizza.

"Are they gone already?" I asked, toweling my hair dry.

"All done," Byron looked up. "Feel better?"

"Some," I said, sitting down beside him and pulling my robe close. "What time is it?"

"Nine. Barker said he'll be in touch."

"Great," I said with a sigh. "Are you believing this?"

He looked at me for a moment, then got up and went into the kitchen.

"Aren't you going to get dressed?" he asked, emerging with a couple of beers in his hand.

"You don't like my robe?" I teased, a little surprised it hadn't occurred to me that I was underdressed. Maybe I'm not turning into my mom after all.

"I like it fine," he growled. I got the picture.

"Be right back," I said, then disappeared down the hall.

Most of my favorite comfy clothes were still in a pile waiting to be washed, so I dug through my drawers and found a pair of cutoffs and a sweatshirt that would just have to do. While I was in there, I ran a comb through my hair and wondered idly if makeup was needed. I decided not. Ok, maybe mascara.

"I'm starving, I hope you guys didn't eat it all," I said, plopping back down on the couch.

Byron scooted the pizza box toward me, then handed me a cold bottle of Coors. "Thanks."

"De nada," he mumbled around his food. When he finished chewing, he said, "I'm thinking maybe we should just back off."

"You're kidding!" I nearly dropped my beer in my lap. "Why?"

He sighed and I watched a muscle working in his jaw. He could use a shave.

"Are you growing a beard?"

"What?" he looked at me like I was foreign or something.

"Just asking," I shrugged, taking another bite. I love pizza.

"You've not been hurt…yet. They're obviously warning you away. Maybe we should just let the police take it from here."

"You're serious," I said in amazement. "Big tough cop."

"Yeah, I am," he almost grinned.

"If they were doing this to you, would you stop?"

He thought about it for a minute. "I don't know. Maybe."

"Liar." No damn way.

He shrugged and sighed again. "Maybe not. But it's not me, it's you."

"And I'm fine," I countered, feeling a little of the anger stir up inside.

"Because they haven't really tried to hurt you yet."

"Unh! Shooting at me in the graveyard? That's not trying to hurt me?"

The look in his eyes gave me a cold chill and shut me right up. "Jesse, I'm just guessing but I suspect if they really wanted to shoot you that day you wouldn't be sitting there now."

"Byron," I wanted to reason with him, but I couldn't think of anything.

"Jesse. Look, we don't have a contract and we don't have any legal reason to be snooping around. I don't want something to happen to you."

"So, be my bodyguard," I smiled. He looked really adorable sitting there all worried.

"Oh, that wouldn't complicate anything, would it?"

"So?" My famous, all purpose answer. "What's life without complication?"

"Would you get serious?"

He looked serious enough for both of us.

"Yes sir," I conceded.

"You beat everything, you know that?" a small grin tugged at his lips, making him irresistible.

I moved the pizza box and scooted over next to him.

"Look," I said, letting my hand rest on his shoulder, "I appreciate your concern and I won't take any foolish chances…" At least not if I know that's what I'm doing. "…but I'll be damned if I'm going to live in fear or let some stranger's actions dictate how I live my life."

"Okay," he said, letting his arm slide around my waist, "then let's forget we ever heard of Beverly Gafford and move on to bigger and better things."

Not at all what I had in mind, but I wasn't stupid enough to argue with him about it at that particular moment. Instead, I leaned over and kissed him softly.

"You know, it's not always wise to get involved with someone you work with," he murmured, distracting me from kissing his neck.

"Wisdom isn't all it's cracked up to be," I mumbled, reveling in the feel of his broad shoulder under my hand and the taste of him on my lips.

"Jesse…" his voice was ragged and I looked up at him, trying to read his eyes.

"Byron…"

He kissed me again.

"Byron?"

"Mmm?"

"Sometimes wisdom is knowing when resistance is futile," I whispered, causing him to chuckle. "What?"

"I can't argue with that," he smiled and I stroked his face with my hand.

"I know this probably isn't wise, but you drive me crazy," I admitted, glad the light was low in case I started blushing.

"Then I guess we'll just have to work through it," he said softly.

"I guess," he stopped me from saying anything else with another kiss. I couldn't argue with that.

"Morning," Byron and Bernice said in unison as I walked into the office. I didn't answer. Must find coffee.

"Not real chatty in the morning, are you?" he grinned.

"No," I agreed, hanging my jacket on the hook by the door.

Everything seemed so perfect when he left last night. I kind of hated to take the relationship back out into the harsh light of day. Too many things could muck it up.

"Got your Glock?" he asked.

"Huh?"

"Your gun?" he said.

"Oh." Oops. "It's in the car. I guess I forgot about it after the flat tire and all."

"Flat tire?" he stopped and stared, obviously waiting for more information.

"Didn't I mention it?" I asked sweetly, suddenly realizing I never did. "I guess the dead flowers in the bathtub threw me off." That made Bernice's head pop up. Now she was listening too.

Hastily, I launched into the condensed version, throwing in the part about the Subaru at the last minute. By the time I'd finished, his face looked like a storm waiting to happen. He got up and headed for the door. "Come on!"

I got up and followed him out the door.

"Open the trunk," he ordered.

I did, watching as he pulled the spare out and examined it carefully.

"Look," he thundered, pointing at something I couldn't see. Moving closer, I peered around his shoulder and followed his finger to a line of tread. "See that?"

I shrugged. Hefting the tire up on end, he pushed in on both sides and I saw what he meant. There was a razor thin cut inside the track.

"I don't suppose I ran over something that did that," I offered.

"What time did this happen?" he asked, dark brows furrowed into a frown.

"Between four and five," I said.

"And when you got home it was what time?"

"About six-thirty."

"Let me ask you this – is it feasible that Subaru man followed you there, slit your tire when you went inside, had time to come here and deposit the roses, then get back there about the time you were leaving?"

"Well, yeah, but he couldn't know what time I was leaving there," I tried.

"No, but he sure knew you'd take longer to get home when you had to stop and fix a flat, didn't he?"

That was logical.

"You go straight to the range," he said, lifting the tire and carrying it to his car. "I'll get this fixed and meet you there, okay?"

I nodded. But why would Subaru man do that? None of this made sense.

"Straight there and don't leave till I get there," he called over his shoulder.

See? I knew better than to come outside.

Byron's friend, John, manned the desk at the range and waved me back before I even had a chance to speak. I'd already exhausted my supply of ammo and John's coffee pot by the time Byron arrived.

"What took you so long?" I asked grumpily, beyond ready to go.

"Sorry," was the only answer I got. "Let's see what you can do."

"I'm out of bullets," I said.

He gave me one of those you-know-better-than-that looks and ducked out, returning a moment later with a new box. "Now."

Knowing there was no point in arguing, I reloaded and set up another target.

He stood behind me and barked out orders: "Left thigh, heart, head, shoot to maim, shoot to kill."

Despite my weariness with the whole ordeal, I felt a little proud that I hit each one right on.

"Good job," he nodded, taking off the earmuffs or whatever they're really called.

"Great. Can we go now?" The place was closing in on me and I really needed to get outside.

"Yep," he said, packing up his gear and mine.

Without a word, I followed him through the door and kept walking when he stopped to talk to John.

"Later, dude. Hey! Call Lonnie and let him know we're on our way, would ya?"

"Sure thing, man," John's answer followed me out the door.

"Who's Lonnie and where are we going?" I asked as we approached my car.

"Pop your trunk," he said, doing the same.

I waited until he deposited my tire back in the trunk then tried again.

"Where are we going?"

"We're going to drop your car at the office, then head out to the academy," he said like I knew what that meant.

"Academy?"

"Police academy," he explained, opening the door for me.

"What for?" Sometimes he was annoying. Just because he always seemed to know what was in my head, he shouldn't assume I knew what was in his.

"I know you can shoot a target, now I need to know if you can determine whether a situation is threatening or not."

It sounded so simple when he said it like that.

"I figure if somebody attacks me, that's threatening," I nodded, feeling pretty sure of that.

"We'll see," he grinned like this happens every day. "I'll follow you."

On the way back to the office, I reminded myself that I determined to get really good at my job. I think what I forgot to tell myself was how lousy I'd feel until I got good. Once I'd parked my car, I waited in the Cobra while he stuck his head in the door and told Bernice where we were.

He talked most of the way about the target course I was about to be tested on.

"Nobody's really going to shoot at me, are they?"

He laughed. "No."

I shrugged. One could never be too sure.

CHAPTER THIRTEEN

I'd like to say I aced the target course at the police academy. In fact, I probably *will* say that, but it isn't entirely true. I only shot one innocent bystander target, though, and I still say she looked suspicious. Who knows what grandma was really toting in that crochet bag? Still, Byron was happy enough to buy me a shoulder holster to celebrate and made a big deal out of laminating my permit while he lectured me about keeping it with me at all times. By the time he dropped me back off at the office, I was glad for a break.

Since he took off to collect some paper from the Dallas courthouse and my desk was reasonably clear, I decided to take myself back to Ellis County. If the guy in the Subaru really did slash my tire, surely somebody in that neighborhood saw him. Hell, if he'd done it in my mother's neighborhood, she could tell you how many nose hairs he had.

Back in the courthouse designated parking area, I slid the car into the first available spot and decided to take advantage of the balmy weather and proceed on foot. Traffic on the side streets moved at a leisurely pace while business types in suits played sidewalk dodge with elderly women in floral housedresses tugging home pull carts of groceries from the corner market. A typical afternoon in a small town. By the time I reached the sidewalk, my shoulder holster pinching reminded me that I was totally conspicuous so I turned back to the car and tucked the Glock, holster and all, under the seat. It wasn't loaded anyway. I was terrified that a sneeze would set the trigger off and the only one who'd get shot was me. Besides, I'd shot one too many grandmas today already.

I started with the street nearest the parking lot since it offered the best view of my car, even though I spotted the truck on the other side. No one answered the door at the first house, but I got lucky with the next three. Or at least I thought I did. The occupants were home and happy to chat but nobody saw anything suspicious.

By the time I reached the other side of the parking lot I knew who did what with whom and which cats belonged to which houses, but nothing about a man in a Subaru, blue or otherwise, and nothing about a flat tire on my car that I didn't already know. I stopped under the corner tree, leaning against the trunk and plotting my next move. Actually, I was breathing a little hard and wondering if the distance I'd save going back to my car was worth climbing a chain link fence.

Deciding it wasn't, I crossed the street and started up the alley that ran behind the shops facing the back side of the courthouse. At least I could save a little distance with a shortcut. Clouds cast a shadow over the thin strip of sunlit ground in between the buildings as I trudged slowly on my way, wishing I was in better shape so my legs didn't ache after walking such a short distance. That thought was replaced by an instant replay of my mother's lecture on how losing five or ten pounds wouldn't be such a bad idea. I argued with myself, but couldn't help wondering if I should take a good hard look in the mirror tonight. Scary thought.

Startled by the yowl of a cat skittering down the alley behind me, my head jerked up and I looked back over my shoulder just in time to see a shadowy figure dart behind a dumpster. I stood, watching for a few seconds, then went on my way, but I was no longer lost in thought. The more I walked, the more I thought it was odd. Not quite dusk, it wasn't like it was late at night and I wasn't sure a town this size had muggers or stalkers or anything like that. When I reached the corner, I went around the building, then stopped, leaning against the building, and waited. A moment later, a tall man emerged from the shadows. His face registered shock when his eyes fell on me standing there.

"Well, well," I said, "We meet again." It was the same guy I'd put on the ground with a bloody nose. "Small world, isn't it?" So my trip hadn't been a total waste after all.

He stood staring for a moment more, like he was weighing his options, then bolted, taking off down the alley the same way he'd come.

"Oh, no you don't!" I yelled, running after him.

No way he'd get this close and I'd lose him before I got some answers. Dodging the trashcan he kicked over in my path, I ran hard and tackled him just before we reached the other end. We both fell in a heap on the ground, but I landed on my elbow, sending a shooting pain straight up my arm. Funny bone my ass! Squirming and kicking, he wriggled out from under me and tried to get back on his feet.

"Hey!" I grabbed at the nearest leg, but was rewarded by a kick in the arm. "Ow!"

Scrambling, I slid in gravel and hit the ground hard again, looking up in time to see him disappear around the nearest corner.

Damn! I took off again but lost sight of him and didn't see him again until I heard tires squealing and turned to the side. There went the tailgate of the blue Subaru fishtailing around the corner.

Damnation!

Muttering all the way back to my car, I headed for home, taking a detour at Frost Farms on the off chance that the Subaru might be parked there. It wasn't. In fact, the only vehicles were the Expedition I'd seen at the funeral and an old woody station wagon. I considered marching up to the front door and demanding that the Brants tell me what they knew, but my confidence level wasn't running very high and my elbows and knees hurt like hell. I opted for a hot shower instead.

The water massage did ease the pain a little, but I suspect the beer I had with my sandwich did me more good. Two or three times I reached for the phone to call Byron, but in my present mood, I figured it would be better to wait for him to call me. As the evening wore on and he didn't call, my spirits sank lower and lower until I found myself muttering at Elvis and sitting cross legged on the floor on front of the TV. Banjo Kazooie didn't even help. I'd been playing the stupid game for months and still hadn't rescued poor Tooty. With that discouraging thought, at half past eleven, I turned everything off and went to bed.

I was just drifting off, hoping for dreams that were more pleasant than real life, when I realized the banging on my front door probably wasn't a dream about the Publisher's Clearing House Prize Patrol.

"Hold on," I grumbled, not caring that Elvis was the only one who'd ever hear me. The banging continued as I trudged sleepily down the hall. "Hold on!" I called a little louder this time. "Byron -" I started the rebuke as I opened the front door, then stopped when I saw it wasn't Byron that stood before me.

It was a very distressed Geneva Grant.

Stunned, I didn't know what to do but let her in. Dressed simply in slacks and a sweater, she almost stumbled making her way to the couch while I stood by the door, watching. When she was seated, her face sank into her hands and her frail shoulders heaved with sobs. Quietly, I took a seat in the chair by the door and waited. After a while I began to wonder if she'd ever stop crying and got up to retrieve a box of Kleenex from the kitchen.

Placing them on the coffee table in front of her, I prodded gently, "Mrs. Brant?"

"Thank you," she mumbled, groping blindly for a handful of tissue to blow her nose.

When she finally looked up at me, her blue eyes were swollen and red-rimmed and her expression was one of sheer panic. "I don't know what to do!" she wailed.

"Can I get you some coffee or something?" I asked, completely at a loss.

"No," she said, mopping her face with more tissue. She was obviously trying to regain her composure. "I'll be fine."

Fine. Right. I sat back in my chair. "What's wrong?"

She looked at me with wide eyes. "Charlotte is gone!" The admission brought a new torrent of tears.

"Gone?" I parroted, not quite awake enough for immediate processing.

"Gone! Someone stole my baby!" her sobs filled the room, echoing off the walls and sending Elvis scurrying back to my room from his lurking place under the sofa.

"Mrs. Brant, are you sure?" I asked, standing up like I needed to do something but not quite sure what to do.

She nodded helplessly, twisting a damp bunch of tissue into a tiny ball.

"Have you called the police?"

Her head jerked up and she looked at me in terror. "No! We can't call the police, oh please!" her voice was swallowed up in sobs.

I stood, halfway to the phone in the kitchen wondering what the hell to do now.

"Mrs. Brant, I really need to call my partner, at least," I edged toward the phone.

"No, you can't tell anyone!" she was nearing the point of hysteria. Scaring me.

"Mrs. Brant," I reasoned, "I can't do this alone. If you want my help, you've got to trust me. I'm calling my partner, not the police."

When she didn't immediately launch into another torrent, I took that as yes and lunged for the phone. I ducked into the kitchen, peeking around the corner now and then to make sure she was still there while I dialed Byron. He answered right away and I wondered briefly why he never sounded like he was asleep when I called in the middle of the night. He said he'd be right over so I took a minute to start some coffee. I needed it if no one else did.

"He's on his way and there's coffee brewing," I told her as I sat back down. As if she cared. All cried out for the moment, she sat staring at a blank space on my wall.

"Where's your husband?" I asked when the silence got too heavy.

"At home," she said sadly, turning to look at me again. "He doesn't think I should panic. He'd kill me if he knew I was here."

"Really?" Odd that he wasn't out beating the bushes himself. "Where does he think you are, then?" A glance at the clock told me it was well past midnight.

"I told him I was going for a drive to clear my head, and that maybe I'd spend the night at our cabin on Lake Ray Hubbard," she made that snuffing sound that happens after you cry a lot.

"And he was ok with that?" I was incredulous. What kind of marriage did they have, anyway?

I left her long enough to get us both some coffee and heard Byron at the door before I got through.

"Hold on!" I called, setting both cups on the coffee table, then turning to answer the door. "That was fast."

He nodded as he brushed past me, a questioning look on his face.

"Mrs. Brant, this is my associate, Byron Montgomery," I said, closing the door behind him.

She looked up at him tentatively, like she wasn't sure if he was real. He sat down on the couch a safe distance from the pile of wet tissue beside her.

"Jesse tells me your daughter is missing and you don't want the police involved," he got right to the point.

Mrs. Brant looked at me, then back at him, heaving a heavy sigh. "I guess I should just tell you."

Once she got started, the words tumbled out in rapid succession. Occasionally, Byron interrupted with a question, but mostly he just let her talk. It occurred to me at one point that I probably should be taking notes, but the whole thing was so bizarre, I was still shaking my head when she left an hour later.

"Well, shit," Byron pronounced, pacing the floor as I locked the door behind her.

I glanced up at the clock on the wall as I headed for the kitchen. Almost three o'clock. More coffee.

"So what do you think?" I asked, joining him on the couch.

"I don't know," he took the mug of coffee I offered. "Weird shit."

That's what I like. Deep philosophical discussions about law enforcement theory.

Unable to have children of their own, the Brants decided to adopt, but his age kept them off the standard lists of potential adoptive parents. Geneva Brant was only in her early forties, but her husband was almost twenty years older. Money was no object, so they opted to go with a private adoption.

The first child they got was a little boy and they loved him dearly, but the birth mother changed her mind and they had to relinquish him nearly six months later. Devastated, Geneva Brant suffered a nervous breakdown and went into a psychiatric hospital for almost a year. When she was finally released, her husband surprised her with a little girl – Charlotte. At the time, she didn't care about the adoption procedure or how he pulled it off.

Assured that there was no way for the adoption to back up like the first one, she poured her heart and soul into their new arrival.

Her new daughter was all she'd hoped for and more. Life was wonderful. Until a month ago when a private investigator showed up at their door saying he'd been hired to find Lawrence Gafford's daughter. Geneva panicked.

Her husband refused to even discuss the matter, hired extra security, and assured her everything was fine. But tonight, when she went to check on Charlotte before turning in, she was nowhere to be found. Bedcovers askew, with her bathrobe draped over the foot of the bed and her favorite teddy bear in the floor, she was gone.

"What are we going to do?" I asked, rubbing tired eyes as I finished my beer.

"Get some sleep," he said, massaging my shoulder with one hand. "There's nothing we can do till morning," he said. "What's this?" he noticed a scratch on my palm.

"Oh," I looked down at my hand. "I haven't even had time to tell you." Seeing oh-no-not-again on his face, I launched into a quick explanation. "I went back to the Ellis County courthouse to see if I could find someone who'd seen the Subaru or someone messing with my tires."

"And?" he prompted, eyebrows on full alert.

"And, the guy followed me down the alley and I had him, too, only we fell on the ground and he got away."

"What?" he thundered, sitting up straight.

I shrugged. "He got away."

"Where was your Glock?" his voice changed to a low rumble.

I cringed. "Under the seat in my car."

"Jesse!"

"I didn't want to scare the old people," I tried to explain.

"That's very noble of you," he rolled his eyes. "So the guy nabs you and you weren't armed."

"No," I was quick to defend myself. "I'm the one who grabbed..." It dawned on me too late that some things are better left unsaid.

"You grabbed him?" he was on his feet now, incredulous. "You were unarmed but you grabbed him and tried to take him down?"

I frowned. How come it always sounded so different when he said it?

"I did take him down."

"Oh you did? Where is he?"

"I don't know, he got back up," I grumbled, "but I bet he's at least as banged up as I am."

"What made you think you could take him?" He was still shaking his head like he just couldn't believe it.

I waited a minute to see if I had a brilliant answer, but I didn't. "He was the guy I kind of punched that day in front of the office."

A wry smile crept across his face. "The nosebleed?"

I nodded.

"I dare say he probably is as banged up as you are." He sank back down on the couch.

"All right," I slapped his thigh. "It was stupid, I know, but all I could think was that I finally found the guy and I wanted some answers."

"I know," he nodded, indulging me, no doubt.

"It would have worked," I argued.

"Yep," he agreed. "If you had your gun."

I shrugged. "Wanna sleep on my couch? I'm going to bed."

"No," he got up and stretched and started moving toward the door. "Too hard to get any sleep around here. See you at the office."

I stuck my tongue out at his back as he went through the door but he didn't see me.

CHAPTER FOURTEEN

After being up half the night, I tried to convince my brain to come up with a suitable 'to do' list on the way to the office, but I wasn't getting much cooperation. All I knew was that a little girl who wasn't Melinda Gafford was missing.

"Hey, Bernie," I waved at Bernice as I passed her desk on the way to my own.

"Hey, yourself," she snapped without even looking up.

My head did an instant replay. "What's up with you?"

She gave an exaggerated sigh. "Nothing."

Oh brother.

"Come on, give it up," I told her, moving a stack of papers out of my chair so I could sit down.

"Perryman's still hasn't paid their last three invoices," she admitted with another sigh.

Perryman's was an investment firm with branch offices all over Texas. They kept us on retainer for background checks on all their new employees, but I guess they weren't all that good at investments. At least they weren't all that good at accounts payable. They never paid their bills on time.

"How much this time?"

"Eight hundred dollars," she answered with a sniff.

"Geez, Bernice, get a grip," I rolled my eyes. "Get me copies of the invoices and I'll take care of it."

Bernice didn't like it when people wouldn't listen to her threats. She slammed a few drawers, shuffled to the copier, then brought me the invoices and tossed them at me like they were painful to touch.

Ignoring the attitude, I asked, "Heard from Byron?"

"Ye-es," she answered slowly, making her way back to her desk and digging for a slip of paper. "He says…he's been detained but he wants you to meet him downtown at The Old Spaghetti Warehouse at 12:30. But he doesn't want you to go anywhere until then."

"Unh." Did he think I was just going to wait around the office all morning because he wasn't here?

"I said I'd tell you but I didn't say you'd do it," Bernice snarked.

My turn to sigh. "Okay," I spoke to the air, "I'll just go ahead to Perryman's on the way since they're close to downtown. At least I can get that out of the way."

"He doesn't want you to go out by yourself," Bernice said, like I'd think it was my conscience or something as long as she didn't look at me.

"He can bite me," I answered the conscience.

Bernice smiled.

I slung my purse back up on my shoulder. "I'll have your money when I come back," I promised on the way out the door.

Perryman didn't take long. A small, weasely man with no hair and glasses so big he reminded me of that brainiac baby on cartoons when I was little, all I ever had to do was show up and smack the invoices down on his desk. He'd shiver and stutter and clear his quivery voice, then tell his secretary to please cut me a check right away. Easy.

With an $800 check in my hip pocket and an hour to kill, I strolled back out into the parking lot and considered my options. I could either visit the Dallas County Courthouse and check a few names, or I could stop in the DPD and quiz a spare officer about locating a hypothetically missing child. As intriguing as that last option was, I decided on the former. Less risky.

And infinitely more time consuming, I discovered when I walked through the doors. Ellis County had one room. Dallas has three floors. With a quick glance at my watch, I dug my spiral notepad out of my bag and dove in. I found nothing on either Gafford or on Bonnie Dean, but I found some nice info on Marcus Brant and on Garfield Archer, the attorney who handled Charlotte's adoption.

Knowing Byron would get antsy if I didn't show up on time, I didn't bother to read it, but made copies of what I found and tucked them into my bag. I had just enough time to dash over to the West End and meet him by 12:30.

Parking in the closest available lot, I rounded the corner and headed for the entrance of The Old Spaghetti Warehouse, already formulating a plan to check out Garfield Archer this afternoon when I got back to the office. Surrounded by the business lunch crowd, I spotted Byron near the entrance, but got stuck behind a huge candidate for the World Wrestling Federation who wasn't inclined to move very fast. Or maybe he wasn't able. When he finally moved out of my way and I raised my hand to wave at Byron, it stopped mid-air.

A petite brunette with curls that reached her waist and a skirt that was trying to do the same stood on tiptoe in three inch heels and planted a ruby red kiss on his willing cheek. I played frozen statue while she reached up a well-manicured hand to wipe the gash from his cheek and he enveloped her in a bear hug that lifted her right off the ground.

"Move it, lady!" a punk with a skateboard tucked under his arm bumped into me from behind.

I glared at him and wondered if he'd ever know how lucky he was that I didn't just grind him into the sidewalk. Probably not. I turned on a dime and steamed all the way back to my car. I'd crossed the Trinity River southbound before I realized that Byron was still expecting me to show up. Tough.

Feeling a little like a balloon full of air let go to fly and bounce off anything that got in the way, I landed at Doug Stanley Ford to vent what little steam I had left on an unsuspecting service attendant. Every time I looked at the bullet hole in my Taurus my blood pressure shot up. I pay insurance. Bout time to get the damn thing fixed. Keeping a furtive eye on me, he wrote up an order from his glass booth, then brought it over for my signature.

"If you'll just sign right here, I'll make arrangements for a loaner," he smiled nervously. I think I looked a little upset.

"A loaner? How long will this take?" I snapped.

"Probably three or four days," he said apologetically.

"For one little bullet hole?" I shrieked. "Can't you just patch it and sand it and use one of those little paint bottles?"

"Not really, ma'am," he gave up smiling but kept the nervous.

"Unh!"

"Yes, ma'am."

A gray haired man with a tie peeked out of the booth. "Problem?"

"Damn right there's a problem," I said. "This guy says you're going to keep my car for three days! It's just a little hole!"

He got off the stool and walked toward us slower than a slug.

"All I want is my car back the way it was before it got shot. Is that too much to ask?"

He looked me over, then his eyes settled on the holster I forgot I was wearing under my jean jacket. "You a cop?"

"No." I didn't offer an explanation. I pouted. And frowned. And pulled my jacket closed.

He looked at my fender. "He's right, it's going to take a few days to fix that."

The nervous one took a step back, looking for a chance to make a break. Sigh. "Well can you at least try to hurry?"

"Three days," he nodded.

"Fine. Get me something to drive, then."

The old guy looked at the nervous one. "What have we got?"

Must have been a hard question, his eyes got big.

"You want another Taurus?" the old one asked me.

I thought about the Subaru following me. "No," I shook my head. "I want a big truck."

"A truck." It was the old one again. Was he deaf? I learned something, though. That evil eye thing my mother does is genetic and she's not the only one that can do it.

"Go get the lady a truck," he told the kid.

Don't let anyone tell you having a tantrum does no good. I drove out of there ten minutes later in a shiny, new Wedgewood Blue F150 pickup. Such power, I was really loaded for bear. Cranking up the radio and loving the surge that accompanied the slightest depression of my right foot, I tooled on over to the DeSoto PD. There was a certain sense of freedom that came with purposely eliminating Byron from my thoughts as though he'd never existed. Time enough to agonize over that later.

That sense of power that came with the truck stayed with me as I walked inside the PD.

"Hi," I smiled at the dispatcher who looked at me suspiciously.

"Can I help you?" she asked in that monotone voice they learn in dispatcher school.

"Barker," I said, like that was enough.

"What about him?" she cocked an eyebrow and rolled her neck.

"Is he here?"

"Is he expecting you?" she countered, looking more displeased by the moment.

"No," I said simply. "Tell him Jesse's here."

She rolled her eyes and turned toward the console, then mumbled something I couldn't hear.

I shrugged and stared at the pictures on the wall. A motley group, all things considered. But then the DeSoto PD wasn't usually the first choice of assignments for heroes.

"Hey, girl, what are you doing here?" Barker's friendly face peeked around a door that led to the inner sanctum.

"Looking for you," I smiled. When I hit my mid-twenties I used to get mad if someone called me 'girl.' Once I headed over the 30 hill, it started sounding kinda good again. Maybe I'd get him to say it in front of Mom. "Whatcha doing?"

He looked relieved. "No more dead things?"

"Only my car," I mused, following him down the hall to a tiny cubicle he called an office.

He frowned.

"It got shot," I explained. "I had to take it to get fixed. Got a badass truck to drive till then though."

"Your car got shot?" his eyebrows jumped up.

My stomach growled and I remembered I was supposed to eat lunch downtown.

"Have you had lunch yet?" I asked.

"Just getting ready to go, actually," he said. "Hungry?"

No. I always go around growling like this. "Yep. Let's do it."

I couldn't convince him to take a ride in the truck, but, since riding in a squad car was still a new experience for me, I didn't argue too much. They have a lot of neat stuff in there.

We decided to try out the newly opened Outback Steak House on I-35. Good choice. I ordered a rib eye, told them not to let it bleed, then dug into a plate piled high with salad. I love those places. When I looked up at Barker, he was smiling.

"What?" I asked.

He shook his head. "Just glad to have a date with a woman who's not ashamed to eat in front of me."

"Unh!" I couldn't believe he said that.

"Hey!" he did the mock surrender thing with his hands. "If you can eat like that and still look as good as you do, I got no complaint."

I'd have said something but my mouth was full.

"So," he said when I slowed down a little, "tell me about your car getting shot."

I frowned. "Do you believe that? Pissed me off. They shot my damn car."

"Who?"

"I don't know." I gave him the Reader's Digest version of my trip to Oklahoma and caught myself before I added Geneva Brant's middle of the night visit last night.

He was still shaking his head when the steaks came. "I don't know what you've gotten yourself into, but you better be careful."

I sighed. Careful wasn't something I was good at. I told him about the guy I chased in the alley.

"You think it's the same guy you cold-cocked in the street?"

"Oh, yeah. It's him."

"Well, shit, Jesse, why didn't you call me? I can pick him up."

I thought about that, pushing my plate away half finished. "I don't know. I forgot I guess."

"Forgot?" he looked like he didn't believe me.

"Yeah... no. I didn't forget it happened. I forgot you could do anything about it. He didn't do anything, really. Not that I could prove, anyway."

"He's stalking you," he reasoned.

"Did I tell you about the dead flowers?"

His face grew a frown as he shook his head.

"In the bathtub last week," I admitted.

"Not good."

"No. See, the problem is – I don't really even have a client." That wasn't entirely true anymore, but close enough. "But it bugs the crap out of me and somebody sure doesn't want us to know something."

"That much is obvious," he agreed. "What are you going to do?"

I shrugged.

"What does your partner say?"

"Who cares what he says?" I mumbled, annoyed that he even brought him up.

Barker leaned forward and stared at me a minute, then backed up. "Okay."

Pretty bright, that Barker.

"How can I help?" he asked.

I thought about it. Then I remembered Archer. "Could you check this guy out for me?" I pulled the copies out of my bag and slid them across the table.

"Who is he?" he glanced over the papers. "Brant?"

"Don't ask me why, just check him out, would you?"

Barker's eyes narrowed but he nodded. "All right. I'll see what I can find."

I waited till he copied the info into his notepad, then stuffed it all back in my purse.

"Where will you be?" he asked as we parted ways back at the station.

Good question. Byron would be on the warpath.

"I'm not sure," I said. "How 'bout if I call you later?"

He pulled a card out of his shirt pocket and wrote something on the back of it. "My home number and my cell," he explained. The card wasn't even bent.

"Barker," I said when he turned to go.

He turned back.

"Thanks."

He waved and gave me half a smile.

CHAPTER FIFTEEN

Four o'clock and Bernice would be worried. Byron would be pissed. Two good reasons not to go back to the office. I pointed the truck toward home, then parked in front of a neighbor's yard. That way, if Byron came looking, he'd think I wasn't home. Feeling like a fugitive, I stuck to the hedges and hurried in the front door, locking it securely behind me.

I stopped in my guest room slash office and turned on my computer, then headed for the kitchen to fix a glass of Pepsi. Steak makes me thirsty. I started to turn on the stereo, then remembered I wasn't supposed to be home and didn't. Instead, I grabbed the portable radio out of my bathroom and turned it down low beside my desk. Too much quiet makes me nervous.

Once I settled in at my desk, I called Bernice, blocking the caller ID and getting ready to hang up if Byron answered. He didn't.

"Private Spies," she answered.

"Bernice," I whispered for no good reason, "pretend it isn't me."

"Okay-y," she said, lowering her voice.

"I just wanted you to know I'm okay," I told her.

"That's ni-ice," she was talking real slow.

"Is Byron there?" I had to ask.

"No-o," she was still doing it.

"Bernice!"

"What?" That snapped her out of it.

"Look, when he comes in, just tell him I checked in and I'm fine, okay?"

"Where are you?"

"I'm...I can't say. Just tell him, will you?"

"Jess, have you been kidnapped and somebody's making you say that?"

I rolled my eyes. "No I haven't been kidnapped. I'm fine."

"Then why are you acting so weird?"

"Because I'm highly pissed and don't want to see Byron right now. Just trust me, will you?"

"He's out looking for you," she warned.

"Well tell him to stop," I said.

"When will you be back?" Now she sounded like she might cry.

"Geez, Bernice, give me a break, will you? I'll be back."

"All right, Mr. Perryman, I'll be sure and tell her," Bernice's voice got all loud and cheerful.

"He's there, isn't he?"

"That's right Mr. Perryman, thanks for calling!" She hung up the phone. Oh well.

I signed on to the Internet and started searching for Garfield Archer. I didn't find much. Maybe Barker did. I reached for the phone to call him, but it rang before I picked it up. Fearful that it was Byron, I waited for it to stop then reached for it again. I'd already started dialing when I realized, if he called back and it was busy, he'd know I was home. I hung up. That's not good.

I couldn't call Bernice back because he was there. I couldn't call Barker or Geneva Brant because it would tie up my line. Duh. I grabbed my purse and pulled my cell phone out of its pocket. Fat lot of good that did. I got voice mail on both calls. Sigh.

I could go visit Archer, but I didn't want to do that until I had something on him, and I didn't want to go back to the PD because I didn't want to see that dispatcher again. It wasn't working out the way I'd hoped. The phone rang again. This time it kept ringing for about a bazillion rings. Somewhere in the midst, I had a brainstorm. Either Byron figured out I was here and wouldn't hang up until I answered, or, he was on his way and Bernice was trying to warn me. Neither option was good. Reluctantly, I gathered my papers, turned off my computer and headed out the back door.

At the edge of the neighbor's hedge, I peeked up and down the street, then, hoping the coast was clear, made a mad dash for the truck. Sometimes, things just suck. Knowing I'd have to get to a grip if I was going to have any luck at all, I did what I always do when I'm desperate. I went home to Mom's.

"Jesse!" she met me at the door, as usual. "What a pleasant surprise!"

"Hi, Mom," I smiled.

"What are you driving?" she asked, ushering me inside.

"It's a truck, Mom," I said, already feeling claustrophobic and I hadn't even sat down yet. "My car's in the shop. It's a loaner." I'm not sure she wanted an explanation, but I gave one anyway.

"Isn't that nice," she smiled.

"Mom, my phone's on the fritz, can I use yours?" Suddenly I was too tired to play the game.

"Well of course," she smiled some more. "Use the one in the den. I'm in the middle of making supper. You'll stay, won't you?"

I sighed. Then I smiled. "I don't know, Mom, I had a late lunch..."

"Good. Your father will be so pleased. He loves when you come over for dinner." Mom has a thing about only hearing what she wants to hear.

I nodded and walked into the den. She was still talking but she'd never miss me.

My enthusiasm for the job had vanished, but I was alone in the den with Dad's TV and newspaper while Mom hummed and clanked around in the kitchen. Might as well make the best of it. Barker was on another call so I left a message, Geneva Brant wasn't home and I didn't leave a message. So much for that. I'm not sure how long I stared at the phone, but when I realized I was doing it, I got up.

"I'm going out in the back yard, Mom," I called, knowing she'd hear and hoping she wouldn't follow me.

The back yard was small, but full. Mom believed in making every inch count. On one side, she had a small vegetable garden, on the other, a replica of an herb garden she saw in Woman's Day magazine. Not that she ever used the herbs, but she could tell her friends she had one. Two giant shade trees covered most of the yard and a wooden swing hung from the eaves at an angle so you could look at the flowerbeds that hid the foundation. Or you could watch the hummingbird feeder, the birdbath, the squirrel feeder or the neighbors working in their garden. Lots of choices.

I sat on the swing, but I chose to look at the tree. Stare at it. Wonder what was going on inside and what I was going to do about it. It's not like Byron broke any promises. Hell, he never made any. Technically, legally, he hadn't done anything wrong. So why did I feel like this? It's embarrassing. I was grown, right? Not in junior high. A modern, liberated woman. If anything, I was the one that screwed up. I flirted with him and let him get close enough to kiss and touch. He didn't promise anything and I didn't ask. Plain and simple. He was my business associate and a good friend. I was the one acting irrationally.

I gave my foot a shove to set the swing in motion and let my thoughts battle it out with each other for a while. Bottom line, my reasonable self told me, I had to stay objective. Someone was stalking me because they thought I knew something I didn't know yet. And a little girl was missing. Thoughts and feelings aside, those two facts deserved my undivided attention. If that meant I had to make nice with Byron even when I wanted to pound him, I had to make nice.

I looked down at my watch. Five twenty-seven. Mom would have dinner on the table in three minutes. Reluctantly, I got up and prepared to practice nice with Mom and Dad. That should get me ready for anything.

Sliding and locking the patio door behind me, I was surprised to hear voices in the kitchen. Mom's was her company voice.

"Jesse, look who's here," she smiled her company smile as I approached the doorway. I put on my company smile and entered the room, then stopped. Nice went away.

"What are you doing here?" I demanded, seeing Byron, gloved in Mom's oven mitts, lifting a meatloaf from the oven.

"Looking for you," his voice probably sounded pleasant to Mom. To me it sounded like fingernails on a chalkboard. "Your mother was kind enough to invite me to stay for dinner."

My eyes darted desperately toward my mom who nodded, still smiling.

"Mom, something's come up... I just remembered... I can't stay," I said, inching toward the door ready to run for it. Byron wouldn't know I was driving that truck out there. Maybe I could hide, then make my escape after he left. Desperation thinking.

Byron's eyes were like ice. "Your mom tells me your car's in the shop," he said. "Nice truck." He knew.

"Of course you can stay, Jesse," Mom said, as if that settled it. "Your father called and he's been detained. I can't eat all of this by myself. Now sit down."

"Yes, Jesse, sit down," Byron agreed. My mother the traitor.

"Let me make a quick phone call," I said, darting back through the door into the den. Ignoring the fact that my hand shook when I picked up the phone, I dialed the DPD and asked for Barker. This time, he was waiting for me.

"What'd you find?" I asked him, stalling for time and painfully aware of Byron watching from the kitchen door.

"Interesting guy, this Archer," he said.

"Barker," I cut him off. "Do me a favor," I kept my voice low, hoping my mother's droning would prevent Byron from hearing what I said. "Can you come to my mom's house right now?"

He was silent for a moment. "Are you all right?"

"No," I said, hoping he'd understand. "Could you?"

"Sure, soon as I wrap up here," he didn't sound sure.

I gave him the address. "Thanks."

I took a deep breath, then walked the plank into the kitchen.

Dinner wasn't actually too bad. Thrilled with a new specimen, Mom gave Byron the third degree. Amazing how she can talk and chew and everything without ever losing that fake smile. I almost laughed when she got around to recommending barbers, but I kept my eyes on the meatloaf I'd pushed all over my plate and managed to stifle it.

Occasionally, when I looked up, I caught a glare, but mostly, I just watched my plate and listened. When the doorbell rang, I jumped like I'd been launched.

"I'll get it," I called already half way down the hall.

"Barker," you'd have thought he just rescued me from certain death. "Thank God you made it."

I felt a twinge of guilt at the concern in his eyes. "What's wrong?"

Byron came up behind me, no doubt followed closely by Mom.

"Nothing's wrong, we were just enjoying dinner with Jesse's mother," Byron answered for me.

Barker's mouth made a little O. I made a face that only Barker could see.

"Well, Jesse," Barker searched for a handle to hold, "I got that information you asked me for earlier. I thought you might need it right away."

"Oh, I do," I agreed, nodding. "Let me get my things." I turned and pushed my way past Byron into the house. "Wait right there!"

When I broke free, I ran to the den and grabbed my purse, then dashed back down the hall, giving my mother a quick peck on the way. Boy would I hear about this later.

"Got it, let's go. Mom, I'll call you, thanks for dinner!"

I fairly dragged poor Barker out in the yard toward his car.

"What about your truck?" he asked when we were a safe distance away.

"Bring me back for it later. Let's go."

He didn't argue and Byron didn't follow us.

Barker drove back into town and pulled into a park not far from my office. "Okay. Spill it." He turned and looked at me with his cop face on.

I squirmed just a little. "I'm sorry," I told him finally. "Can we get out?"

He nodded and I opened the door and got out. I walked to the nearest picnic table and perched on top of it.

"Are you going to tell me or do you want me to guess?" he asked.

I took a deep breath then covered my face with my hands. Like when I uncovered it, everything would be different. It wasn't.

"He makes me crazy."

"I gathered that much."

"Look, it's embarrassing, I don't want to talk about it."

He shuffled his feet, staring at the dirt for a long time before he looked up. "Jesse, I'm not going to pry, but you know there's a lot going on in your life right now. You can't afford to let your guard down."

"You're right," I said. "I don't know what's wrong with me." I sighed. "Take me back for my truck. Maybe if I can get some sleep -"

He nodded, then walked with me back to the car, but didn't say anything else. He didn't say anything all the way back to my mom's house, either. Not until I got out.

"You call me if you need me," he said soberly.
I nodded, then got in the truck to go home.

CHAPTER SIXTEEN

Even with Billy Joel blaring from my stereo, the house seemed incredibly quiet. I can't remember when I'd felt so alone. Or maybe I could. Maybe the day of Joey's funeral. I thought about that for a minute and a tear slipped down my cheek. I miss you Joey. I could still hear his voice in my head. *You're a nut, Jesse. When are you gonna grow up?* That lopsided smile always softened any criticism and I knew he loved me even when I screwed up. That's what was missing. I wanted Byron to be Joey and he's not. Worse, he never will be. I'm afraid I'll screw up really big and he'll go away and then I won't be able to handle the office and Mom and Dad will say I told you so. Epic fail.

Wow. I wasn't mad because some bimbo kissed Byron and he didn't tell me about it. Well, maybe a little. But that wasn't the problem. The problem is that somebody came in *my* house and put a dead guy in my tub. Worse, they're following me, and shooting at me and leaving me other dead things and I'm scared. So I don't want Byron kissing people. I want him to pay attention so I don't get dead. Holy smackers, Batman. I really do need to grow up!

I'm a full grown business woman. And I'm working on a case. I grabbed the papers Barker gave me and started looking over the info Barker dug up on Archer. Seems he'd been questioned about a number of things through the years, but never actually charged. The word "seedy" came up a couple of times. The phone that had rung so insistently when I was home earlier was eerily silent. Not even a telemarketer called. Too bad for them. I might actually have bought something in my present state.

When I fed Elvis, I noticed he was almost out of cat food. Probably the ants were eating it when he wasn't looking. In a sudden burst of inspiration, or maybe desperation, I took off for the grocery store and spent over an hour there buying all sorts of things I'd probably never use. The frenzy continued when I got home and before I'd finished, my house was spotless, my kitchen cabinets rearranged and even lined with shelf paper. Elvis was stunned.

"What?" I asked, slumped in a heap on the couch.

"Naoooooowwwwww" he said, jumping up on the arm and staring down at me like I was pitiful.

"Keep your hateful opinions to yourself," I muttered, getting to my feet again with great effort. I dropped a load of clothes in the washer, then took a long, hot shower to wash away all the crud. Unfortunately, the water didn't reach the stuff inside and I took it to bed with me. And it didn't matter how incredibly tired I was, I just laid there in the dark, fast awake.

"Naowwwww," Elvis jumped on the bed and announced at a quarter to one.

He was right. It had gone on long enough. I reached for the phone beside my bed and dialed Byron's number.

"Yeah," his voice sounded so close, like he was here with me in the dark.

"Byron?" Like I wasn't sure it was him.

"Yeah."

I don't think he was glad to hear from me.

"I want to apologize for the way I acted," I said.

Silence, then, "Okay."

"It wasn't very nice and I'm sorry," I added, at a loss for words now that I had him on the phone.

More silence. Well, not exactly. There were TV sounds, then a woman's voice whispering, "Who is it?"

Great.

"Can we talk about this tomorrow?" he asked.

"Fine," I lied. Not tomorrow, not ever. I hung up the phone.

Nyquil works wonders when you can't sleep, even if you don't really have a cold.

"Morning," Bernice looked at me warily when I entered the office.

"Morning," I answered, heading straight for my desk.

"I'm glad you're here," she got up and shuffled toward me. "Some woman's been calling you every ten or fifteen minutes for an hour now."

"Really?" I looked up from the computer screen. "Who?"

"Wouldn't say, but she sounds frantic," Bernice laid a stack of messages on my desk.

"Odd," I mused. Probably Geneva Brant. Hopefully.

"Mr. Montgomery won't be in till afternoon," she continued, standing in front of me with the distinct look of a messenger bearing bad news.

"Good," I said without giving her another glance.

I cleared my desk, then spread out everything I had on Garfield Archer. Male, age fifty-eight, divorced three times, same office address for the last seventeen years. Nothing to go on there. He passed the bar on the third try in 1978 and his practice seemed pretty eclectic. Divorces, bail jumpers, contracts, a smattering of corporate cases, some misdemeanor offenses, personal injury, you name it, he'd done it at least once. What was I missing?

Duh. I turned back to my keyboard and navigated to a site Joey set up. I'd never asked because I suspected it was one of those we weren't really supposed to be able to access, but it might be helpful. Yeppers. There it was. I brought up a list of every case Archer filed in Dallas County since 1978, then narrowed it down to adoptions. Amazingly enough, there was just one. Charlotte Brant.

I was still staring at the screen, trying to figure out exactly what that meant when Bernice informed me my mystery caller was on the phone again.

"This is Jesse," I answered the phone.

"Oh, thank God, Miss Morgan," Geneva Brant's frantic voice came through the phone.

"Mrs. Grant, I'm glad you called. What's going on?"

"I can't talk here. Can you meet me?"

"Of course," I told her. "Where?"

She gave directions to a park not far from her house and I agreed to meet her there in half an hour.

"I've gotta go out," I told Bernice, gathering my things and stopping beside her desk.

Mid morning traffic was light and I got to the park ahead of schedule but Geneva was already there looking remarkably conspicuous in a tightly belted trench coat and huge sunglasses. Too many spy movies.

"How are you?" I asked when I got close enough.

She sighed.

"Let's sit down over there," I pointed to a picnic table nearby. Fortunately, I didn't see anyone else around. There was only one car in sight and it was too far to tell if anyone was inside. Otherwise I'd worry they'd suspect some kind of shady drug deal or something.

"What have you found out?" she asked nervously once we were seated.

"Not much, Mrs. Grant," I said. "It's not easy when I can't question anyone who was in your house when it happened. Are you sure you don't want to go to the police? I know someone who'd be glad to help."

"No!" Emphatic.

"Mrs. Brant," I leaned forward and looked at her intently. "Would you take off those glasses so I can at least see your eyes?" We were sitting beneath a huge shade tree, for God's sake. And they hardly disguised her anyway.

Reluctantly, she did and I saw why she wore them. A huge purple bruise started about an inch below her right eye and extended around the side and up over her eyebrow disappearing under her hair.

"What happened?"

She looked down at her lap, ashamed. "It's not important."

Like hell. "Mrs. Brant, I'm going to level with you," I leaned forward and looked at her intently until she met my eyes. "Something is very wrong and it bothers me a great deal that you know things you're not telling."

Tears filled her eyes, but her expression was one of defiance. "I can hire someone else," she said, but the quiver in her voice told me she knew better.

"It wouldn't change anything," I said. "I'm in it. A dead guy in my bathtub, a dead duck on my porch, my car shot, dead flowers, my tires slashed, I'm being stalked, and one way or another, it always leads me back to your house. You can work with me or not, I don't care. I'm going to get to the bottom of this. But I'd think you'd want someone helping you, if your daughter is really missing and you're really concerned about her. Whoever it is behind all this, they play for keeps."

I let that sink in a minute.

Reaching a hand into her coat pocket, she withdrew an envelope and passed it across the table to me. She looked as if she knew she was signing her own death warrant. "Please, find my daughter and make sure she's okay."

I took the envelope and opened it. Inside, I found a little over four thousand dollars in cash and a folded piece of stationary. I looked up at her.

"My husband gave me that note this morning," she said.

It read:

Mrs. Brant,
Don't worry – Charlotte is safe. She won't be harmed unless the police get involved. Trust your husband to work out the details and she'll be home safe and sound before you know it. Don't call the police!

"That's it?" I looked up.

She shrugged.

"Have they asked for money?"

"I think so, but he won't tell me," she said.

"This doesn't make any sense," I said, shaking my head and hoping something would fall into place. Granted, I was inexperienced with kidnapping procedures, but this didn't look like any ransom note I'd ever imagined.

"Can you find her?"

Good question. "I can sure try. Tell me again, everything you know."

She went over the scenario again, answering my questions honestly the best I could tell.

"Okay," I said when we were through. "Here's what I want you to do. When your husband comes home tonight, try to convince him that you're trusting him with this." Looking at her bruise, what I really wanted to tell her was to have the jerk arrested for assault, but I figured we could do that later. "If you can make him believe you, maybe he'll slip and tell you a little more. I need to know if he's getting money together to pay them and when."

She nodded, but didn't look too confident. That made two of us.

"What are you going to do?" she asked.

"I'm going hunting," I got up and got ready to leave. "How can I get hold of you?"

"Oh!" she dug around in her purse and came out with a card. She wrote something on it and handed it to me.

Cell phone. I found a card and wrote my number on it for her.

"Call me tonight when you get a chance," I said, then headed back to the truck. I waited until I saw Geneva get in the white car I'd spotted earlier and was surprised to see there was someone else in the car. From the shoulder length blonde hair that whizzed past as the car drove by, I'd guess it was a woman but I couldn't really tell. Maybe Geneva had a friend. In any case, I didn't have time to worry about it. I had miles to go before I could sleep.

Back in the office, I spread my info out on the desk and jumped on the keyboard again. Time to explore Marcus Brant. After about an hour of wading through society pages and articles that told me nothing aside from his propensity to act charming and give the glad hands to socialites and politicians. I began to get the idea that he was the kind of man who said what people wanted to hear, then did whatever he damn well pleased when they weren't looking. Just a guess.

I reached for the phone and called Barker.

"Barker," he said. I got his direct number.

"Hey, guy."

"Jesse," he recognized my voice. I heard 'what now?' in unspoken.

"How come you're not out beating the streets?"

"It's called everlasting, never-ending paperwork," he groused. "How are you?"

"I'm good." All things considered. "I do have a tiny problem, though."

"Hah," he snorted. "Let me guess. There's a dead elephant in your kitchen."

"Very funny Barker," I rolled my eyes. "Can you check someone else out for me?"

"It'll cost you," he warned.

"Name your price."

Silence. "I'll have to think about it," he said, finally. "Who is it?"

I gave him the details.

"I've heard that name. Isn't he a politician or something?"

"Something," I said.

More silence.

"Let me see what I can do. Where will you be?"

I looked at my watch. It was still early enough to pay Archer a visit. "I've got a few things to check out. Call my cell."

"Gotcha. Be careful, Jesse."

I smiled and hung up the phone.

"I'm gone," I told Bernice after I shut my computer down. "See you tomorrow."

She gave me I-don't-know-what-you're-up-to-but-I'll-figure-it-out. I shook my head and smiled again. Nice to be loved.

I took a minute to look up Archer's address on my Mapsco and pointed the truck toward Oak Cliff. Good thing there's lots of daylight left. I don't do Oak Cliff after dark. Odd, as I remembered it, Archer's net worth would have afforded a much better location for an office. I guess maybe his typical clientele were more comfortable on their home turf. All the more odd, then that Brant would ever seek him out as an attorney.

I've always been amazed how two different worlds could exist in such close proximity with neither of them aware how the other side lived. Maybe that wasn't entirely true, I corrected myself. There were quite a few who lived in the slums that knew exactly what the inside of a $500,000 house looked like. Sometimes they worked in them. Other times, they robbed them. Still, it was sobering to think of the thousands of people that traveled down I-35 every day with no concept of the reality that was everyday life for those that lived alongside.

Brant struck me as one of those. I wondered if he'd ever been tempted to steal food because it was the only way he could feed his children. I exited the freeway at Ledbetter and turned right. It was like an invisible filter covered the sun and everything was a tiny shade darker, even though there was no visible reason why. I scanned the street numbers until I got close, then parked in the nearest available slot.

The office was once a tan brick building but most of the bricks had collected an assortment of spray painted graffiti through the years. Iron burglar bars guarded the windows and litter covered the cracked sidewalk in a breadcrumb trail to an empty, crumpled trashcan chained to the corner of the building. Like someone would steal that rusty, battered old can. The only greenery visible was a small crop of weeds growing through cracks in the asphalt. Nice place.

A black iron burglar door clanged against the building in the wind. Since lawyers don't typically keep a lot of cash or jewelry in the office, I wondered what he went to such lengths to protect. But, as I scanned the street, I thought again. Maybe it was just standard. Some neighborhoods have trash pickup and garbage disposals. This one had burglar bars. I reached for the doorknob and wondered briefly if I should cover it with something first. A suspicious substance stuck to the door at eye level and traveled down over the doorknob in streaks that were probably slimy once. I hoped it was only an egg.

When I opened the door, I was surprised to find a waiting room filled with people and an obnoxious odor I couldn't really define. I looked at the door again before I shut it, just to be sure. It said "Gar ld cher" in peeling yellow paint. Close enough.

Nobody paid any attention to me that I could tell, and I crossed the room swiftly. A large, black woman of indeterminate age sat behind a broken desk with a broken phone. She was turned sideways with one foot propped on her knee and looked like she missed her last few hairdresser appointments. The nails were good, though. Long as her fingers and bright red with slashes of white lightning. Interesting.

I cleared my throat.

She looked over at me without turning her head. "What you want?" Customer service at its best.

"I need to see Garfield Archer," I told her.

"You got a pointment?"

"Nope, but I need to see him now," I handed her a card that wasn't bent.

Miss Congeniality turned to get a better look at me, then stared down at the card and shrugged. "Better sit down, you gone be a while."

Not if I can help it, I thought, turning to look for a seat. On second thought, maybe I'd just lean on the wall. The waiting room was tiny, maybe ten by ten. A couch that might have been floral once had a distinct sag in the middle and was covered with a tired looking woman in denim overalls and three children who might have been triplets. They were all about the same size, but they didn't hold still long enough to get a good look. Next to the couch was an orange armchair with stuffing spewing out of one arm. It had a variety of stains, but the dark one in the middle of the seat that ran down the front was the most suspicious. It seemed about the same size as the one on one of the triplets' red shorts.

Another armchair sat in the corner, full of a man whose stomach wouldn't stay in his pants or shirt. I couldn't tell if that bothered him much. His cap covered his face and muffled the snoring sounds he made. The other wall had three metal folding chairs that looked like they'd been run over by a truck. Every few minutes, a woman sitting in one of them seemed in danger of sliding out and shifted so she wouldn't. Maybe it was the blue satin dress. I wouldn't have chosen those green disco ball earrings to go with that particular shade of blue, but I'm not much for fashion. I probably wouldn't have picked those shoes either. Four-inch acrylic heels with something floating in them that moved every time she kicked her foot.

The man that sat beside her kept staring at her cleavage until she slapped him on the arm and told him, "You look you pay."

I looked at my watch and tried to imagine the Brants sitting in here. Couldn't. A few minutes later, the door behind Miss Congeniality creaked open and a tall man with greasy red hair and a pencil thin mustache ambled out. The plaid suit was too short for both his arms and his legs. A real thrift shop special. I followed him to the door with my eyes, wishing I could escape into the sunshine.

The sound of a door slamming took my attention back to the desk. Archer's door was closed again. But the waiting room occupants were all still there. When another ten minutes passed with no word from the inner chamber, I approached the desk again.

"How long is it going to be?" I tried to sound pleasant, but firm.

"Shit," she snorted. "I tole you to sit."

I waited. Somewhere inside me, impatience would win. The stomach was still snoring, the kids still climbing, the peeker still peeking and the hooker still slapping. I wasn't inclined to wait any longer. I leaned over the desk, careful not to put any pressure on it in case it caved in, and made sure my holster was visible underneath my jacket.

"Listen, I have an appointment at the police department when I leave here. I suggest you get your butt in there and tell Archer I'm waiting. He won't be happy if I talk to them first. Know what I mean?"

I'd seen that expression on a mad dog that tried to tangle with Elvis until I went after him with a big stick. I suspect that dog saw the same look in my eyes that Miss Congeniality did. She got up and slithered through Archer's door.

"He'll see you now," she snarled when she came back a moment later.

"Thanks," I told her.

His office had the same decorator as his waiting room, but at least it had a window. The little bit of sun that leaked between the burglar bars made a nice sheen on Archer's greasy head. And apparently he shopped the same place as the red haired man. He was more creative though. The plaid of his pants was a whole different pattern than the one on his suit coat that hung from the back of his chair and trailed on the ground.

"Garfield Archer?" I asked roughly, flipping one of my cards on his desk. "I'm Jesse Morgan."

I gave the chair in front of his desk a quick check before I sat on it. I didn't bother to shake his hand.

"What can I do for you Miss Morgan?" His voice was as slippery as his hair.

"Well, it's like this, Mr. Archer. I'm working a case that's creating a problem for me and your name cropped up. What can you tell me about the adoption of Melinda Gafford?"

In my mind, I expected him to start looking nervous about then, but he didn't. He looked sleazy, but he was already doing that when I walked in.

"I don't know," he said. "Don't recall the name."

"Really? That's odd. I've done some checking. In all your years of service, you've only filed one adoption proceeding. I'd think that would stand out in your mind."

"Think again, Miss Morgan. I have clients in and out of here all day six days a week. When I get paid, I put a case away and move on to the next one."

I had to think about that for a minute. This wasn't going the way I imagined. Of course, that wasn't really anything new. "Too bad. I'd have thought a man like you handling such an important case for a man like Marcus Brant would have a hard time forgetting." His eyes might have narrowed, but they were already so squinty and beady it was hard to tell.

"I'm a busy man, Miss Morgan. What do you want?"

When I'm put on the spot there seems to be a short-circuit in my wiring somewhere. My mouth goes into motion without consulting my brain. "That little girl is missing, Mr. Archer. I thought maybe I should look here."

I tried really hard to believe he looked nervous, but he really just looked annoyed.

"Do you see any little girls lurking around in here?" he made a sweeping gesture around the cluttered office with one sweaty arm.

"Guess I'll just have to keep looking." I got up and walked slowly to the door.

"Miss Morgan?" his voice followed me.

I turned to look at him.

"Better be careful. Streets around here just aren't as safe as they used to be."

"Ya think, Mr. Archer?" I smiled. "You be careful too. Sometimes things we forget come back to bite us on the ass."

CHAPTER SEVENTEEN

"There," I told Elvis, dropping a slice of brisket in his dish. "Now play nice."

Barker's idea of payback for his research efforts was a home cooked meal so I stopped at the Longhorn BBQ and bought him one. Somebody cooked it, I figured. We'll eat it at my house. Hope that counts.

"Come on." Oops. When I heard the knock on the door, I assumed it was Barker. It wasn't.

"Expecting someone else?" Byron asked.

"Well, yeah."

"Smells good, what is it?" he asked, looking over my shoulder.

I moved so he wouldn't strain himself, then shut the door behind him.

"Hmmm," he popped a piece of fried okra in his mouth. "Good."

"Byron."

"Jesse," he turned to look at me and his smile wilted. "Want me to come back later?"

At this point, I didn't want him to come back ever, but I couldn't say that. Not without ruining what was left of my evening.

"I know we need to talk about Geneva Brant," I compromised. "I asked Barker to run Brant through his system and see what he found."

"Good idea," he nodded. "The guy's a crook."

"And a wife beater," I added.

That shot his eyebrows up. "Oh, really. What else have you found out?"

Business, I could talk about. I sat down on the couch. "Garfield Archer is a sleaze."

"Been to see him, have you?"

"Yes," I said, annoyed with his attitude. "We *do* have a case, you know."

"You sure? Have we been formally retained?"

"To the tune of four smackers, we have."

That surprised him and I smiled. I like it when he doesn't know everything.

"I guess you have been busy," he admitted, perching on the edge of the chair by the door. "Sorry I've been out of pocket, then."

I nodded but held my tongue. That was an odd way to describe busy with a secret lover who wears red lipstick and short skirts and whispers in the middle of the night.

"I won't stay. Let's go over all this in the morning, ok?"

I nodded back at him and followed him to the door but he was already outside. Barker passed him on the driveway and nodded at him. Byron didn't stop.

"I come at a bad time?" Barker asked, handing me a bottle of wine as he walked through the door.

I shook my head, but I suspect my face told a different tale.

"Man, that smells good," Barker said, shrugging out of his jacket. "Cooked it yourself, did you?"

I grinned. "Of course."

I let him open the wine while I retrieved the only two goblets I own, then we sat down to enjoy the feast before Elvis beat us to it.

Barker knows more about wine than I do. It was good.

"Well, Ms. Morgan, I salute your culinary endeavors," he teased, pushing away from the table.

I made a face at him. "Go have a seat on the couch and I'll put this stuff away."

When I joined him in the living room, he had papers spread all over the coffee table.

"Wow," I said. "Anything good in all that?"

He turned toward me. "Depends on how you define good."

"You know… like… has he killed anybody or embezzled any large sums of money? Things like that."

Barker laughed. "The real question is – has he ever been caught?"

"Oh," I nodded. "So you think he has?"

"I think he's probably capable of almost anything. But he's good, and he's got good attorneys. He'll never do time."

I sat in the floor by the coffee table and scanned over the papers. "Hmmmm. Never say never. Find anything about Garfield Archer in all this?"

"Archer?" he looked surprised. "Isn't he that shyster I ran yesterday?"

"Um hmm," I nodded.

"What does he have to do with Brant?" his eyes narrowed and I had to decide just how much I was going to tell him.

"Let me ask you something. Hypothetically," I posed.

"I'm listening," he agreed. "Hypothetically."

"How do you interpret RTB?" I loved that it sounded like I knew what I was talking about. In reality, I'd only found the acronym on the Internet earlier while I was researching my options.

"Reason to believe?"

"Yeah."

"In what context? Reasonable doubt? Suspicion?"

"In the context of…" how should I word it? "…welfare of a child."

He frowned. "That's tough, Jesse. I don't play with that."

"I know," I nodded. "But, how do you know if there are extenuating circumstances?"

"According to who?"

"Me."

"Is the child in danger of losing his life?"

"I hope not." How could I say it? "Okay, let's go another way. There's no law that says a parent has to report a kidnapping to the police, right? How does RTB work with that?"

"Jesse."

"Hey! I looked it up, Barker. So what if you knew somebody's kid was taken and they got a note that said don't tell the police so they didn't. Is there a law that says you have to tell?"

He sighed. "No. There's no law. But you know it's -"

My mind raced, trying to think of a way to tell him without telling him. A way that he'd respect, because he already suspected. "Look. I know the law requires me to report if I suspect a child is being abused. And I know that kidnapping could righteously be considered an abusive situation. But, the law doesn't require the parents to report it, so how could they require that I report what the parents don't?"

"You're right," he nodded, rubbing his hand over his eyes. "It's a loophole."

"So," I continued, feeling a little better, but not much, "if I know that little Johnny has been kidnapped and his parents want me to help find him, but absolutely refuse to go to the police and I tell you about it, what happens then?"

He leaned back against the back cushion and rubbed his temples with his hands. "Well. Assuming I went to my supervisor and made a report that the parents would deny, there's really nothing I could do. Child Protective Services wouldn't even be involved at that point."

"Good," I nodded again.

"So, are you going to tell me what the fuck is going on?"

My turn to sigh. "I don't know Barker. It's so convoluted. I need help but I don't want to screw things up."

"Okay," he said, finally, leaning forward and resting his elbows on his knees. "No names. Just tell me a story."

"But you'll know who I'm talking about," I argued.

"Supposition," he said.

I sat there, thinking, for a long time. Somehow, I feared if I told him, all hell would break loose and it would be my fault.

"Jesse," he said, waiting for me to look up at him. "Have you told your partner everything you want to tell me?"

"No," I admitted.

"Why the hell not?"

"It's a long story."

"Well, you know what? If you're working a case that has dead guys showing up in your bathtub and strangers stalking you all the way to Oklahoma and kids in danger, you damn sure better be able to talk to your partner or get the hell out of the business."

I didn't move, a little surprised to see him get so angry. But what he said was the first thing that connected with something inside of me. He was right.

"What?" he asked when I didn't say anything.

I shrugged. "You're right. I need to talk to him."

He shook his head and a tiny smile skipped around his mouth. "Why is that so hard? He was a cop longer than I've been one and he seems like a pretty decent guy."

"He is," I agreed, getting up to go to the kitchen. "Want a beer?"

"Sure," he called. I got us both one, then sat down on the couch.

"I need a therapist," I mused, half out loud.

Barker laughed. "I doubt it. Time heals all wounds."

"Yeah, well, I'm a little short on time right now."

"You want to tell me?"

I smiled. "I don't even want to tell me."

"Thanks for dinner," he smiled as he got up.

"I'll get it sorted out," I promised, getting up to follow him to the door.

He picked up his jacket and slung it over his shoulder, then opened the door. He was almost to the driveway when he turned back. "You know I'm here for you if you need me."

"I know," I smiled. "Thanks, Barker, you're a good friend."

He smiled back and saluted.

CHAPTER EIGHTEEN

Morning brought a whole new sense of determination. I was up before the alarm went off and on my way to the office early enough to beat Bernice. With coffee brewing and light rock playing on the radio, I was ready to sort my day.

The first thing on my list was to find Geneva Brant. She'd promised to call last night, but I never heard from her, even though I'd paged her several times. I tried her pager again, then, when she didn't return the call in fifteen minutes, tried her cell number. I nearly dropped the phone when a man answered.

"What's wrong?" Byron sauntered through the door and caught me staring at the phone with my finger holding down the receiver button.

"A man answered Geneva's phone," I said, replacing the handset.

He shrugged. "She's married."

"I know, but it's her cell phone. She said it was safe to call her on that because she always keeps it with her."

"Maybe she's in the shower," he offered, dropping his briefcase beside his desk and moving toward the coffee pot, mug in hand.

"Maybe," I said, not believing it.

He took his time with his coffee, then sat down at his desk and swiveled around to face me.

"Why don't you tell me why that bothers you?"

I realized how much he didn't know yet. "Guess there's a lot I better tell you, huh?"

I gave him a condensed version. Byron was quiet for awhile after I finished and I felt like I'd been to confession, only I left out a few secrets that would probably send me straight to hell. But I could only deal with one crisis at a time and my personal problems with Byron fell pretty far down the list.

"So, where do we go from here?" I asked when his silence started to make me nervous.

He sucked in a big breath, puffed out his cheeks and blew till it was all gone, then rubbed his nose. Thinking, I presume.

"I know what I'd do if I was still with the PD, but I'm not."

"Well, that's all kinds of helpful," I observed.

"I guess the first thing we have to know is, do we have two cases working here, or just one?"

"Okay," I agreed. That made sense. "But how do we find that out?"

"That's not too tough," he said. "The first one is a given. There's no question that a dead guy wound up in your tub and all that followed. The question is, is Charlotte Brant really Melissa Gafford and is she really missing? Come on," he got up and grabbed his briefcase, heading for the door.

Bernice pulled up in the parking lot just as I was locking the office door.

"It's open, Bernie," I called as Bernice ambled slowly across the lot with a coat and purse slung across one hefty arm and a box of donuts on the other. "We'll be back later."

"Where will you be?" Bernice called as I opened the door to climb into Byron's car.

"I don't know. Call me if you need me."

"Wait!"

I heard her voice as I slammed the door behind me, so I rolled down the window. "What?"

"I don't think I've got the right number. I called you all evening yesterday and you never answered."

With a frown, I pulled my phone out of the case and stared at it. Nothing. Byron reached over and flipped a switch on the side of it.

"Why'd you do that?" I turned to face him.

"You have to charge it now and then," he nodded.

"Sorry, Bernie, I forgot to charge it," I offered. "What'd you need last night?"

"Some woman called and said you weren't answering the cell phone and would I try it. So I did."

"Unh! Who was it?"

Bernice shrugged. "She wouldn't leave a name or number. Sounded kinda nervous, too."

"Thanks," I told her as Byron started the car.

"Plug it in to the car charger and check your voice mail."

I was still trying to figure out how when Byron stopped at a red light and took the phone, then dialed a series of numbers and handed it back.

Following the instructions, I pressed the right buttons until Geneva's whispering voice sent a chill up my spine.

"Miss Morgan, I only have a minute. I confronted Marcus like you told me and he wants me to get Charlotte's teddy and pack some of her things, then meet him at the office tonight. He says he'll explain everything over dinner. I'll call you back just as soon as I get home."

"Oh no," I groaned, pressing the replay button and handing the phone to Byron.

His lips formed a tight, thin line as he listened.

I looked over at him. "I guess I got busy last night with dinner and all. I forgot."

We drove a while in silence. "Hey," I said, finally, staring at the face of the phone. "This thing has caller ID?"

"Yeah, why?"

"Do they all?"

"All the good ones. Why?"

"Because I called her cell phone from the office this morning and that man answered."

"So, if it's Brant, he knows you were looking for her," he finished the thought.

I nodded. "What now?"

"We go to her house and see what's there," he said, keeping his eyes on the road.

When we arrived, Byron trolled slowly along the side of the house first, checking the garage for vehicles. The stable office area had a few people moving around but the garage behind the house was empty and there was no sign of life.

"You wait here," Byron said, getting out of the car and retrieving a briefcase from the back seat. "They've seen you but they haven't seen me. I'll see what I can find out."

Knowing he was right and feeling generally bummed out about the whole situation, I slumped down in the seat and tried to keep an eye on him inconspicuously. I didn't have to wait long.

"What?" I prompted as he slung the case back in the car and slid behind the wheel.

"According to the housekeeper, Mrs. Brant took little Charlotte to visit with her grandparents. She's not expected back for weeks."

The vise around my chest tightened a notch. "You know better."

"So do you."

I stared at him while he stared at the steering wheel. Neither of us spoke for a few minutes. Then we both started at once.

"Byron -"

"Jesse -"

He looked over at me. "Ladies first."

Oh sure. Now he's a gentleman. I sucked up my courage and tossed pride out the window. "Look, I've been acting like an ass for a couple of days. I can't help feeling like if I'd been less focused on my own stupid self and more focused on this case, we might not be here right now."

He looked over at me, but didn't comment.

"It won't happen again," I told him, and meant it. If I hadn't been so full of my own hurts, I'd have talked to him. I wouldn't have avoided him, and maybe, just maybe, he'd have known what to do about Geneva Brant before she disappeared.

"Fair enough," he nodded. "You know we still need to talk, but now isn't the time." As he watched my face, miserable as it probably was, his expression softened. "Still partners, then, huh?" he asked as he started the car and eased out on the road.

I smiled. That sounded good. "What do we do now?"

"Regroup," he said, pointing the car back toward the office.

When Byron suggested I stay behind at the office while he visited Marcus Brant at his office, I didn't like it much, but figured I wasn't in a good bargaining position. So, I booted up and set my computer bloodhound on the trail of any and all information I could retrieve on Geneva Brant in hopes of locating the alleged visitees. I did it, too, three hours later. Geneva's mom lived in South Carolina and she sounded a lot like mine. She was thrilled to hear that maybe Geneva and little Charlotte were on their way for a visit and promised to call me back when they arrived. I didn't have the heart to tell her they probably wouldn't.

"Why don't you go get some lunch or something?" Bernice suggested. Guess I was starting to bug her.

"I don't know. You want something?" I was frustrated that I hadn't heard from Byron and couldn't shake the feeling that there was a huge clue staring me in the face and I was too blind to see it.

"I'll eat something if you'll go," she said, rolling her eyes when she thought I wasn't looking.

"Then I'll go," I made up my mind. At least a breath of fresh air might clear my head some.

But when I got back to the office with a bag of tacos in hand twenty minutes later, I was just as puzzled as I'd been when I left. I sat the bag on Bernice's desk and collected a Pepsi from the refrigerator.

"Thanks," she said, handing me the bag, considerably lighter, as I passed on the way to my desk.

"What am I missing, Bernice?" I asked rhetorically as I opened the bag.

She swiveled around to face me and gave me that you-don't-really-want-to-go-there look.

"Not a man," I assured her. She rolled her eyes again.

"But think about it," I persisted, thinking out loud. "It all hinges on the girl." At least I could figure out that much. I finished my taco and cleared my desk, then spread out everything I had on Charlotte aka Melinda. Then I stared at it, hoping something would jump up and announce itself.

"What do you know about adoption?" I asked Bernice when nothing happened.

"I know I don't want to," she said.

"Something is wrong with this. Archer is a sleazo, big time, and it's the only adoption he's done in all these years."

"Black market," Bernice shrugged. "Probably kidnapped her in the dead of night and sold her to strangers."

"Right," I chuckled, "then went downtown and filed a report about it. "I don't think so."

"What better way to throw them off the trail?"

"You watch too much TV. Bonnie Dean signed the papers."

"Uh," Bernice snorted. "So who is she? Who died and made her God?"

I stopped. "Oh my God. Bernice, that's a good question." I rifled through the stacks until I found what I wanted. The copies of the adoption files listed both parents as deceased and Bonnie Dean as the sole guardian. Where was the record of Lawrence Gafford's death?

My hands flew across the keyboard and I spent the next hour looking everyplace I could think of, but no death certificate. Lawrence Gafford hadn't filed a tax return in seven years. No reported income on his social. Nothing. I picked up the phone and called Candace in Oklahoma who was more than happy to be enlisted again.

I'd just hung up the phone and started looking on my own again when Byron dragged in, looking disgusted.

"Took you long enough." I twirled around in my chair, following his progress across the room to his desk. "What'd you find?"

"Shit," he plopped down in his chair and shoved a stack of papers over so he could rest his arm.

"There's a lot of that out there." I waited to see if the mood improved.

"How 'bout you?"

"Well, I've done a lot of thinking and that's pretty much what I see too." Suddenly, the mind I couldn't keep clear of thoughts flying free like hungry vultures went almost totally blank.

"You track down Geneva Brant's parents?"

"Oh, yeah!" I remembered. "She's not there."

"Big surprise," he offered.

"Yeah. But I got to thinking – why didn't Lawrence Gafford become Melinda's legal guardian when Beverly died? Isn't that the way it usually works? I mean, I can't find any record of divorce or anything…"

He perked up just a little. "That's true, so that's where you've been looking?"

I nodded. "No income, no taxes, nada for the last seven years, but no legal explanation. I called Candace and she's going to Oklahoma City tomorrow to check it out."

"I guess that's about all we can do today."

"Are you okay?" I didn't remember seeing him quite so subdued before. He nodded.

"Jesse? Line two," Bernice called across the room.

"You leaving?" I asked her as I reached to pick up the phone.

"Yep," she stood and wrestled her purse out of the drawer she kept it in.

"See you tomorrow," I told her. "This is Jesse," I told the phone.

"Jesse," Candace's voice was vibrating with excitement. "You're not gonna believe this!"

"I thought you weren't going till tomorrow," I quizzed, putting the phone on speaker so Byron could hear.

"I didn't have anything else to do so I called over there just to see if they'd do it and save me the trip. You're not gonna believe it!"

"You keep saying that," I chuckled. "So tell me already!"

"Okay. Get this. I called the OKC office just to see if they'd maybe fax it to me. At first, she didn't know when she'd be able to pull it, being so old and all, but *then* when I gave her his name, she said the file was already on her desk!" She paused. For emphasis, no doubt.

"And?"

"Well, the file was already *on* her desk because some insurance guy came in looking for it just this morning! Is that a coincidence, or what?"

Byron had gotten up and come over to perch on the corner of my desk. He looked a little impatient.

"What for?"

"You're never gonna..."

"Candace!" I cut her off. "Could I get the condensed version?"

"Oh. Ummm okay. Two months before Beverly croaked, she filed a claim with Aetna for a $250,000 life insurance policy on Lawrence Gafford..."

"So, he's definitely dead?"

"No, that's the deal. She said he was in a plane crash and died, but the body was never found."

"Well, how bout that?" I looked over at Byron.

"But that's not all I found," she said. "I checked the dates and got some newspaper clippings and she faxed me the file, including an old denial from Aetna. As long as there's no body, they can't declare him legally dead for seven years."

Byron and I both caught that one at the same time. "What's the date?" I asked.

"It will be exactly seven years in five days," Candace crowed. "But get this…the newspaper said it was suspected that Gafford was making a drug run and about five hundred grand disappeared with the plane!"

"Oh, Candace, you're an angel!" Finally, at least a partial explanation for all the confusion. "Fax me everything right now!"

"Don't you love it?"

"I do. I love you!" She was right. I couldn't believe what she'd turned up.

"On the way. Anything else I can do?"

"Give me tonight to go over what you send, then I'll call you in the morning," I promised.

The fax machine whirred to life minutes after I hung up the phone and Byron stood in front of it like it was about to give birth. There was something appealing about a man so concerned about a missing woman and child, to see compassion in one so primally male. I'd almost convinced myself to invite him home to go over our findings over dinner and let the night lead where it would when his cell phone rang and he got suddenly secretive, turning his back while he whispered at the phone. So much for that idea.

I stalked over to the fax and snatched up the papers, then made copies and thumped his pile on his desk on my way out the door. He might have called my name, but I couldn't hear him because I was running to the truck.

CHAPTER NINETEEN

After a quick stop at the grocery store, I headed home prepared for a long night of strategy. Wounded pride and hurt feelings wouldn't interfere with the case, but I didn't have to like it. Diligence, that's what it was. Diligence and productivity. I even remembered to charge up my phone.

Candace had stumbled across a gold mine, to my way of thinking. The fact that Lawrence Gafford had been missing for almost seven years answered a lot of questions and posed a few more. For once, my naturally suspicious mind was worth something. By midnight, I'd lined out several new possibilities. I debated taking a quick trip out to the Brant's just to see what kind of activity I'd find, but my more practical self ruled it out and sent me to bed.

Unfortunately, sleep wasn't on my agenda. I was tired all right, and the room was dark and Elvis curled up on my feet, but my mind was too busy. For a long time, I heard every noise, every grasshopper and cricket that denied winter's approach, every sweep of the tree branch across my bedroom screen when the wind forced northern skies a little farther south. About the time I'd start to doze off, another sound jerked me back and I'd stare again at the digital clock beside the bed, wishing the rhythmic flip of the minute cards could move a little faster and maybe hypnotize me to sleep.

It worked, at least for a while. I opened my eyes and the clock read 2:47. It was 1:12 when I closed them. Suddenly, my senses went on alert. Every other time I'd woken, I immediately pinpointed the culprit. This time, there was pure, concentrated silence. As if on cue, Elvis raised his head and looked at me. I lifted my head off the pillow, hardly daring to breathe. Listening. Something was wrong.

Sometimes, silence is the sound of loneliness. Or maybe aloneness would be more accurate. A dark, vacant place, so still it's like your soul is drawn to diffuse through the pores to fill the void. Then there's the pregnant silence that screams of an unseen presence. A tangible, palpable heaviness that sends the soul scurrying deep inside, hiding from horrors not yet realized. The silence that wrestled me from my sleep was the latter variety.

Wishing I'd taken the time to burp the waterbed last time I'd filled it so it wouldn't make those sloshing sounds when I moved, I eased myself to the edge and slid over. Hitting the ground on my knees, I considered my options. I could call the PD and tell them I don't hear anything but I doubt they'd be real worried about that. Or, I could pick up my cell and my Glock and go look around myself. Yikes. Feeling a little foolish, I crawled on hands and knees to the door, then stood up and listened to see if heard anything. Nope. Tip-toeing softly, I turned right down the hall and circled the inner perimeter of the house, checking every door and window. Not once did I hear a sound.

For nearly an hour, I patrolled the premises, persistently resisting the idea that I might look like Barney Fife. Even Elvis left his post in the bedroom windowsill and curled back up on the bed. At 3:39, I joined him. The waves were rocking me back to sleep when a crunching sound propelled me right up out of the bed like a fast motion levitation act. I hit the ground running and zeroed in on the window nearest the sound – the one in my office. What I saw made my skin crawl. There, in the shadows cast by my porch light on the F150, I could barely make out the shadow of a man scooting out from under the huge truck. I stared, frozen to the spot as he wiped his hands on the front of his thighs, cast a quick look around, then jogged off down the drive and into the night.

I'm not sure how long I stood there like that, but Elvis rubbed against my ankle and said, "Naaoooooooowwww," in a quieter than normal tone. Right. I picked up the phone and dialed Byron's number, never taking my eyes off the spot I'd last seen my visitor.

"What?" He didn't sound so fresh at four something.

"Byron," I whispered. "A man just crawled out from under my truck."

"What?" More awake now.

"A man just crawled out from under my truck," I repeated, still whispering.

Byron didn't say anything for a moment. "Call Barker, I'll be right there."

Barker. Where did I put his number? Unwilling to put the lights on and become a target with a spotlight, I ran to the kitchen and fetched a flashlight out from under the sink, then hurried back to the office where I dumped my purse on the desk and sorted through the resulting pile. Not an easy task in the dark with trembling hands trying frantically to keep the flashlight from pointing directly at the window and the Glock from disappearing beneath the waistband of sweats with elastic that gave up a long time ago. Why didn't I just put the number in my phone when he gave it to me? Found it! Now if I could just dial. Propping the flashlight on the purse debris, I hitched up the Glock with one hand and dialed with the other.

"Barker?" I asked when the ringing of the phone was replaced by heavy breathing.

"Yeah. Who's this?"

"Barker, it's Jesse. A man just crawled out from under my truck and Byron said to call you."

There was a sound that might best be called a groan.

"Barker, is that you?"

"Mmff yeah. Hold on…"

I shut off the flashlight and moved back to the window, just in case I missed something.

"Say that again, would you?" He sounded a little more human this time.

"A man just crawled out from under my truck," I repeated.

"Just now?"

"Well, no." I looked for the clock. "About ten minutes ago." Was that all? It seemed like hours.

"Are you all right?"

"I'm not dead." How the hell was I supposed to answer that?

"Is your partner on the way?"

"Yes."

"Don't touch anything. I'll be right there."

Don't touch anything. I hung up the phone. Like I was about to run outside and crawl under the truck to see what he'd left behind.

"Maybe we should make some coffee," I told Elvis who'd curled up in my chair.

I approached the kitchen cautiously, stopping before every corner and listening with scenes from every teenage horror movie I shouldn't have watched flashing in my head. I needn't have worried about Byron sneaking up on me. I heard the squeal of tires turning the corner and the spray of gravel even with the water running in the kitchen sink.

"Hey," I said when I met him at the door. His expression was grim.

"Barker on the way?"

I nodded. "He told me not to touch anything."

Byron didn't respond to that.

"What do you think he was doing under my truck?"

"Got a flashlight?"

I frowned and went to get it.

"What do you think…?" I started to ask again, holding the flashlight for ransom.

133

"I don't know. That's why I want to look."

"Don't touch anything," I warned his back as he headed out the door. He ignored that too.

Too nervous to just wait inside, I hurried back to my room and exchanged my drooping sweats for jeans and pulled on my Reeboks. A passing glance in the mirror caused my hands to shoot up and run through my hair. That would have to do.

When I ventured out on the front porch, I saw that Barker had arrived and the two men were conversing quietly beside the truck. I joined them just in time to hear Barker say something about bomb squad into his phone.

"What?"

"Let's get back inside," Byron took my arm and herded me that way.

"What did he say?" I twisted around and tried to see Barker over my shoulder.

"Come on," he tugged. "I'll tell you inside."

"What?" My heart was starting to pound again.

"We don't know that it's a bomb, but there's been a small box attached under your axel. I'd hoped maybe he'd just cut your brake line…"

"Oh!" I laughed, but not really. "That would have been so much better."

"Sit down, Jesse. In this case, yes it would have been. You saw the guy; you wouldn't have driven the truck. We'd have found the line cut, case closed."

"Aren't you forgetting one tiny little thing?" My voice was starting to do the mom thing again. "You don't have a suspect!"

"You didn't recognize the guy?"

I stared at him, open-mouthed.

"Did you get a good look at him?"

"Well, geez, Byron, it was so dark and it all happened so fast. Never mind that it was almost four o'clock in the morning! Did I forget to get his name? Where are my manners?" Full-blown mom now.

"Coffee," he said, moving toward the kitchen.

I didn't speak again until he returned with mugs in hand. I took one from him, glad for something to hold. Elvis disappeared at the first sign of reinforcement. Traitor. Byron took a seat in the chair by the door and looked at me intently.

"I'm fine," I told him, thankful to hear my normal voice had returned.

He nodded.

"I'm not liking it much, though."

He almost smiled at that. "Where's your sense of adventure?"

"Asleep."

There was a knock at the door and Byron reached over to open it without getting up.

"Coffee, man?" Byron asked as Barker walked in.

"No," he shook his head and looked over at me.

"What?"

"We're waiting for a team from Dallas," he said, sinking wearily onto the couch.

"Is that bad?" I asked.

Barker rubbed his face with one hand. He still looked half asleep. "Well, our guy says it's live and he doesn't want to mess with it."

"I don't blame him," Byron said. "It's not like DeSoto gets bombs every day."

"I don't think they've ever had one. Mitchell said he saw something like this when he was with San Antonio. Homemade but powerful."

"So," it was starting to sink in, "somebody put a bomb under my truck. They shot my car and now they want to blow up my truck."

Both men nodded.

"Great."

"Good thing you saw him," Barker said.

"What happened, anyway?" Byron asked. "You weren't still up, were you?"

"No. Something woke me up about 2:30 and I got up and walked around for about an hour. I never heard anything else so I went back to bed, then something woke me up again."

"What?" Byron asked.

I shrugged. "I don't know, a sort of a crunching sound."

Byron and Barker exchanged glances.

"Like maybe a car door slamming?" Barker asked.

I shook my head. "No, I don't think so. It was more like..." I tried to think of something that would make the same sound, but drew a blank.

"And you say the first time you woke up was over an hour before?" Byron asked.

"Yeah. I was watching the clock."

Barker got up. "Maybe we better check the rest of the house."

"You coming?" Byron asked, pausing beside the front door.

With half the police force in the front yard, I was starting to relax and feel the lack of sleep. Still, with most of the lights out and my companions disappearing, sitting in the living room in the dark didn't seem too welcoming. I decided to join them.

"Let me get my jacket," I told him.

By the time I'd wrapped myself in denim, they were both outside and I caught up with them going around the south side of the house. Not wanting to be in trouble, I had my gun and my phone in hand. I walked slowly, right behind them, ignoring the swarms around the truck in the driveway. The grass in the yard was dead from consistent lack of watering and made a soft, swooshing sound beneath our feet. No place to find a footprint here, especially not in the dark. I watched as they examined the holly bushes that lined the foundation. Prickly. To discourage burglars.

They rounded the corner, flashlights sweeping, with me right behind them. Barker's beam stopped on the floodlights mounted under the eaves.

"Isn't that a motion sensor?" he asked, shining the flashlight on the two dark bulbs, angled to illuminate most of the back yard, including the porch and kitchen door.

"Yeah but it's burnt out," I said, wishing I'd remembered that fact sometime before now.

"How long's it been out?" Byron asked. "It was on the night we found the dead guy."

"I don't know," I said, remembering. I don't spend a lot of time walking around in the back yard in the dark for some reason. "I think that's the last time I saw it."

Byron mumbled something and Barker ducked around the corner and whistled at somebody. I moved on before they thought of any other embarrassing questions. The back door looked untouched, at least to me, but a few feet past it, I saw the screen from my bathroom window on the ground.

"Didn't you just put that back on?" Byron snuck up behind me.

"Yeah," I reached for it but he stopped me.

"Don't touch it!"

"Maybe it was just loose and fell off," I said, wishing I could believe that. A sudden gust of chilly wind caused my hair to flutter against the back of my neck, sending a shiver down my spine. "I'm going back inside."

"Jesse," Byron tucked a warm hand under the arm I held clenched against my side, "it's okay. We'll get this guy."

All I could do was nod and look down at the ground. Not soon enough, we wouldn't. I should be tucked in my warm bed. Instead, I stood in a dark yard in the pre-dawn hours with cold wind rippling my hair and my heart. I stepped back as Barker returned with reinforcements, then followed Byron around the other side of the house. Nothing unusual there. We wound up in the front yard again, watching serious men with serious weapons maul a truck that wasn't even mine.

"Let's go inside and get some coffee," Byron suggested, like I hadn't been ready to do that years ago.

Before we turned to go, the two officers beside the truck reached down to help another officer who'd been looking under the carriage. As they walked back toward the other officers on the lawn, Byron and Barker headed toward them, motioning for me to go on inside. Curiosity got the better of me and I waited.

I couldn't make out much of what they were saying but they started moving back toward the house and I thought I heard something about the

Dallas Bomb Squad. Before I could ask, I heard a loud click and somebody yelled, "Take cover!"

There was no time to respond. An explosion followed and knocked me back a few feet. I landed on my butt and fell back into the dirt that was intended for a flower bed beside the front door. For a moment my ears were stopped up like I'd been swimming and I heard shouts that seemed far away and a loud ringing noise. My attention was drawn to the street where my rental truck was laying on its side and flames shot up from the bottom. Oh my God! Just like a Die Hard movie. Sirens blared in the distance and people were running toward the truck from both sides of the street. Firemen on both sides of the truck motioned them to stay back and I just sat and watched. It was so surreal.

I looked over where the group of officers had been and saw them scattered around the yard. Everyone was on the ground, but most appeared to be moving and a couple had started to stand up. There was smoke all around that made it hard to see clearly. I reached up and felt my cheeks were wet but I wasn't sure if that was from the smoke in my eyes or from crying. Maybe both.

"Byron!" I called, doubtful that anyone would hear me. "Barker?" The truck was surrounded by firemen now and it looked like the flames were out. An ambulance had pulled in behind it. It looked as though the EMTs were checking each officer in the yard. I finally spotted Byron standing beside one of the EMTs and pointing back at me. At least he's ok. I just sat there. This couldn't be real.

One of the EMTs walked toward me. He looked like he was barely twenty and accompanied by a female officer who couldn't have been much older. Her blonde hair was in a ponytail. I felt ancient.

"How are you feeling?" he asked. Randall was on his name tag.

I looked up at them both, wondering what you're supposed to say to that in this situation. Fine? "I'm ok."

Blondie said something to him and he extended a hand to me. "Let's see if we can get you inside and check you out, ok?" He smiled.

I took his hand and let him help me to my feet, feeling a little shaky but otherwise ok. They led me in and had me take a seat on the couch. Elvis was there, watching it all from his perch in the windowsill.

"I'm surprised it didn't break the windows out," I said, for no particular reason. Maybe just to feel normal.

"Yeah, that's lucky," Blondie observed. "Actually, they said the bomb wasn't very big. It could've been a lot worse."

I sat still while Randall poked and prodded and measured and finally pronounced me ok, albeit with my blood pressure a little elevated. Understandably so.

I guess I still looked a little stunned so Blondie stayed with me when Randall went back outside. I was grateful for the company, especially when she seemed good at making small talk and didn't seem to mind when I didn't answer. I don't know how long it was before Byron and Barker came back inside but neither one of them looked good when they did.

"Are ya'll ok?" I hated that my voice sounded a little quivery.

"We're fine. You?" Byron asked.

I just looked at him. He didn't define okay. "Thanks for staying with her," Byron told Blondie as she went back outside.

Barker sat down on the couch beside me and leaned forward with his elbows resting on his knees. "Talk to me, Jesse."

I shifted my gaze from Byron to Barker and stifled a chuckle. Like I've been withholding evidence, right? "What?"

"Who wants you dead?" he asked.

"Gee, Barker, didn't I mention that?" I know it sounded sharp, but did he honestly believe I knew the answer to that question? I looked at Byron. "How's the truck?"

"Let's just say it's a good thing you weren't in it," Byron sounded like the voice of reason.

I didn't really want to think about that. "I guess they got tired of warning me, huh?"

"Looks like," Byron nodded his agreement.

My first thought was that I should go get my gun. My second thought was that a gun wouldn't have helped much if I'd been in the truck. I wasn't sure where to go from there.

"Well," Barker raised his hands, "maybe not. It wasn't hooked to the starter. They'll have to go over the pieces in the lab but as far as I heard, they didn't see a remote detonator so it may have been on a timer set to go off in the early morning hours when no one was around. We're not sure yet."

I looked at him in amazement, not sure what to think. Somehow the idea that somebody thought it logical to plant a bomb under my truck on purpose was terrifying, no matter what time it was set to go off. What if I had to run out in the middle of the night for Pepsi or something? "Unh! Does that really make a difference?"

"It could," Barker looked like he was trying to convince himself. "It might have been set to go off before you got up…you know, to scare you."

I laughed. "Well, then, it worked."

Byron shook his head. "I don't think so. It's too much. I mean, Greaves, a dead duck, dead flowers, those were to scare her. Bombs blow shit up."

The numbness was starting to wear off and in its place, I felt a growing sense of panic. Or maybe anger. Or a little of both. I got up.

"Do me a favor, will you?" I looked at Byron, hoping he'd understand. "Stand guard while I get some sleep, okay?"

CHAPTER TWENTY

Of course I didn't sleep much, with all the noise, both in the yard and in my head. I did get a shower though and a nice purring from Elvis. With those two things under my belt, I was ready for anything. Byron drove me to the Ford dealership and explained the situation. They didn't like it much but at least I got my car back. Minus the bullet hole.

"Straight to the office," Byron ordered with one foot inside his Mustang door, "do not pass go, do not collect $200."

I made the appropriate face when he turned his back, then did exactly what he said. I might be headstrong but I'm not totally stupid. Someone tried to blow me up. Target practice wouldn't have saved me. I needed to think about that for a while.

As soon as I reached the highway, Byron fell in behind me and tailed me into the office parking lot.

"Morning, Bernice," I mumbled, heading straight for my desk when I got inside.

"Good morning," she chirped. "Coffee's ready."

I changed my course and headed for the pot. "What's new?" I wanted to hear something normal for a change.

"Huh?" Obviously, Bernice wasn't into it.

I rolled my eyes and schlepped to my desk. "What now?" I asked Byron, dropping into my chair.

"I wish I knew," he said, following suit.

"Something's wrong, isn't it?" Bernice asked, slowing her shuffle toward my desk. That Bernice. She doesn't miss much.

"Someone kind of blew up my rental truck this morning," I mumbled.

Her eyes popped open wide, shoving the eyebrows back under the bangs again. "Blew up?"

"Yeah, well, pretty much."

She looked at Byron for confirmation. He didn't have to nod, it was all over his face.

"Look," I leaned up and looked over at him, "this is insane. So I might have been blown up by a bomb," I shrugged. "I might have been hit by a bus downtown yesterday too, but I wasn't."

"Nobody planted a bus on your truck," he had that sarcastic look that made my eyes want to roll. I resisted.

"You know what I mean. I'm not going to be all scared to death and stop living. I want to go out and find these idiots and make it stop. They're starting to really tick me off."

"Jesse, you can't just run all over town like a moving target," he said, shaking his head emphatically.

"Well I can't just sit here like a sitting duck either!"

He sighed. Loud.

"What'd Barker say?" I asked, knowing he must have said something about all this.

"They'll have someone on your house twenty-four seven," he said. "I've got custody of you."

"Oh, lucky you," I tried to grin.

He glared at me, then got up from his chair. "Come on, then."

After a quick stop to gas up the Cobra, we headed for the gun range where Byron strapped me mercilessly into a Kevlar vest. Those things are heavy but I didn't have to worry about getting cold.

"What do I need this for?"

"To stop the bullet."

I looked down, then frowned at him. "A lot of my good parts are still hanging out."

He gave me exasperated. "Want a suit of armor?"

"I was kidding, Byron." The man has totally lost his sense of humor. "What's that?" I asked when he picked up a box from John and slid it in his jacket pocket.

"Insurance," he said.

Right.

Our next stop was the Brant estate at Frost Farms. Mostly I just followed him and watched while he scared the phooey out of a couple of stable hands. Unfortunately, they were pretty stupid and didn't have much to tell.

"What now, Sherlock?" I asked when we got back in the car.

Byron looked at his watch. "We've got two choices," he said. "Archer or Brant."

I looked at him long and hard for a minute. "Why not both?"

"You know why."

"Byron, I'm fine. Drop me at the office to pick up my car. I'll go for Archer, you go get Brant." Seemed simple enough to me.

"That's not smart," he shook his head, putting the car in gear and pulling back out on the road.

"Hey, I'm bullet proof, remember? And a little lumpier than I used to be."

He didn't think that was funny either.

I watched the scenery as we drove, wondering how things could look so normal when obviously the whole world had gone mad. But the sun kept shining and the trees swayed in silent rhythm while the wind blew the leaves in swirls to litter the ground below. It all looked so peaceful, I almost bought it.

"All you have to do is tell me what to do. You know I can take care of myself," I reasoned, surprised he seemed like he was actually considering it.

What do you know? It worked. Although Byron did look at me a little like one of us had lost all sense of good judgment and I'm not sure which one he thought it was.

It was good to be back in the golden, fits like a glove, Taurus, with a bullet hole you almost couldn't find anymore, unless you're like me and see it there glaring at you anyway. I was also a little surprised how fast the day sped by, even though my mother warned me that would happen once I turned thirty. *Especially* if I was still single by then. Her emphasis, not mine. Funny how my eyes start to roll when I ponder Mom's pearls of wisdom. If I didn't start hanging with a different crowd, they were likely to roll away one day and leave me blind. Speaking of Mom, I better make time to stop by later. That short, "Don't believe anything you read in the paper about me," wasn't going to work for long.

Gliding along I-35 North with the radio blasting oldies from KVIL, I wished Ron Chapman, the deejay of deejays, wasn't only on the air in the early morning when reasonable people were fast asleep. The music of my teenage years makes me feel more invincible. Even more than the stupid flak jacket Byron made me swear I'd leave on. Straightjacket was more like it. Those things are heavy and they hardly bend! Still, when I exited the freeway and headed east into never never land, I have to admit, it did make me feel a tiny bit safer.

When I pulled up in front of Archer's office, I was surprised to find the parking lot empty except for a beat up Buick on two wheels that wouldn't be going anywhere under its own steam for awhile. At least I could park off the street this time. Reluctantly, I got out, locking the door behind me. Even with cars alternately whizzing and sputtering down the street, the place had an air of desertion. Like one of those ghost town movies without the swinging saloon doors. I glanced at my watch. It was only a little after three. Kind of early for the place to be empty.

Nervously, I tried the door. It was unlocked, but as I stepped into the waiting room, all I saw was dark, a little lighter in the general vicinity of the one lone window. With the front door propped wide open, I looked around for a light switch and found it, but it was already turned on. Maybe Archer forgot to pay the electric bill. Slowly, I let the door swing shut behind me and stood still, waiting for my eyes to adjust to the darkness.

A little carpet fresh, or maybe some Lysol spray, would be a worthwhile investment I determined, wrinkling my nose at the subtle stench that crept up at me from the filthy upholstery. Even stale cigar smoke would be better. As I acclimated to the dimness, I edged on over by the front desk and called, "Hello!" Quiet as a tomb. I started anticipating that horrible music from scary movies.

That prickly, oh-no-something's-wrong feeling started in the pit of my stomach as I ventured down a short hall that led to an appallingly filthy unisex bathroom. If the used condoms in the vicinity of the overflowing trash can were an indication, the room was a multi-function facility. Ugh. I closed the door and used the bottom of my sweater sleeve to wipe my prints off the knob. I didn't want anyone to know I'd ever been in there. Probably I should start carrying latex gloves if I'm going to be a real PI.

I walked back to the desk and glanced around again, envisioning the room as it was on my last visit. Full to overflowing and cranky. Only one other door, the one into Archer's office behind the desk. I found it odd that they'd be closed at this early hour, and stranger still that they'd leave the place unlocked, what with the burglar bars and all.

Taking as deep a breath as I dared, I stepped behind the desk and knocked tentatively on the door. No answer. I knocked again, a little louder this time. I'm not sure why. Maybe because I was beginning to regret coming here by myself, not that I'd ever admit it. It was absolutely silent, except for the filtered noise from the street. A little voice inside kept telling me to get while the getting's good.

I stood and stared at the door for a while, then let my sweater slip down over my hand and turned the knob. I'm not sure if it was the visual impact or the stench that knocked me back a step, but what I saw was enough to make me wish I'd followed my instincts. I'm not sure how long the screaming lasted before I figured out it was me and stopped.

Garfield Archer was laid back in his chair, eyes wide open and a small dark hole in the center of his forehead with a tiny trickle of blood that traveled down beside his nose, across his mouth and chin and disappeared into the dark fabric of his leisure suit.

I forced myself to take a few steps closer to the desk, squinting through a grimace like it would soften the effect any. Strangling noises popped out of my mouth every now and then, letting some of the pressure off I suppose. It was kind of like when a field mouse got loose in my house only much, much worse. The screaming just happened, separate from my brain. You see a dead guy – you're supposed to scream. Archer was definitely dead and considerably puffier than the last time I saw his scrawny self. The question was – who did it and what do I do now?

Get the hell out of there and call Byron, the little chicken voice screamed in my head. But I needed answers and I didn't want to leave without them. Besides, a dead guy couldn't hurt me, right? When I took another small step toward the back of the desk, out of the corner of my eye I spied a mess behind Archer's chair that I suspect was the best part of his brain. I didn't really want to examine that any closer.

The cell phone in my pocket rang and I swear I had a close brush with the ceiling before I tripped and landed flat on my butt in the floor. Keeping an eye on Archer like he might actually do something, I fished the phone out of my pocket and answered it.

"What?" Professional, I know.

"Jesse? You all right?" It was Byron.

"Sure," I lied, wondering if he'd known me long enough to know "sure" means "anything but" in Jesse-ease.

"Where are you?"

"Archer's office."

"Get any answers from him?"

I looked around. "Not exactly, no."

"Jesse, what's wrong?"

I'm really going to have to work on my acting skills. "He's………. kind of ……dead."

"What?" I held the phone away from my ear for just a second while he did the Damn-it-I-knew-I-should-never-let-you-go-over-there-by-yourself drill.

"Are you done?" I asked when he got quiet.

More quiet.

"Byron?" For once, I sounded like the sensible one. I got up off the floor, still clutching the phone in my hand.

"Are the cops there?" he asked, finally.

"No-o. I don't think they know."

"Jesse…" he started the talk-to-Jesse-like-she's-a-moron-or-a-small-child drill. I was getting a lot better at reading him.

"Byron," I cut him off. "I promise – he's completely dead. He's not going anywhere. I just wanted to look around a little before I called them, that's all."

"Oh, now *there's* a good idea." Sarcasm. "Get your prints all over everything so they'll have a good reason to hold you."

"Unh!" I cradled the phone with my shoulder while I tried to keep my sweater over my fingers and open the file cabinet that stood next to the desk. "Like I don't have better sense than that! I'm not leaving prints on anything."

"Are you wearing gloves?" he sounded surprised. Gloves. Sigh. I was almost fast enough.

"No," I admitted. "I'm covering my hands with my sweater."

"Great. Then you're leaving fibers all over everything."

I didn't have an answer for that and the files were jammed full. If Miss Congeniality from the other day filed things, I might never find what I needed. Especially while I was trying to hold the phone to my ear with my shoulder. And the damned vest was starting to itch.

"Jesse, you've got to get out of there. Now."

"Ten minutes," I bargained.

"Now," he insisted.

I didn't answer, using a pencil to try to separate the files enough to see the names on the tabs. No Brant. Damn.

"Jesse?"

"What?" He was getting annoying.

"How did you get in?"

"The door was unlocked."

"Did it ever occur to you that someone else might come in and find you in there with a dead guy?"

Oops. Good point. "But if I leave, I won't get to look at his files."

"And if you don't and the killer sees your car there..."

He didn't have to finish that thought. I shut the file drawer and headed for the door.

"You win. I'm gone. Where are you?" I said, peeking out the window in the waiting room before I opened the front door.

"On my way but I want you out of there."

"Hold on," I told him, slipping the phone back in my pocket so I could wipe my prints off the front door knob after I closed it behind me. I didn't retrieve it until I was in the car with the doors locked. "Okay. So where do I meet you?"

"Why don't you head back to the office? I'll call you there."

I frowned but couldn't think of a better idea. This wasn't the sort of neighborhood to hang around in. "All right."

I was back on the freeway headed south before I figured out that he was just as much a sitting duck there as I was. We should have gone together. At least I could keep an eye on his Cobra while he was inside. That decided, I got off at the next exit and headed back. Knowing it would take him awhile to get through late afternoon downtown traffic, I stopped at the Jack-in-the-Box on the corner and got a soda.

Drink in hand, I drove slowly back toward Archer's office, taking careful note of the neighboring blocks. There was no sign of Byron's car and mine would be too conspicuous parked out front so I made the loop around the block and settled for a spot around the corner in front of a garage. I could still see between the buildings to the front corner of Archer's office parallel parked on the street in front of JJ's Automotive, sandwiched between a primer red Oldsmobile about fifty years old and a car of questionable lineage with rear tires big enough for a Monster truck and leopard skin seat covers. Mom would call it a pimp-mobile but there were no dice dangling from the rear view mirror, so it wasn't, really. Actually, I didn't see a rear-view mirror at all.

I let the seat back a little to allow for slumping and settled in to watch, feeling very much like a private eye from television. What a life. It didn't take long to get bored. I left the radio off so I could hear things and I think I was still numb from the day's shocking surprises. I hadn't been doing this long enough to be desensitized. An occasional car trolled down the street, but nothing extraordinary. They hardly noticed me.

When the digital clock flipped to 5:00 I wondered if I should worry. Byron had plenty of time to get here by now but there was no sign of him. Unless he parked somewhere besides in front of the office. Aha! Rule number one. Private investigators never announce their presence by parking in plain sight. They skulk around. How could I forget that?

I debated whether I should surrender my perfect hiding place for a quick pass around the block, or get out and go for a walk. It wasn't dark yet, so I opted for the latter. After all, I had on a flak jacket and a big gun, right? I could load it in a hurry if I had to. No. Better load it first. I stopped and loaded the Glock then adjusted the shoulder harness as best as I could with the flak vest on. Nothing is easy.

I eased out of the car and closed the door as quietly as possible, then headed for the fence that circled JJ's. I hadn't seen it yet, but the loud barking that erupted inside made me think I didn't want to go in there. Hoping there was no one home armed with lethal weapons, I skulked through the side yard of the house next to JJ's and emerged in a tiny alley that ran beside Archer's office and curved behind. With gravel crunching persistently beneath my feet, I snuck around the front corner of the building and peered out, looking for Byron's car. No sign of it. I checked my watch. Five fifteen. He should have been here a long time ago.

I leaned against the wall and waited for inspiration. Going back inside Archer's office was not an appealing thought. But maybe Byron was already in there, or worse yet, maybe he'd already come and gone and I missed it. The sound of a boom box blaring rap music accompanied by teenage voices scooted me around to the back of the building to avoid being seen. When I spotted the burglar bars on what must be Archer's office window, I decided to peek. Maybe I'd find Byron in there.

146

Walking slowly to minimize crunching, I realized as I approached the window that the ground slanted downward and I wasn't tall enough to see inside. Jumping high enough to catch a glimpse would require more effort than I was willing to invest.

I trudged on down to the other end of the building thinking I might get lucky and catch a glimpse of Byron or his car. Instead, I spied a plastic milk crate in a pile of trash beside the dumpster. I could climb on that.

I chanced a peek around the front of the building but still saw no one moving around. Ducking back into the alley, I gingerly wrestled the crate out of the pile, trying hard not to make too much noise. With my trophy in hand, I made my way back up the slope to the highest point beneath the window and planted it there, kicking gravel out from underneath to help prevent myself from teetering over once I'd climbed up. As I'd hoped, the step up afforded me a perfect view. Bizarrely framed in an eerie parallelogram of the day's last light, the first thing I saw was the mess behind Archer's chair.

Swallowing hard, I forced my eyes up and squinted trying to see if there was any sign of movement beyond the office door I'd left open. The sun was already setting and the dusky light didn't penetrate far into the darkened rooms. The only thing moving was my own shadow. So much for good ideas.

Holding tight to the building, I lowered my right foot, feeling for the ground, then stepped down and turned around. I didn't see him at first, standing in the shadows, but when I did, the message was clear. Caught.

CHAPTER TWENTY-ONE

Maybe I'm lacking in spontaneity, but staring into eyes that look colder than the Arctic ocean backed up by two hundred muscled pounds of a six foot hulk dressed in commando clothes makes me speechless. At least at first.

"What the hell do you think you're doing?" Byron asked.

I swear he crossed the alley in one giant step.

"Looking for you," I offered in a wobbly voice. I cleared my throat.

"You're supposed to be at the office."

"Yeah...well..." Good argument, Morgan. That's telling him. I shuffled my feet and felt my heart start beating again. "I just figured you might need some backup."

He snorted. "Right."

I glanced at the shadows we both cast on the alley. His was at least twice the size of mine. Some backup. I shifted and stood a little straighter. "You never know. One day, you'll be glad I'm here."

He kept glaring. In all honesty, he didn't look like he'd need much protecting.

"Did you go in?" I asked.

Nodding his head, he took my arm and led me back to the end of the building. "And I called the cops. They'll be here in a minute."

"Oh."

He almost grinned. "Can you lie convincingly?"

"Why?"

"Because I found him," he explained. "I came over here to ask him a few questions and there he was."

I just stared.

"And there you weren't," he added, obviously aware that I didn't get it.

"Oh." I tried to picture it. "No, I don't think I can."

"Good," he said. "We finally agree about something. I don't think you can either. You look suspicious when you're telling the truth. Where's your car?"

"Next street over," I nodded in that direction.

"Why don't you go there now and go back to the office like you were supposed to?" He started walking that way, keeping a firm grip on my arm.

He left me at the back yard of the house next to JJ's and I started skulking back through, trying to ignore the barking dog. I'd just emerged in the front yard when a loud bang scared the shit out of me and dropped me to the ground.

"Jesse!" Byron's voice came thundering up behind sounding far away, displaced by the loud ringing in my ears.

"Oh, thank God!" he dropped to the ground beside me and hugged me close.

"What the hell was that?" I asked when I could pry my mouth away from his vest.

"God," he shook his head. "I thought it was your car!"

"My car!" I scrambled to my feet, ignoring the siren that roared up the next street over. Two steps further down the fence line and I slowed again. "My car. MY CAR!!" It was a rerun from the early morning. My beautiful golden Taurus was still kind of parked where I left it, but now it wasn't golden. It was on fire. I couldn't believe it.

Byron came up behind me and wrapped me in his arms. I never even heard the officer approaching.

"Good evening officer," Byron said over my head, muffling my mouth with his forearm. "I'm Byron Montgomery. I called about Archer."

Taking the hint, I peeked up at whoever Byron was talking to. A tall, black man in DPD uniform glared down at me. "Who's this?"

"Jesse Morgan, my partner," Byron said. "That's her car over there." People were coming from all over the block, forming a semi-circle around the Taurus until another officer started moving them back to make room for the fire truck rolling up.

The man kept staring. "I need to see identification. Both of you."

Byron eased away from me. "We're both armed," he said, moving slowly with his hands up in plain sight. "My ID's in my inside pocket."

I stood completely still, waiting. The officer didn't look too concerned. Trimmed like a mountain, he might even have an inch or two on Byron. I guess he didn't think we'd try to take him. Or maybe things blow up around here every day.

"Where's the weapon?"

"Left shoulder," Byron eased his jacket back so he could see then pulled his vest open so the officer could see him reaching into the pocket and removing his wallet. With slow hands, Byron removed his driver's license, his PI license and his conceal and carry, handing them over.

The officer stared at them, then back at Byron. "Okay," he handed them back and turned to me.

"Left shoulder," I repeated what Byron said and reached in my front right jeans pocket for my wallet. Occasionally uncomfortable in tight jeans, it's the safest place I can think of for my wallet. Well…really it's a business card holder with just enough room for my licenses. I stick any money I have in my pocket. I'd have to be dead for a pickpocket to get it there. Even then it would take some effort.

"All right," he said, handing them back to me. "Now tell me what the hell happened here and keep your hands where I can see them."

I looked up at Byron. Cops know how to talk to cops. Even coming from him, the whole thing sounded bizarre. I hate to think what it would have sounded like if I'd said it.

Hours later, we were parked securely in a back booth at El Chico's finishing our dinner when Barker joined us.

"You two are getting quite the reputation," he remarked, sliding into the seat next to me.

"Not exactly the kind I had in mind," Byron answered.

"You okay?" Barker looked over at me.

I glared at him. "They blew up my car."

Barker sighed and looked back at Byron. "What's the plan?"

Byron shook his head. "I don't want her to go home."

I glared at him too.

Barker agreed. "Not safe, Jesse. Somebody means business. That bomb on the truck this morning was one thing, this was another. We can't assume they're trying to scare you anymore."

"Yeah, well, they're not safe either…not if I find them. If it's that scrawny little weasel who's been tailing me, I wish I'd made a smear in the alley with his lousy ass. You know what really pisses me off?" I asked. "I wasn't out of the car for more than half an hour this afternoon. They were there watching the whole time and I never saw them. They blew up my car!" I still couldn't believe it.

"You got a line on who this might be at all?" Barker asked Byron.

He shook his head. "Nothing I can run with. I know what it's linked to, but I'll be damned if I know who's behind it."

"Look," Barker leaned forward earnestly, looking at each of us in turn. "I know you're trying to protect a client, but this has to stop. You're not safe anymore. You've gotta tell me what's going on."

I shrugged at Byron. Barker was right. Who was I trying to protect?

"You'll take the report?" Byron asked.

Barker nodded. I waved at the waitress. I needed another beer.

Byron did the telling, he knows all the right words. I interjected occasionally but mostly just traced designs in the condensation on my mug of beer and ate chips and salsa. The bomb in my car threw me into serious overload and I wasn't feeling much of anything anymore. The thought that I couldn't go home to my own house pissed me off, but if Byron had suggested a quick trip to Alaska I wouldn't have argued. I felt like I'd entered the twilight zone and the whole world was going on around me but I was sealed, separate from everything, and about that vulnerable. Not a good feeling and not one I intended to keep.

"I'm tired. I need to sleep," I said suddenly, interrupting whatever they were saying.

"Yeah, you're right," Byron said, gathering his jacket from the booth beside him. "Come on, let's go."

I followed him outside and stood beside the car, vaguely aware of him giving directions to Barker.

"We'll stop by your house to pick up what you need," he said, glancing over at me from behind the wheel after we got in the car.

"Elvis," I said.

He nodded. "Elvis, too."

I sighed. This was all too strange.

I moved through the house like I was in a fog, stuffing things in a duffel bag. Byron gathered a litter box and a bag of cat food and helped me carry everything to the car. Elvis growled at both of us from my lap as we pulled away from the curb. Probably thought it was a midnight trip to the vet.

Mornings are scary. Rudely awakened out of dreamland, hours after the last coffee or Pepsi or hamburger. No idea what's been going on in the world while you sleep so you never know what horrible news will greet you and spend all day playing catch up. Besides, your hair looks like crap no matter what and you have that funny taste in your mouth and feel like your teeth are wearing little sweaters. Not good.

Byron's guest room looked like a prison cell. One lonely bed, one nightstand, one lamp. No pictures on the walls. All it needed was a stainless steel toilet in the corner. Elvis glared at me from his post in the windowsill. I considered glaring back. If Byron thought he was going to keep me prisoner here, he better think again. Still, where else could I go? I didn't want to go to Mom's. What if they followed me there and something happened? I couldn't risk that.

I shuffled out into the hall in search of a bathroom. There must be one here somewhere.

"To your left," a disgustingly cheerful voice called from what I presume was the kitchen. Cooking sounds were there.

"Unh."

My eyes worked better after I washed my face, but the rest of me still didn't feel too good. I had vague memories of Archer's dead body and Arnold Schwarznegger and my car blowing up. No. I had vivid memories of my car blowing up. Must call insurance man. A hot shower and clean clothes made me look considerably more presentable, but inside, I was still a wreck.

I wandered back into the hall and headed toward the kitchen in search of coffee. Coffee first, insurance second.

"Here," Byron came toward me with a steaming mug in his hand so I sat on the nearest object of necessary height. Fortunately it was a chair. "Hungry?"

"Unh."

Byron smiled. He was too far away to smack.

"How's that?" he joined me at the table and slid a plate full of eggs and hash browns at me. I have to admit it smelled really good.

He gave me time to eat and drink my coffee in peace. I guess he knew me pretty well. When I finished my food, he refilled my coffee and sat back down. "Sleep okay?"

"Fine, thanks." See? Autopilot does work sometimes. The real answer would have been more like "Hell no and why would you even bother to ask you two-timing traitor?"

He sat and looked at me with a sad dogface and didn't say anything until I started to squirm.

"Byron," I sighed.

"What do you want from me, Jess?" His face was so serious and so concerned, I started to feel really bad about being angry with him.

"I'm sorry." I couldn't tell him exactly why, but I was.

He stared some more. Finally, he asked, "Are you ever going to tell me what went wrong?"

I thought about it. I really did. But rejection is something I'd rather do than have done to me, so I smiled. "Nope. You're the big, bad detective. You figure it out."

I left him sitting there, staring, while I went back to gather my things. When I came back out, he was still there. "Get the rest of my stuff, would you?" Elvis was not happy and I didn't know how long I could hold on to him with a duffel bag in my other hand.

"What for?" he jumped up in utter amazement.

"Because I don't live here, that's what for," I propelled myself toward the front door, Elvis in tow.

"Jesse…"

"I mean it, Byron," I told him, struggling to open the door without setting Elvis free, "I was too tired to argue last night and I appreciate your hospitality and all but I'm going home. Well not home, exactly…" I kept chattering while I maneuvered the knob on the deadbolt. "I'll go home and take Elvis, then I'm going to get another car and run by the office and go out and locate some scum to sweep off the streets…" I kept talking all the way to the car. He followed me, like I knew he would.

I looked up at him expectantly, waiting for him to unlock the door.

"You know this isn't smart," he said.

"I've been accused of a lot of things," I retorted, "but smart isn't usually one of them."

He didn't argue with that. I wondered if I should be offended. Dropping the duffel bag on the ground beside the car, I wrestled with Elvis and waited impatiently for Byron to fetch the keys he'd left in the house.

"You forgot this," he flung the Kevlar vest in the back seat after he opened the door to stash the rest of my things.

"It makes me itch," I frowned.

The way he jerked the car into reverse, I figured he was a little pissed so I sat quietly and waited. When we pulled up in front of the house, it looked so abandoned, except for the DeSoto squad car parked across the street. Byron wandered over to chat while I carried Elvis in then went back for the rest of my things. By the time I had Elvis fed and locked the front door, Byron was back behind the wheel.

He didn't get any chattier while we visited the Ford place and got me a new car. Worse, he tossed me the Kevlar, got in his car and drove away before I'd even cranked up the engine in the rental they reluctantly gave me while they waited for the insurance payment to replace my Taurus. And, I suppose, their truck. Some people are so picky.

I drove back to the office and settled into my desk to sort mail and try to decide what my next move would be. Honestly, I never thought Byron would leave me alone but he wasn't at the office and Bernice said he hadn't been there. Once I had my emails answered and my desk squared away, there was nothing left to do but start back at the beginning.

"I'm going to the Brant's," I told Bernice, "and if I don't get any answers there, I'm going downtown to his office."

Ever diligent, Bernice nodded but didn't look up from her filing. "Try not to get killed."

I appreciated the encouragement.

My rental was another Taurus, only a dark green one. Kind of like Byron's Cobra color, only not nearly as much fun. I did suggest that they rent me a Cobra, but they didn't like that idea much. On the drive out Pleasant Run, I considered whether I should replace my car with a Cobra even better than Byron's. That thought caused my foot to press down even harder on the accelerator. By the time I pulled up beside the Brant house, I was practically soaring and fully convinced that I could afford the increase in payments, no matter how much it was. After all, I was a business owner now and every good PI should have a hot car. Now if I could just convince Ford Motor Credit of the same thing.

Feeling much better about my immediate future, I parked the car on the side of the road beside the stables, far enough that it didn't attract attention, but close enough to run to if I got in trouble. I'd even opted for my Reeboks instead of my trusty boots. Is that good planning, or what?

This was the first place I came when the investigation started. It was where I was supposed to find Lawrence Gafford but found Gary Greaves instead. It was also where little Melinda disappeared and her mother soon after. I suspected it was where I'd find the little weasel who'd been tailing me in Greaves' truck. And, it was where I fully intended to get some answers or die trying.

Since I'm not entirely without common sense, I'd slipped the Kevlar vest on under my jacket before I headed over. The way the wind was whipping across the open field, I was grateful for any warmth I could find. It didn't seem to bother the horses that were milling around inside the corral.

I assumed that meant there were people present. As I approached the stables, I felt the first twinge of nervousness and hastily checked to see that my Glock was still in shoulder holster where I put it. I hoped it wouldn't accidentally go off and shoot me before I had a chance to use it. Kevlar wouldn't help where it was pointed.

When I reached the end of the stables, I kept close to the wall, trying to be inconspicuous even though I knew anyone within shouting distance could see me skulking along the side of the huge white building. A black jacket and jeans might be good in the dark, but it wasn't much camouflage in the daytime, especially with the sun almost directly overhead. About halfway to the front entrance, I decided maybe I didn't want to waltz right through the front doors. I stopped and thought about it for a minute. No. Definitely not.

Turning, I eased back the same way I'd come, then ducked around the end of the building and slipped between the slats in the fence. Horses don't chase people. Besides, the building was shaded on this end. Much easier to hide. Feeling considerably more at ease, I headed on around the end, pausing long enough to peek in the windows. No one in sight. At the corner, I peeked around the other side and spied that little blue Subaru parked in the front parking area. Eureka! That little weasel must be here somewhere.

Carefully I removed the Glock from my holster and took off the safety. I had no intention of shooting anyone, mind you. But I sure as hell wouldn't let him know that. Like a lioness stalking her prey, I crept silently along the far wall toward the front entrance, momentarily aware of how ridiculous I'd look to anyone who happened to see me. I'd circled the entire building before I realized the only ways in were on either end and the back end had been locked up, or at least closed. Guess the front door entrance was my only option, unless I wanted to break out a window and climb through. But, since the front door *was* open and breaking the glass would alert anyone inside, I chose the front door. Great detecting, huh?

Careful to keep the Glock close to my side, I edged through the front door and was greeted by an overwhelming stable smell. Natural bodily functions for a horse, perhaps, but it made my eyes water. Promising myself never to grumble about litter boxes again, I inched my way forward, hurrying past the open stalls that had horses in residence. I wondered, idly, why they didn't all get to go outside to play.

Stalls lined the front end on both sides, and I walked down the center corridor lined with hay and mud and other brown stuff that was probably the reason it smelled so bad. Hammering from inside a stall up ahead on my left was the first sign I had that the place was even occupied. Fortunately for me, the hay was so sogged it didn't make a sound when I walked. Well, maybe a little squishy sound, but it wasn't very loud.When I made it to the stall beside the one the hammering came from, I stopped and waited, listening. There was no sign of any other person and I could see past the office in the center, if you could call it that, all the way to the doors on the other end. I thought for a moment about dashing back to the front door to see if any other vehicles were parked where I'd spotted the Subaru, but talked myself out of it. The only thing I remembered was the truck because it was the only one there, not because I'd been so excited to see it that nothing else registered.

Holding my breath and my Glock, I risked a peek around the wall separating the stalls. The weasel! I jerked my head back and tried to think. What now? Shoulda had a plan, Morgan. Before I could think of one, the hammering stopped and he stepped right in front of me. A whistle died on his lips as he saw me standing there, mouth open and eyes wide.

I mirrored his stunned expression, I'm sure. In a split second, I knew he'd bolt and my arm acted of its own accord, I swear to God. With the Glock pointed smooth at his mid-section, I warned, "Don't even think about it." It would have sounded tough except for the squeaking and quivering.

"Hey, lady," he narrowed his eyes, trying to decide if I was really dangerous or not.

I wasn't really sure myself until he decided I wasn't and started to turn around. Knowing it was my moment of truth, I shifted my aim and fired a shot into the muck right beside his filthy boots. He must have jumped at least a foot higher than I did.

"See?" I screeched. "I told you!"

"Lady, you're crazy!" He looked at me, wild-eyed, but he didn't move again.

"That's right. Write that down! And you're the one that's making me crazy!" I told him, warming up to the cause. He watched me warily while I tried to decide what to do next. When he started looking restless, I said, "Now move back in there," I jerked my head toward the stall he'd just exited. "Move!"

So what if he was going because he thought I was a crazed woman with a gun? He was probably more right than wrong. I positioned myself so I could keep the gun on him and still watch the door, just in case the sound of my shot brought the cavalry from parts unknown.

"Jesus, lady! Whadda ya want?"

"I want…" What *did* I want? "I want to know why you've been following me…and why Greaves ended up dead in my bathtub while you tool around in his truck. And what you know about Lawrence Gafford and where Geneva Brant and the little girl are…and why you blew up my car!"

He tried to stare me down through squinty eyes, then spit on the ground by his feet. "I ain't tellin' you shit."

"Oh, really?" Wrong answer. Hmmm.

"You might as well shoot me now," he smirked, knowing I wouldn't. "Isn't this where you're supposed to tell me you're a marksman?"

I thought about that for a minute. "No. This is where I tell you I'm not a marksman. In fact, I usually hit the things I'm not trying to hit."

He looked a little unsure about that.

"But I'm not trying to hit you right now, so I guess maybe you should worry. I don't want to shoot you. I just want some answers." With sudden inspiration, I took a step toward him. "Why don't you just tell me?"

He didn't flinch. I took another step, keeping the Glock pointed right at his heart.

"You're not gonna kill me right here in cold blood," he growled, not looking quite as sure as he had a second before.

"You're right. I'm not going to kill you. But that doesn't mean I won't shoot you," I nodded. "Ever see *Guarding Tess*?"

He gave me a blank look.

"It's one of my favorite movies," I explained. "See, Nicolas Cage is a Secret Service Agent. And the lady he's assigned to guard gets kidnapped and he just knows the chauffeur knew who did it, but the chauffeur's not talking. Remember that one?" I was really getting into it by then.

The blank look gave way to disbelief and his eyes darted from my face to my gun, then back again.

"You're not paying attention," I charged. "Anyway, Nicolas tells the chauffeur that he's going to count to five, then he's going to shoot off a toe. Well, the big, bad chauffeur doesn't believe him. But you know what?

156

He did it. My absolute favorite part." I nodded and gave a pointed look down at his feet. "But, I don't know if those are steel toed boots so I'll probably aim a little higher. You won't die from it, but it'll hurt like hell. Ready?" I lowered the Glock and aimed at his right knee.

He didn't look too sure.

"Should I back up a little first?" I asked, like I was really considering it while he stood there, probably in some warped, distorted kind of shock. There wasn't another noise in the stable and it was a big gun, even if I did look a little crazed. I took a step back and considered the angle. "That should do. Should I count?"

Weasel still had that bug-eyed I-can't-believe-this-is-really-happening stare and I was beginning to wonder how far I'd really have to go when a familiar voice sounded from somewhere near the front door.

"Jesse?"

Oh thank God! I jerked the Glock back up to point at Weasel's chest when he looked like he might make a run for it. "I'm here, Byron. I trapped a Weasel."

A few moments later, he was behind me, no doubt wondering what the hell was going on.

"So this is your weasel," he leaned against the door behind me and I could hear the smile in his voice.

"Yep, but he's not talking," I answered without letting my eyes stray from his face. "I told him I'd shoot him if he didn't start."

"Hey mister, this lady's wacko. Get her off me!" Weasel pled with Byron.

"I don't know, Weasel. Seems to me she's got a point. You know something you're not telling. Why don't you just give it up? Tell her what she wants to know and she'll leave you alone."

"Maybe," I wasn't ready to go that far just yet. "Look," I tried to reason with the guy, "I know you're not the one I want. But I've had a dead guy in my bathtub and you're driving his damn truck. Somebody shot a hole in my Taurus, then they blew up the truck I was driving while I got it fixed, then they blew up my Taurus. I'm getting really ticked off about all this. And you know what? The police know who you are and they know you've been following me. We could make a citizen's arrest right now and you'd go down for all of it. Is that what you want?"

Weasel turned a ghostly shade of pale.

"I didn't really think so. I don't want you either. I want to know who hired you so I can make all this stop. I mean…what's the point of getting a new car if someone's just going to blow it up again?"

"See?" Byron eased through the door of the stall and stood beside me. "She may seem a little crazy, but she's got a point. And you've got three choices. Tell her, get arrested, or get shot."

When Weasel still didn't move, Byron looked over at me. "What do you choose?"

I gave him a wicked grin. "I say let me shoot him first, then arrest him."

"Hey! You can't just shoot me!"

I laughed and took a step closer. "Oh, I think I can. I've been practicing on the target man. Big strong guy like you with a hammer and nobody around for miles," I tried on my sister's whining voice. "All I did was come out here looking for Geneva, but you're the same bad man who's been following me and my car just got blown up. I think you might hurt me. What's a girl to do but defend herself?"

Byron shook his head and sighed. "I think she's got you, Ace. Jesse, I'll leave you to do your business and I'll wait for you out front." Without another word, Byron walked away.

Of course, I knew he'd never go far, but you don't have to tell everything you know.

"Wait! Shit!" Weasel gave up. "He'll kill me, too," now he was the one who was whining.

"Who?" I waved the Glock for effect.

"Gafford."

CHAPTER TWENTY-TWO

"How'd you find me, anyway?" I asked Byron while he walked me to my car.

He smiled. "Even a blind squirrel finds an acorn sometimes."

"Unh! Everybody's a comedian."

"Bernice told me," he admitted.

"Better."

"I have my moments." He opened the car door for me and waited while I got in.

"Want me to drive you to your car?"

I guess he did. He got in.

"You're hungry, right?" he asked.

"Famished."

"I told Barker to meet us at Outback after he gets the weasel squared away."

I smiled. Steak sounded good about now.

"You play a mean game," he studied my face as I eased out on the road. "What'd you say that shook him up so much?"

I smiled again, remembering. "I told him what Nicolas Cage did to the chauffeur who wouldn't talk in 'Guarding Tess'."

He laughed.

"I love that part."

"Would you have shot him? If I hadn't come, I mean?" he sounded like he was half afraid of the answer.

I looked over at him for a second. "I don't honestly know. Maybe. He blew up my car."

"Damn, woman. You scare me sometimes."

I shrugged. "Sometimes I scare me."

I let him out beside his car, then followed him back to town and wiggled out of the Kevlar before going inside. Damned if I was going to eat in a straight jacket.

I ate like I hadn't seen food in days, then shoved the plate away and wished I dared unsnap my jeans. Maybe this was why so many older ladies wear stretchy pants. "What's taking Barker so long?"

"With any luck, that weasel is singing like a bird," Byron pushed his plate back too, then motioned for the waitress to bring coffee.

"Gafford hired him," I shook my head, still not sure what to make of that.

"Still too many pieces missing, but it's coming," Byron said, accepting his coffee gratefully.

I noticed that "ladies first" didn't apply with waitresses when the man looked like Byron.

While I finished my iced tea, Byron talked through the possibilities without arriving at any good conclusions.

"Let's go," he said finally. "We can stop by the PD on the way back to the office."

"Nah, you stop by the PD," I told him. "I'll meet you at the office." I didn't want to be stared at by an assortment of cops who didn't know quite what to make of me.

"Did he find you?" Bernice asked as I entered the office.

"Hello to you , too," I teased.

Bernice scowled at me.

"Yes, he found me."

Since Bernice didn't seem inclined to be chatty, I decided to take advantage of the quiet and clear up the paperwork I'd been avoiding. Instead of feeling bored, the monotony and impersonal nature of the work was a welcome relief for a change and before I knew it, a couple of hours had passed.

"There you go," I plopped the last file on Bernice's desk. "Someone else you can bill." She lives for it.

Returning to my desk, I reached automatically for the Gafford file that was getting too fat to fit in the slot anymore and pulled up the corresponding notes on my computer screen. After entering a shortened version of the morning's activities, I alternately scrolled, flipped and stared. There had to be something we'd missed. As far as I could tell, neither of us had ever really considered that Gafford might still be alive.

A little annoyed that Byron hadn't returned, I flipped to a clean page in my notepad and started playing with the possibilities. Nothing made sense at first, but the more I scribbled, the more I saw. Finally, I reached for the phone and called Candace in Oklahoma.

"Got a minute?" I asked her when she finished telling me how thrilled she was to hear my voice.

"Always, for you," she enthused. "When are you gonna hire me full time?"

I laughed. "When I'm a lot richer than I am now."

"Hey! I'd bring in more business than we could handle!"

"Give me a few months and we'll see if you still want to," I offered, hoping she didn't really mean it.

"I'm gonna hold you to that," she warned. "Whatcha need? On a new case?"

"Nope, same old one, I'm afraid. But listen, I just got word that maybe Lawrence Gafford is still alive. Can you give me the name and number of that friend of yours we talked to about that life insurance?"

I waited while she looked it up. "Thanks!"

"You call me and let me know how this turns out, hear?"

"Will do," I smiled. She was starting to grow on me.

It took a few minutes, but I finally got the information I needed and tracked down the representative from Aetna who'd been researching the case. Just like I suspected, he got real interested when I told him Gafford might be alive.

"Hold on a second, Ms. Morgan," the man's voice was immediately replaced by a generic woman's voice extolling the virtues of Aetna's many customized health and life insurance plans. By the time he came back on the line, I was almost convinced to ask him about additional insurance for myself, but what he said stopped me cold. "Ms. Morgan? The payment has already been authorized."

"What does that mean?" I jerked up straight in my chair. "It's already been paid?"

"No ma'am, but it's been authorized."

"Well, if the check hasn't been written, you can still stop it, right?"

"No, ma'am."

"Unh! I don't get it. What if the guy's not dead? Surely you don't want to pay all that money if he's not dead! Isn't that fraud or something?"

"Well...yes and no," the guy was really beginning to jerk my chain. "The authorization is based on a death certificate signed by the court. If it's not right, they're the ones you need to talk to."

"Well, can you tell me who it's been issued to?"

"No, ma'am."

"I don't believe this!" I slammed down the phone.

"What?" Bernice looked up from the stack of envelopes she was sealing.

"I just told the insurance company that Gafford's not dead and they don't care."

"Morons," she resumed her licking.

"What do I do now?"

Byron was fortunate enough to walk in about then. I unloaded on him before he made it to the desk.

"You don't even look surprised," I griped.

He shrugged. "I'm not. It's the law. Law says he's dead, he's dead."

"That's a crock!"

"Yes," he agreed. "But that's the way it is."

"So nobody cares that they're paying out hundreds of thousands of dollars and the guy's not even dead?" It was beyond my comprehension.

"Oh somebody cares. A lot of bodies care." He looked like he was considering something.

"Did you find out anything at the PD? You've been gone forever."

He sighed. "Nothing that really matters. Your weasel didn't really know much about Gafford, or anything else for that matter. It seems he's just one of bunch of thugs," he offered a weak smile.

"Okay," I got up and walked over to his desk, scooting his in-basket out of the way so I could perch on the corner. "Let's think about this, then. Beverly Gafford was to inherit the life insurance money, then she died and left everything to Melinda."

"Right," he nodded. "Which means that Bonnie Dean would have been the guardian, but she gave her up for adoption…"

"Sold her, you mean."

"Whatever…" he sat up and grabbed a notepad then started writing something down. "So the real question is – what happens to the money when the child's been adopted."

"Garfield Archer," I nodded.

"But Archer's dead," he gave me a steady look. "What if Archer filed something else we don't know about yet?"

"Huh?" I knew he was on to something, but it made no sense to me yet.

"For instance," he continued, "what if he doctored the adoption papers to retain guardianship or made himself the child's trustee or some shit like that?" He was grasping for the legalese but I began to get his drift.

"He could have done that, couldn't he?"

"Sure could. Would have too, I'm betting. Come on," he got up and grabbed his jacket and I followed suit.

Byron's car flew down the freeway. This time, he parked in front of the house beside Archer's office. Out of bomber territory I assume.

"Just act like you know what you're doing," he mumbled, hurrying me down the sidewalk.

The neighborhood was pretty much deserted, even though it wasn't five o'clock yet. Apparently most of the traffic I'd seen other days had been coming and going from Archer's office. Ignoring the crime scene tape,

Byron had Archer's front door opened as fast as if he'd had a key. I made a mental note to get him to show me how to do that later.

"Stay in here and watch the window," he ordered, crossing swiftly into Archer's office. From the sounds coming out of the back room, he wasn't worried much about leaving a mess.

"Find anything?" I asked when he emerged with a disgusted look on his face.

"No."

"Think the cops got it?"

"No. Probably kept it at home or in a safe somewhere," he said, peering out the window then easing the door open. "All clear outside?"

"Looks like," I shrugged. Nobody came near that I saw.

He motioned for me to follow him and we made our way back to the car without incident.

"You know the number to that friend of yours in Oklahoma?" he asked as he slid behind the wheel.

"Yeah. Why?"

"Call her," he looked at his watch. "Find out if she can find anything on the adoption up there."

I did.

"What?" Candace left me on hold while she looked, then came back with news that Byron must have suspected. I covered the phone and turned toward him. "She says there's an addendum that gives Bonnie Dean visiting rights and makes her trustee of Melinda's estate until she turns twenty one."

"Bingo!"

"Is that all you want?" I asked him.

"That's it."

"Thanks, Candace."

"You owe me, Jesse," she chirped.

"Right." I hung up and turned to Byron. "So what does that mean?" I hated to sound stupid but I still didn't get it.

"It means Bonnie Dean is expecting a large payment from Aetna very soon," he said grimly, turning the car back toward the freeway.

"I still don't get it. What does that have to do with the girl being missing?"

"Well," he said, watching the traffic over his shoulder as he merged into the nearest lane of rush hour traffic, "it doesn't have to have anything to do with it, but I'm betting it does."

"Oh, that's deep," I scoffed.

"Think about it," he said. "Maybe someone's using the girl to get the money from Dean, or... maybe Gafford's decided he wants the money and his daughter."

"Oh," I hadn't thought of that. "That's not good."

"Maybe it is."

I looked at him like he'd lost his mind.

"Seriously," he reasoned. "It tells us where to look next. Maybe we can find her before Aetna cuts the check."

Now, that made sense. Ten minutes later he pulled up in my driveway. "Go feed the cat and get a bag of clothes together while I walk around the house," he ordered.

I was surprised to see him in the kitchen when I emerged from the bedroom.

"Got everything you need?" he asked.

"How long will we be gone?"

"Dunno. Maybe a day, maybe three or four."

"Be right back," I ducked back in my room to grab a few more things. Three or four was more than I counted on.

"Better grab a couple of books," he called from the front room. I did.

"Okay," I met him at the end of the hall and handed him my bags.

"Listen," he looked down at the floor, suddenly uncomfortable, "why don't we take Elvis back to my house?"

That scared me. "Why?"

"Just call it a hunch," he shrugged. "We know they've been here, whoever the hell they are. We don't know they've been to my house and I've got an alarm... I'd just hate to come back and find out..."

He'd said enough. I headed for the kitchen and started packing a bag. Elvis would hate it but I'd rather he hate me alive than love me dead.

Byron stowed my bags in the trunk then came back for the bag of cat food and litter while I coaxed Elvis out from under the bed. Good thing he trusts me. We didn't talk much on the ride to Byron's house, and when we got there I tried to comfort Elvis while he glared at me from under the end table beside the couch.

"Okay," Byron came from his bedroom with a duffel bag slung over his shoulder, "I've got the timers set so there'll be television and radios on till late, lamps and all that. Maybe he won't hate it so bad," he smiled. I probably looked as discouraged as I felt.

"And maybe pigs can fly," I muttered. Elvis was still glaring when I walked out the door.

As beautiful as the Cobra was, the buttery soft leather seats I fell in love with weren't nearly so comfortable after I sat in them for hours without relief. The two-hour trip from Dallas to Sherman wasn't so bad. We'd pulled in to the closest Holiday Inn around nine and grabbed a bite to eat then retired to our rooms to make a plan. Although Byron was pleasant, he was distant and I missed him. We slept late, in separate rooms, then spent most of the day waiting. We already knew we needed to watch Bonnie

Dean, but when we located her house, it was miles from anywhere and there weren't many good places to hide a shiny green Cobra in broad daylight. I should've had a clue when I saw the address included a rural route number. I was so surprised to see that it was in Texas and not Oklahoma I guess I just didn't notice anything else. I still need to fine tune my observation skills.

At Byron's suggestion, I tried to take a nap late in the afternoon but failed miserably. Around five, we headed out, stopping at a convenience store about a mile from her house to stock up on snacks and coffee. From that time, we'd been parked around a curve from her driveway watching nothing but an occasional bird or rabbit or other crawling critter until it got too dark to see anything. The last time I forced him to turn the car on so I could see the clock, it read 2:21.

"You wiggle too much," his voice broke the stillness.

"Tough," I told him.

"Why don't you put the seat back and go to sleep?" It was eerie, the way his voice came out of the darkness. With clouds covering the moon, I couldn't even see his face two feet away.

"I don't get paid to sleep."

He chuckled. "I told you to stay at the hotel."

"And miss all this fun?" The word sounded foreign when I spoke it. Fun.

"You're insane, you know that?"

I sighed and let my head roll back against the seat for a moment. "You know? I've always had a problem with that word."

"Come up often, does it?" he teased.

"No," I sat up. "Really. Think about it. The opposite of clean is unclean, right?"

"Right."

"The opposite of happy is unhappy."

"Okay…"

"The opposite of believable is unbelievable."

He laughed. "The opposite of right is wrong…"

"Play fair," I tried to nudge his leg but hit the console instead. "So where do they get INsane? I mean, shouldn't it be UNsane? Or even out of sane?"

He laughed again. "Jesse, you've got too much time on your hands."

"Doesn't it make sense? If you're out of gas, you're not in-gassed, so if you're out of sanity, where the hell do they get in-sane? And who are 'they' anyway? Ever think of that?"

"Think of what?"

"Who makes all this up? Is there some guy sitting in an office somewhere thinking up what words are right and what words aren't? Is it the same guy who decides what month Easter comes in?"

Silence.

"Don't you ever wonder about that?"

"Easter?"

"Yeah. Sometimes it's in March, sometimes it's in April. You can never tell unless you look at the calendar. Does a bunny come out of its hole and see a shadow or something?"

More silence.

"Stuff like that really bugs me."

"Ever consider getting professional help?"

"Unh!"

I shifted in my seat again. I have good kidneys, but the coffee was starting to get to me.

"You're wiggling again."

I sighed. "Have you done this a lot?"

We'd already talked about every movie and television show we'd ever seen. All the memories we dared think about, much less say out loud. We'd even played twenty questions until it made me too uncomfortable. He wouldn't turn the car on because the sound of the motor carried in the night. He wouldn't let me play the radio because that would run down the battery. So here we sat surrounded by nothing but cold and dark and rustling sounds in the night.

"Yep."

"Is it always this bad?"

He chuckled. "I'm not having a bad time. I've had worse."

"We don't even know if she's in there."

"She's in there."

"How do you know that?" I already knew the answer, but the sleepier I got, the more aware I was of his close proximity and a nagging desire to feel his arms around me again. To fall asleep in his lap. "Maybe her lights are on a timer like yours."

"Don't think so."

Damn. I felt like I'd been talking non-stop for hours. My mom would never believe it but I was actually running out of things to say. Appropriate things, anyway.

"We could talk about us," he did that mind reading thing again.

That shut me up.

"You never have told me exactly what I did that made you so mad." In the dark, his voice took on definite intimate overtones. Or was that my hormones kicking in?

"I thought you were having a good time," I hedged.

166

"How come you won't talk to me?"

"Byron. I have to go to the bathroom." Desperate times need desperate measures.

"Coffee can in the back seat." I could hear him smile.

"I don't think so."

"Too much coffee."

"How else was I supposed to stay awake?" The good thing was, my plot to change the subject worked. The bad thing was, I really did have to go to the bathroom.

"Well, if you won't use the can, what do you suggest?"

I'm supposed to have all the answers? "That little store is open twenty four seven."

"And?"

"It wouldn't take that long. She's not going anywhere in the middle of the night."

"She's not the one I'm worried about."

"Byron…"

"Jesse. I'm not leaving."

I thought about that. He sounded pretty sure.

"Okay. Then you get out and I'll go."

I heard him shift in his seat. "You want to drive my car?"

"No, duh. I thought I'd push it."

"Jesse, you're dangerous."

"I drive fine," I was offended at the thought he didn't trust me with his car.

"Your car just got blown up!"

"Well, Byron, I didn't blow it up! And I wasn't driving it at the time!"

He sighed really loud. "You really have to go?"

"What do you think?" He'd taken a trip out in the trees hours ago.

"You know where it is?" his voice sounded flat, tight.

"How could I miss?" As I recalled, it was right on this same road.

He opened his door. I opened mine too, then leaned on the side of the car while the feeling rushed back into my legs.

"I'll be right over there," he motioned to a darker spot in the dark.

"You'll see me before I see you," I whispered as I passed him on the way to the driver's side.

"As soon as you see the house, kill the lights and motor and coast in," he instructed.

"You want anything?" I had visions of Ding Dongs and didn't want to come back empty handed. Breakfast was a long way off.

"Coffee," he yawned. "Two coffees. And hurry," he added as I slipped into the car. "It's cold." No kidding.

I started the car and drove off, wondering if this was how it felt to get out of prison. Never in all my life have I been so glad to see the welcoming lights of a Chevron Mini-Mart. It even overshadowed the thrill of driving my dream car, which quickly regained that status once the heater and radio were on and I was tooling down the road. Drove like a dream. A magic carpet ride. The trip was way too short.

Savoring the feel of the sleek vehicle, I whipped the wheel and slid right into the front parking space. No customers at this hour. It even seemed warmer under the flickering fluorescent lights when I got out to go inside. A tiny woman looked moderately annoyed when the bell on the door rang, signaling my entrance. I guessed her to be thirty-five going on ninety, maybe a hundred pounds soaking wet. Her hair had been bleached a few times judging by the broken ends and the rainbow of blonde shades next to brown roots. Miss America she wasn't.

"I sure hope you have some fresh coffee," I told her over my shoulder. First stop – rest rooms.

I guess she didn't because when I came out of the bathroom feeling considerably relieved, there was a pot brewing. I lined up four of their largest cups in anticipation. The pot wouldn't fill much more than that. With that done, I made several trips, filling the counter space with an assortment of packaged sandwiches, chips and chocolate. Necessities of life.

"Got the munchies?" the clerk offered a crooked smile that revealed crooked yellow teeth and tiny lines around her mouth.

Up close, I wondered if there'd be any face left if she washed off the layer of Cover Girl. The ring of black eyeliner was so thick it overflowed the boundaries and filled the little wrinkles, traveling south like tiny tributaries eroding away the carefully sculpted landscape of pale foundation that covered her face. I decided to invest in a brighter light for my bathroom mirror lest the same thing happen to me.

"Yeah," I nodded, filling the cups. "Could you tuck these in the bag?" I handed her some sweetener and cream. While she started ringing it all up, I dashed back to the refrigerator and grabbed a couple of bottles of Pepsi, just in case. It took two trips to get it in the car. I sat in the parking lot long enough to unwrap a Ding Dong, then put it in gear and hit the road. Byron was probably frozen by now.

Driving away was like passing through the slit in a black velvet curtain into another realm. Following the curve of the road, I watched in the rearview mirror until the lights from the gas station faded out of view, leaving only the faint glow of the earth barely visible somewhere between the tops of the trees and the sky. They say the earth gives off light of its own but I'd never seen anything that remotely resembled that until now. Keeping an eye on the odometer, I eased off the accelerator as I got closer to my target. When it hit the right number minus one, I dimmed the dash lights, put on the parking lights and slowed to about ten miles an hour. Right on target, I saw Dean's house up ahead through a break in the trees and turned all the lights off. Instinctively, I pressed on the brake, praying that my eyes would get accustomed to the dark in a hurry. They didn't.

Thinking it might help, I rolled down the window and tried to ignore the cold wind in my face as I drove slowly keeping the edge of the road in sight. When I reached what I thought was the spot, I edged the car off the road and shut off the motor. If I was right, Byron should be knocking on the window any second.

He didn't. Oh no. What now?

CHAPTER TWENTY-THREE

We really should have had a better plan, I told myself as I got out of the car. I swear it felt ten degrees colder out in the trees than it had at the Chevron. All in my mind, probably. Keeping to the edge of the road, I walked slowly toward where I thought we'd been parked before. Ignoring the wisps of frosty breath that puffed out of my mouth, I kept my head tucked low and scanned the trees, hoping for a sign of movement. Familiar movement, that is. As the car faded into the darkness, the road curved slightly to the left and Bonnie Dean's house began to take shape. Too far. I stopped walking.

I don't know how long I stood there, but soon I was shivering. The silence was so thick I thought maybe I could touch it. No wind. No birds or crickets. No cars or airplane. No sign of life at all. Where would Byron have gone? I could understand walking around a little to keep warm, maybe, or to get a closer look at the house. But I'd been gone for more than half an hour. Surely he'd seen enough and was ready to get in out of the cold.

Figuring maybe I'd been closer than I thought and that I'd find him in the car, I headed back that way. He wasn't there. Not knowing what else to do, I got in and warmed my hands on my coffee cup. This couldn't be happening.

I couldn't see the face of my watch so I gently turned the key far enough to turn the dash lights on. 4:13. Not good. More than two hours till daylight and no sign of Byron. I sipped at my coffee and tried to think of something but the coffee didn't taste as good as it had earlier and my mind seemed to be freezing up too. Lack of sleep or lack of partner, or maybe a little of both. Staring at the clock, I ate half a pimento cheese sandwich and wondered how long I could keep this up before I dozed off. Actually, I think I did.

With that jerking feeling you get sometimes when you dream you're falling, I sat up straight and opened my eyes wide. Did something wake me?

Or was I just drifting off? I turned the key again and saw that it was now 6:37. Yikes. Some detective. My partner's missing and I'm dozing off in the car.

There was no doubt anymore. Something was very wrong. Seemed like my theme song. I got out of the car and stretched and was surprised to see that the sky looked just a tiny bit lighter on the left. Must be east. Sliding my hands back into the gloves I'd stuffed in my pockets, I trudged across the road to the trees on the other side. With every step it seemed the darkness gave way to a little more light. Finally, it occurred to me to look up and I saw that the clouds had cleared out and the last of the stars were being chased from the sky by the encroaching light of dawn.

When I reached the clearing that led to Bonnie Dean's house, I stopped and leaned on one of the trees that lined the road. I really had no idea what Byron would want me to do. I could stay and look around, or I could just walk up to the house and see if he was there. Or, I could go back into town for help. I sighed and tried to think like a PI. It gave me a headache. The crackling of a twig underfoot chased every trace of sleep from my brain and I stood up straight and took a step forward, every sense tuned to hearing. Somebody was out there. Byron would have spoken and I didn't make that noise. If I needed to confront some unsavory character, I wasn't about to do it in the middle of the woods. Heading for the house, I heard it again and knew someone was following me. It also occurred to me that I should feel scared, but I was too cold and too confused and starting to get a little pissed. Ready to just find the little girl and go home to sleep for a year or so.

At the tree line, I paused and considered my options. There weren't many. Front door or back door. Since there seemed to be someone watching, I decided the back door would give me more cover and darted out into the open half expecting to hear a gunshot mid way across the yard. That was the first time I remember thinking fondly about the flak jacket Byron insisted I wear. Ducking around the corner I stopped and waited, hoping I'd hear something to tell me what the hell was going on. It was nearly daylight by now, and the whole area behind the house was barren aside from dead brown grass cut close near the house and jumping to knee height about twenty yards back. An old sofa was overturned beside the garage, which was separate, and slightly behind the south side of the house. I shuddered to think what I might find under that. Three wooden steps with rails that didn't look too steady led down from what I presumed was the back door. The windows were too high for me to peek in. This was just great.

I didn't hear a sound so I started moving, along the wall, around the steps toward the other side. At the corner, I paused again, wondering if my stalker had decided to catch me coming around the other side. I pulled my hand out of my pocket and reached in my jacket for the holster, bringing the gun along for luck. No sounds came from around the corner so I took a chance and darted over to the garage door. It was locked up tight with a padlock. The sight of a window around the far side made my heart jump, but it needn't have bothered. The inside of the window was covered with sheetrock. This was crazy. Tiptoeing around out in the middle of nowhere.

I took a quick peek around the back of the garage, more because it was there than because I expected to find anything but dead grass. I was right, there was nothing there. Deciding I'd just march right up to the front door, then go to town for help if I didn't find Byron there, I headed that way and ran smack into a man I'd never seen before going around the front corner.

"Unh! Who the hell are you and what are you doing out here?" The words popped out before I could stop them. If I'd waited a minute I wouldn't have had to ask. It was Lawrence Gafford, a little older than the picture, but definitely him.

Probably five eight and maybe a hundred and sixty pounds, he looked a little worse for the wear. Heavy lines creased his face in a permanent scowl and a lock of hair kept falling in his eyes. He'd push it back and it would fall again. I bet that got old. A slow, wicked smile made his face scarier still. He was an ugly man, but not as ugly as the rifle he had in one hand. "I been looking for you."

"Well, I've been looking for you, too. What do you want?" I kept my right hand behind me, not sure I was ready to meet his rifle with my Glock. The words sounded strange, coming from a face that was going numb from the cold wind. Time seemed to slow and I was oddly, suddenly aware of everything around us. The wind, the sound of branches scratching against the garage, the crackling of the grass as Gafford shuffled his feet. My heartbeat.

"Look," I decided to ignore the rifle. I tried to appear casual, keeping the Glock behind my back. As numb as my fingers were, I'd probably shoot myself if I tried to use it. "I don't have a lot of time. Say something or get out of my face."

His smile got bigger but I could tell he didn't mean it. Guess I wasn't going to catch him off guard.

"Lady, you ain't going anywhere but with me," he growled.

Funny how time seems to go in slow motion when you get scared. I was suddenly aware of just how far we were from anywhere and wondered how fast and how far I could run. Not fast or far enough with that rifle in his hand for sure. I tried to think back to the last karate class I'd had and all the things my sensei used to repeat about facing an opponent. Nope. And I'd have sworn I'd never forget. With the heels on my boots, I could look the man square in the eye. He didn't outweigh me by much either, not something I'd admit out loud, but the mean on his face made him seem bigger.

"Gafford, my partner will…"

"Your partner is tied up," he cut me off with a snarl.

My blood turned cold at the sinister tone and I reminded myself that this man was probably responsible for the dead guy in my tub. He might just be desperate enough to kill Byron and me, too. I glanced at the rifle he still held loosely, but it was pointed at my midsection. Wouldn't he have to cock it or something? I suspected the Kevlar wasn't worth much at point blank range. I wished I'd asked someone before now but I didn't really have time to worry about it.

"Not so chatty now, are ya?" he took a step toward me and I knew I had to move fast.

Locking my eyes on his lower throat like I'd learned in self defense classes years ago, I took shallow breaths and watched for peripheral movement while I slowly shifted my weight to my left foot and eased up on my right.

"Drop your gun on the ground and kick it over here," he ordered.

How'd he know I had a gun? I frowned, bringing my right hand and Glock around slowly, trying to buy some time.

"Hurry up!"

"Un uh," I shook my head, raising the Glock to point at his chest and praying his gun wouldn't move. I remembered Byron saying never, ever give up your weapon. I hoped I wasn't confusing it with something else. But if Byron was lurking around the edges waiting to save the day, I thought he would have done it by then. I was on my own.

I was rewarded with a flash of uncertainty and it was all I needed. With all the force I had, I stepped forward, jerked my right foot straight up into his groin and used my left hand to sweep the barrel of the rifle away. With a loud grunt, he doubled over and grabbed his crotch, dropping the rifle in the process. I'd expected that, but I didn't expect it to go off. The sound scared me so bad I tripped on Gafford and both of us fell to the ground in a heap. Thank God, the Glock seemed frozen to my glove. Fortunately, I fell on top and was able to get to my feet in record time without dropping it. I couldn't jerk the rifle out from under him, however.

"Get up!" I yelled at his writhing form. Since I wasn't facing down the barrel of the rifle anymore, my anger was kicking in. I gave Gafford a swift kick with the toe of my boot "Get up or I'll kick you again."

The moaning and writhing continued, but I noticed one hand snake out toward the rifle and fired a shot into the ground about three feet from his head.

"You think I'm kidding?" I screamed, noticing that my voice seemed magnified to the point of echoing in the frosty morning air. Even the short bursts of smoke that accompanied my words seemed angry. This was asinine and I was fed up. That and more scared than I'd ever been. Except maybe for the dead guy in the bathtub. "Get up now, Gafford, before I get really pissed!"

He must have believed me; he rolled away from gun and gave a half-assed effort to get up. Keeping the Glock pointed in his general direction, I circled his feet and stooped over, collecting the rifle in one quick move and tucking it under my arm.

"Let's go," I told him as he struggled to his feet. There are many good reasons to wear cowboy boots. No doubt the metal guard on the pointed toe made an impression on Gafford this morning. "Who's in the house?" I asked when he got unsteadily to his feet and I motioned for him to move that way.

He didn't answer but he didn't have to. Before we reached the back stairs, the door swung open and Byron emerged.

"My God, what happened to you?" The whole left side of Byron's face was a gruesome palette of blue and black and purple color, not to mention that it was swollen so bad I couldn't even see his cheekbone on that side.

"My guess would be him," Byron nodded his head slightly toward Gafford. From the sound of his voice, there was quite a bit of swelling inside as well. When he stepped out on the landing, I saw that his hands were still bound with duct tape.

"You idiot!" I smacked Gafford in the middle of the back. "Get that tape off him!"

I'm not sure, but I thought Byron's good eye twinkled at me as Gafford stumbled to the stairs and started fumbling with the tape around Byron's wrists.

"Is there anybody else in there?" I asked Byron while Gafford continued to pick at the tape.

Byron nodded. "Dean, but she's dead."

"Oh, really?" my eyes turned back to Gafford. I was glad I didn't know that earlier. I'd best not underestimate this man. "You got a knife in your pocket?" I asked Byron, knowing he usually did.

Byron nodded, shifting his hip so I could slide a hand in. Good thing his pants weren't quite as tight as mine.

"Back up and stand still," I ordered Gafford, who glared at me but did as I told him. A minute later, Byron's hands were free and we walked Gafford down the driveway and back to the car. It seemed a lot shorter than the circuitous route I'd taken through the trees earlier. Byron retrieved a pair of handcuffs from the trunk and put them on Gafford's wrist then sat him down in the back seat of the car while we stood outside. Now what?

It was pretty dark by then and more than a little cold. Byron got in the car and started it and pulled it forward to just outside the gate that would close on the driveway. Looking at his bruised face and disheveled hair, it wasn't hard to figure he was as exhausted as I. It had been a long sleepless night last night, a longer day and now this.

"Try it again," I begged, meaning I wanted him to try and get a signal on his phone. Mine was dead.

He pushed a button then held it out for me to see. No bars showing. Nothing. "We can't leave here and we've got to call the Sheriff."

I thought about that. I know it was right, but my mind was having trouble coming up with a solution. One that I could live with, anyway. I desperately feared that it meant one of us would have to stay here while the other went for help. I covered my eyes and groaned. "Just tell me. Just tell me what to do."

I thought I saw a tiny smile on his face for a second, but it was dark and I might be hallucinating by now. He reached over and opened the back door. "Get out, Gafford!"

Gafford looked up at him like he thought Byron was insane. I wasn't going to quibble.

"What are you doing?" I tried to speak softly so Gafford couldn't hear me.

There was that smile again, although I don't believe he meant it. "I'm going to keep him here with me while you go back to the gas station and call the Sheriff. Simple."

"Ok." I wouldn't argue with that. I didn't want to stay here and I didn't want to be alone in a car with Gafford. Problem solved.

I pulled in to the parking lot and considered going inside for coffee before I made the call, but thought better of it. There was a pay phone mounted on the wall beside the door and I dialed 911 and told them what had happened. I had no clue of what address to give them but they had the location of the phone I was calling from and they agreed to send someone to meet me there.

Once that was settled, I went inside to get some bottled water and two cups of coffee. I hoped there'd be real food in the not-too-distant future, but figured we could make do with what was left in the car until the cops got through with us. That could be a long time.

I sat back in the car to wait, and raided the snack bag. I didn't realize I'd dozed off until a loud bang on my window jerked me up. I rolled down the window. "Evening officer."

He didn't seem inclined to chit chat so I revved the engine and he followed me back to where I'd left Byron. I tensed up for a minute, not seeing him when I pulled around the bend, but they'd moved and were sitting by the side of the gate. I parked the car and when I got out, Byron was already filling the officer in and another Sheriff's car pulled up and parked behind the Mustang.

Thinking it best that I say nothing, that's what I did. When they seemed to finish talking, the deputy took Gafford and put him in the back seat of the car and got on his radio.

"They'll have to talk to you, you know," Byron said.

"Yeah," I nodded. "There's fresh coffee in the car."

I think he smiled but he headed for the car so fast it was hard to tell. "Can I sit in here till they're ready for me?" I asked when I caught up with him. It was cold outside.

"Go ahead," he said. "It's gonna be awhile."

Not what I wanted to hear, but not a surprise either. Another car arrived, then another. Before long they had halogen lights all up and down the drive and people in little scrub like suits with gloves, flashlights and bags picking up all kinds of stuff I probably wouldn't even have seen if I'd been looking.

As if one night sitting in the car wasn't enough, we spent most of another night, then continued our sit-in at the local Sheriff's office. At least they had heat and a bathroom. I think Byron made a couple of life-long friends. If he hadn't we might still be there. As it was, the Sheriff himself didn't seem too fond of either of us. The way I understand it, they could let us go because we were both duly licensed in Texas, because Byron had been on the force so long, and because there wasn't any evidence that made us look guilty of anything but doing our jobs. It might take time for all of that to sink in. Regardless, when Byron said, "Let's go," I got up, headed for the door and didn't look back.

"All in all done," I told Byron, slamming the car door hard after I slid into the passenger seat. I know I should have been grateful the country bumpkin deputies didn't put our asses in jail, but I was just tired. "Let's make tracks before they change their minds."

"We've still got a problem," Byron looked over at me from behind the wheel.

"Oh, just one?" I chortled.

Bonnie Dean was a weak lead at best and now she was dead. The Sheriff didn't act like he believed us when we explained about Geneva Brant and her missing daughter. He made sure we knew he'd be just 'spittin' happy' to talk to the officer in charge of the investigation back home. Meantime, we could just hotfoot it out of his county and stay out. We didn't bother to enlighten him that we were the only ones on the investigation since Brant claimed his wife and daughter were happily visiting relatives.

Byron headed straight back to the motel where we crashed for a few hours. Sleep sometimes makes things seem more logical.

"What now?" I asked Byron, stumbling through the adjoining door to our rooms when I heard him moving around the next morning. The sight of his half naked form, still damp from the shower, was almost enough to stop me where I stood, but the scent of fresh brewed coffee from room service tempted me on in. With a cup in hand, I perched on the nearest chair and watched him gathering his things and stuffing them in the duffle bag on the bed.

"I called Barker," he said, "he's got nothing. They're going to lean on that weasel a little harder and see if there's a name we've missed. Right now, I figure all we've got to go on is the lady who claimed to be Mrs. Gafford."

"Great," I meant not great. "She could be anyone anywhere."

"You got a better idea?" He pulled on a sweater and sat down on the edge of the bed.

I made a face at him.

"Gafford knows who she is," he said.

"Ya think? I bet he just forgot to mention it when they questioned him." I was getting the distinct feeling that a few hours of sleep weren't helping as much as I'd hoped they would.

Once we got home, I moved Elvis back to the house and slept like a baby with a cop parked in the front yard. After an early breakfast of coffee and a semi-stale hostess cupcake, I was back at my desk raring to go. Bernice had a pile of background checks she needed me to sign off on. While we were going through them, Byron came in.

"Not his usual chipper self," Bernice mused.

"No," I frowned as I watched him sit down at his desk. "Morning!"

He waved but didn't turn around.

"Probably needs coffee," Bernice diagnosed. "I'll get it."

I nodded and kept signing. I'd just finished the stack when she stopped back by my desk. Now I could get busy looking for the elusive Mrs. Gafford, whoever she was.

Emily Marshall was Gafford's secretary all those years ago. She was also, if we could believe him, a lying, bitching gold-digger. We'd managed to locate a couple of old acquaintances in Tulsa who remembered Gafford feeling differently. According to them, the relationship was hot and heavy and Gafford thought Marshall had hung the moon. Funny how opinions change over time. Unfortunately, nobody had any idea where the woman was now. I booted up my computer and determined to find out.

Sometimes, when I get on the Internet, it's like time stands still and I enter another zone. When the persistent growling in my stomach finally got my attention, I came out of computerland and stretched, looking over at Byron's back. When he hung up the phone, I said, "I'm hungry."

"Find anything?" he swiveled his chair around to face me.

"Lots of stuff, but nothing that helps much," I told him. "Did you?"

He shook his head and rubbed a hand over his eyes. "Come on," he got up and grabbed his jacket off the back of his chair.

We'd called a truce of sorts and indulged in small talk and speculation over lunch. Neither of us mentioned a personal relationship at all, although a couple of times I'd looked up to see something in his eyes that made me squirm. Confrontation would come. Hopefully, by the time it did I'd know what to say.

With little to go on, we did what we always do. We went back to what we knew. A trip to the Brant's told us that the household help were still sticking to the story that Geneva and Melinda were visiting relatives and Marcus Brant was at the office, as usual. So Byron pointed the car downtown.

On the best of days, downtown Dallas is a dark place, with tall buildings that line the streets blocking the sun. When there is no sun, it's even darker. Walking down the sidewalk from the corner parking lot, I tried not to cringe and wonder what would happen if a nearby building suddenly decided to cave in. One way streets that confused the hell out of me when I drive were wall to wall cars, all of them in a hurry. I wondered why all those people weren't in an office somewhere instead of cluttering up the streets.

"Come on," Byron reached back and grabbed my arm because I kept lagging behind.

"Your legs are longer than mine," I muttered, keeping my chin low to help block the frigid wind that took my breath every time it gusted.

Finally, he steered me into a revolving door in the front of a mirrored building and a gust of hot air greeted us on the other side. It was the plush, mauve lobby of BankOne. Byron led the way to the elevator and we squeezed in. He pushed the twelve button and we waited quietly as it stopped on almost every floor and people got out. By the time we hit the twelfth floor we were the only ones left.

If anything, the interior was even more elegant than downstairs. Glass partitions lined the hall where I could see a bevy of people busy at work. At the end of the hall, two glass doors awaited with "Brant Enterprises" painted across both in flowing script. Byron paused outside the doors.

"Just let me do the talking," he looked down at me to make sure I understood.

I shrugged, avoiding his eyes. His eyes narrowed like he was trying to decide if he'd said enough. I guess he thought he had. He opened the door and held it for me to pass through. The carpet felt cushy beneath my feet and I suddenly felt underdressed. Everything in the place screamed money.

Fancy potted plants, brass fixtures, paintings that belonged in museums all over the walls. Whatever Brant did, he must do it well.

Hanging back a little, I watched as Byron approached the receptionist and murmured something too low to hear. A look of surprise crossed her face and she reached for the phone while he waited patiently in front of her desk.

She was probably in her forties, although she didn't show age. Perfectly groomed brown hair framed a carefully painted face and she dialed the phone with manicured nails on hands that wore more jewelry than I'd ever owned. I tried to superimpose a picture of Bernice behind that desk but it just wouldn't focus. The woman replaced the phone and said something to Byron with an expression that looked a little stern. I took a step closer as Byron stood a little straighter and made a show of pulling his jacket open by sliding his left hand in the pocket of his slacks. Uh oh.

It worked. The woman's face blanched under her makeup as her eyes lighted on the gun in the shoulder holster. Handsome is one thing. Heavily armed is another. She reached for the phone again and I smiled. He's good. A moment later, I was following him down yet another hall that led to Brant's private office. Another perfectly coiffed, blanching secretary was just setting the phone back down when we entered.

"Mr. Brant will be with you shortly," she told us in clipped tones.

As Byron sat down, I wandered around the room, studying the paintings on the walls and wondering if they were the real thing or just expensive forgeries of some sort. Art isn't my thing. I noticed the secretary pretended to work but kept a steady eye on Byron. Guess she didn't want to get shot. Somehow, surrounded by all the opulence, I didn't think we were going to get much information there.

"Would you sit down?" Byron told me in a hushed voice.

Since I'd seen everything there was to see, I did. "You really think he's going to tell us anything?"

He shrugged. The side door opened and I looked up to see Brant standing in the doorway. He must have a perfection clause in his employment contract.

"Mr. Montgomery, I presume?"

We both stood up. Somehow, I'd pictured Brant as bigger. Brant was a handsome devil though, with silver hair, a deep tan, and sharp brown eyes that looked like they could see things that weren't even there. I knew he was in his sixties, but he sure didn't look it. Unless you think about Sean Connery, then maybe.

Brant's eyes narrowed slightly as I preceded Byron into his office but he didn't offer to shake my hand.

"I've told you all I can," he said sharply after he shut the door behind us. "I don't appreciate you coming in here and terrorizing my employees."

I snickered at that. He hadn't seen terrorizing yet. Byron sat down in a chair facing the desk and I took another stroll. The office was much larger than the others and the walls were half glass, providing a lovely view of the surrounding buildings. I wandered over to one of them and peered down at the street below, feeling the cool air that hugged the glass.

"I'll keep coming back until you start telling the truth," Byron said evenly.

I turned back to see Brant's response. He was seated behind a skinny desk that was really a table with a sleek black top. There was one inbox on the corner, empty, a phone, a rolodex, a computer monitor and a pencil holder. It didn't even look like anyone worked there. Brant's expression was blank, too, tinged with slight annoyance. He sighed.

"What is it you think I'm lying about?"

"Where are your wife and daughter?" Byron answered immediately in those same even tones.

More annoyance. "I told you, she's visiting her parents. Not that it's any of your business."

Suddenly, I was tired of all the waiting. I remembered the look on Geneva's face that day I met her in the park. The swelling, the bruises, the fear about her daughter.

"Why don't you get her on the phone?" I suggested. Both men's heads snapped around to look at me in surprise. You'd think they didn't even know I was there until I spoke.

"Well?" I prompted when he didn't answer. I walked over to the side of his desk and looked down at him. "Why don't you? Let me talk to her and we'll go away."

He looked, for a moment, like he didn't know what to say, then snapped, "I don't need to interrupt her vacation just to prove something to you!"

"Well you know what?" I shoved the inbox over and perched on the corner of his desk, "I think maybe you better because I'm not giving up until I find out where she is!"

"This is absurd!" he got up from his chair. "I don't have to put up with this!"

"Too bad she didn't tell you the same thing when you hit her, isn't it?" I retorted, pleased to see him freeze in place. "Or did she? Is that what happened, Brant? I saw the bruises. I know what you did and I've talked to her mother," I jumped down from my perch and took a step toward him. "Now where the hell is she?"

Out of the corner of my eye I saw Byron get up. So much for him doing all the talking. At least he didn't try to stop me.

"That's ridiculous! I never hit my wife!" he backed up a step but there was a growing panic in his eyes. Gotcha.

"You're a liar," I told him. "And I'm fed up with this. Call the police, Byron. Call them right now."

"You don't know what you're talking about," Brant sniped, stepping around me and moving slowly toward the door.

I cocked my head to the side and looked at him. Something in my expression must have caught his attention because he stopped and stared back at me. I wish I knew what it was. He was calling my bluff. "I may not have all the answers yet, but I'm going to be like gum on your shoe," I assured him.

He didn't answer but he didn't move either. I looked over at Byron and shrugged then turned back to Brant.

"She's right, Brant," Byron stood and stepped over behind me. "This one's not going away. And if that little girl isn't alive, I'll be your worst nightmare."

I reached for the door handle and Byron joined me. I turned back before I opened the door. "Sure you don't want to talk?"

"You can't prove anything," he snarled.

The look in his eyes was frightening.

CHAPTER TWENTY-FOUR

"Well, that was fun," Byron observed once we were back out in the hall.

"Wasn't it? What now?"

"Well. We can tail him again, but so far that hasn't helped much. Or we can hang around here and see if we can find out anything from someone who works here," Byron said, pushing the down button on the elevator.

"When you were here before, did you talk to any of them?" I nodded at the perfect employees behind the glass. The only one who looked out of place was a scruffy young man pushing a mail cart between the rows of desks.

"No, why?"

"Who do you think knows all the dirt on the boss?"

"I agree. But neither of us will turn up much here, in Brant's front office. We'd need to catch them off guard."

I looked around at them then at Byron. "Off guard? Like in a lunch room or something?"

He shrugged. "Maybe. Or leaving the building."

I looked at him again to see if he was serious. I think he was. "Really? Do you know how many people work in this building?" I didn't, but there were probably thousands and most of them didn't work for Brant.

"Nobody said it was easy."

When we got back downstairs, Byron posted himself by the bank doors and I headed for the exit to the left of the elevator. Lucky for me, there was a snack bar there and I got some coffee and cheesecake to help take the edge off the waiting. When I'd finished the cheesecake, I got up and walked over to the nearest trash container and noted that it was beginning to rain outside. Great. There was a rule about downtown traffic and rain. Everyone had to be absolutely cranky and the cars in the outside lanes were required to hit every puddle and splash as much water and mud as they could on nearby pedestrians.

As I wandered back to my chair, I looked up in time to see the scruffy young man from Brant's office mosey off the elevator. He didn't seem to be in any particular hurry and stopped in front of the snack bar where I joined him.

"Hi, don't you work upstairs at Brant Enterprises?" I asked cheerfully.

He looked over at me with a surprised but not unpleasant expression. "Yeah, why?"

"I thought I saw you there earlier," I gave him my best and hopefully youngest smile. "Coffee break?"

"Nah," he accepted the coffee the snack bar attendant handed him and waited for his change. "I get off at 3."

"Wow, is it three o'clock already?" I looked at my watched and grasped at straws. "Damn."

"Late for something?" he asked, ambling slowly toward the exit.

I looked up at him with as much phony earnestness as I could muster. "Hey, maybe you could help me. You got a minute?"

He didn't look too sure but after he glanced out the door at the rain pounding the sidewalk he followed me to the chairs and sat down beside me. "Who are you anyway?" he asked.

Good question. Not one I cared to explore at that moment, however. I just did what my Dad always said I did best, back in the day when his nickname for me was Motormouth. Half an hour later, I had exactly no more pertinent information than I'd started with. That was a total waste of time.

I don't know how long I sat there after he walked out the door but my legs felt wobbly when I got up. I made my way back to the bank to find Byron. He was sitting half hidden by a potted palm looking like he was waiting for someone.

"Give up so soon?" he asked, surprised to see me.

"Yeah. Come on," I tugged his sleeve until he got up.

"What?" he followed me out the door.

"I just know we can figure this out. There's got to be something we already know. We're just not looking at it right."

Byron didn't look convinced, but it was kind of hard to see his face since we both pulled our jackets over our heads as we ran to the car.

For once in my life, I didn't even want to stop for something to eat. Byron insisted though, telling me it wouldn't take us any longer considering rush hour traffic. My mind was racing, asking "what if's" and "how about" until something started to make sense. I waited until the waitress at the Cracker Barrel had filled our coffee cups and taken our orders before I unleashed on Byron. I loved the feeling that I might figure it out before he did, but I'll admit there was a little hesitancy that he might just see all kinds of holes in my theory.

"Okay. Get this," I told him, leaning forward and nearly wiggling with anticipation. "Gafford's a sleaze, right?" It was a rhetorical question. "And he's cheating on his wife with his secretary. Beverly figures it out, but before she can divorce him, he disappears in a plane crash with loads of drugs and money."

"Whoa! Aren't you assuming? There's no record of her planning to divorce him."

I shrugged. "Bear with me. Of course she was. Why else would she change her will to make her sister Melinda's guardian?" It made perfectly good sense to me.

"Circumstantial," Byron said.

I made a face at him. "Anyway, he disappears but he's not really dead and Emily figures that out but there's nothing she can do about it. He probably told her they'd live happily ever after with the money only he cut out on her, too."

Byron rolled his eyes. "You're assuming again."

I ignored that. "It's all in the news how the money was never found and even that Beverly can't get his life insurance money because he can't be declared legally dead."

"Well, that part's true enough," he conceded, moving aside when the waitress arrived with our plates.

"Exactly. Now. The longer he's gone, the more ticked off Emily gets and she's watching Beverly just to see if there's any word or maybe any way she can get some of the money he's cheated her out of. When Beverly dies, it gets a little trickier because now she has to keep up with Melinda. Are you even listening to me?" He seemed more interested in his hash brown casserole than in anything I was saying.

"I'm listening," he mumbled around a mouthful. "I'm just not sure I'm buying it."

"Why not? Byron, she was his secretary. His lover. She must have known something about the people he worked for, right? Who else would have called me and pretended to be Beverly Gafford?"

"I don't know," he said tersely, "and I'm not saying you're wrong. But you've got no proof."

"Unh! Would you just eat and listen?"

He smiled.

"Okay. What if…" I paused long enough to take a bite of eggs before they got too cold, "…what if Emily tracked Melinda down here to the Brants, then decided to put the moves on Brant?"

"What for?"

"Unh! To get the life insurance money, of course!"

Byron put down his fork and studied me for a minute. "Like he's just going to give it to her? And he doesn't get it, anyway. Bonnie Dean does."

I frowned. "So? Maybe Emily doesn't know that? Or maybe…maybe she …yeah! Maybe Emily and Gary Greaves were in cahoots to kidnap Melinda in exchange for the money!"

"But, there's no ransom note," he argued.

I frowned again, then suddenly had another idea. "No! Hey – the ransom note went to Bonnie Dean!"

Byron looked surprised, but he didn't argue that time. "Oka-ay," he said. "Then why didn't the police find it and why is she dead?"

"Because she wouldn't pay! Gafford probably took the note when he killed her! Oh." I realized that up to that point, Gafford hadn't figured into my theory. "Gafford."

Byron nodded, looking far more amused than I thought was necessary.

"Soo-oo, Gafford's been watching all this time," I improvised, "and he figured out what Emily was up to…" I had trouble thinking that fast. "Damn! I don't know. Your turn."

Byron moved his empty plate and motioned for the waitress to refill his coffee. I decided to eat the rest of my food, even if it was a little cold by then.

"I think you're probably not too far off base," he said.

"Really?" I mumbled, surprised.

"Really. It's entirely possible that the woman Brant is involved with is the same woman who posed as Beverly Gafford. And, it's also possible that all of this hinges around that insurance money and the little girl. I just don't really understand Brant's involvement in the whole situation. He's a wheeler, dealer, true, but he's also a stickler for reputation. I can't see him getting involved in anything that might tarnish his good name."

"Yeah, but By, you forget. When he was desperate, he wasn't above using Garfield Archer as his attorney even if he was a sleazebag."

Byron seemed to consider that. "That's true, but even if that hit the press, he was just trying to adopt a child for his grieving wife. That kind of press wouldn't kill him."

"Who killed Archer, anyway? And why?"

He shrugged. "My guess is Gafford had it done, but the "why" escapes me."

"It's too complicated," I complained, moving my plate away. Nothing like congealed eggs to scare away your appetite.

"It doesn't really matter," he said, waving at the waitress again. "Our job is just to find the girl and Geneva and make sure they're okay. The cops can sort out the rest."

"You think she's okay?"

"The girl?"

I nodded.

"Yeah. At least until they get the insurance money. After that, I don't know. We really need to find out who has her."

I stifled a shiver. "Well, we know it's not Gafford, but I'm not sure that's a good thing. I just hope the little girl and Geneva are all right."

"Yeah, me too," Byron said, getting up and pulling his jacket back on. "Let's get out there and see what we find."

"Where are we going?" I was running out of ideas.

"You remember that night Geneva Brant came over to your place?"

I nodded.

"You said she mentioned a cabin on the lake. I thought we'd just drive out there and take a look. Maybe Brant's hiding them out there."

"How do you know where to go?"

He smiled and patted his jacket pocket. "Bernice."

I followed him, shrugging into my jacket on the way to the cashier. Moving on through the front door, the bright, aromatic interior of the restaurant gave way to dark gray drizzle suspended in a cold wind. Bleak was the first word that came to mind and I drew the collar of my jacket up around my neck and hurried to the car. Not the best PI skulking weather.

While Byron navigated the freeway, still packed with cars trying to find their way home, my mind wandered back over the visit with Brant. He was definitely hiding something, but what? Could the man who'd pay any price to adopt a baby for his grieving wife just a few years ago be the same man who beat his wife and kidnapped that same child? It didn't quite make sense.

"Do you think Brant's involved in all this?" I asked when traffic thinned out a little.

Byron paused a few moments before answering. "Involved?" he shot a sideways glance my way. "He's definitely involved, but I'm not sure how and I'm not sure it's by his own choice."

"That's clear as mud. What do you mean?"

"I mean I think he's hiding something. I think he knows where his wife and daughter are but I'm not sure he's the one that put them there."

I exhaled loudly. "You think someone's holding him up for ransom too? It's not just the insurance money?" That thought hadn't occurred to me before.

He shrugged, keeping his hands firmly on the wheel. The swooshing of the tires on the wet road played in a steady rhythm that threatened to put me to sleep. I shifted and sat up straighter, turning my attention to Byron and trying hard to concentrate.

"It could be something like that, although I really didn't get that feeling from Gafford. It may just be that Brant beats his wife and he's got a mistress and doesn't want anyone to find out."

I let my head roll back against the headrest to think about that, but it popped back up again pretty soon. "But even if it means his daughter is in danger?"

Byron shot me a look. "Your guess is as good as mine."

We drove the rest of the way in silence until I was numbed by the road sounds and the brain cramps from trying to figure everything out. Byron talked like he knew right where the secret cabin was located. By the time we pulled off on the gravel road he'd described, I wasn't so sure. There were no street lights and the only natural illumination came from an occasional flash of lightning.

"Maybe I'll wait in the car," I told Byron when he finally settled on a parking spot under a couple of big trees about a hundred yards from the house. As soon as he turned off the car I felt the cold and I wasn't even wet yet. The drizzle had turned to rain that was so steady it covered the windshield immediately and I could barely see the porch light from the house. This was a night for a fire in the fireplace and an afghan on my lap. Not a night to go sloshing around in the cold rain in darkness so dense there was a chance I'd end up in the lake.

Byron looked over at me and sighed. "Nasty night, isn't it?"

"What do you want to do?"

"I want to wait for it to stop raining but I don't think that's the best idea. We need to know who's in that house."

I dug my gloves out of my jacket pockets and put them on. Like they'd really keep my hands warm. Byron groaned and got out of the car, returning a minute later with Kevlar vests and rain ponchos.

"Shit!" he said as he slammed the door.

"What?"

"Damn cold," he shook his head then pulled his hair back into a ponytail. As he pulled off his jacket and started to put on the vest, I reluctantly did the same, feeling its cold through my sweater as I slid it on and buckled it. Not an easy thing to do in the front seat of a Mustang but I'd be damned if I was going outside to do it. Grunting and wiggling, I got my coat back on and snapped it up then slipped my Glock in the front coat pocket.

"You ready?" he turned to face me.

"Ready as I'm going to get," I smiled and wished like hell I'd brought a hat. I hate that his hair always looks better than mine.

We got out of the car and I gave it a fond last look before following him to the road. Loud sucking noises beneath my feet reminded me of the horrible things mud can do to a good pair of boots. Too bad I didn't change. The rain wasn't coming down too hard, but it was steady. Cold drops hit the top of my head and ran down beneath my hair, collecting around the collar of my coat. A chill danced up my spine.

"Let's make this quick, shall we?"

A clap of thunder pushed me into Byron's arm. Unfortunately it also landed me in a puddle and I shivered again as the water seeped into my boots and my teeth began to chatter. I tried to watch the ground a little more closely but it all looked wet. The only thing that identified a puddle was the splash of my feet once I'd stepped in it.

"All right," Byron pulled up short as we crossed the road and came to the edge of the trees around the house. "I'll take the back from this end, you take the front and I'll meet you on the far side," he said.

"Great," I said, not meaning it at all.

"Watch the road and watch your back," he warned before taking off across the yard.

I stood watching for a moment, a little surprised how quickly his dark form vanished from sight. Following his path the best I could, I sloshed my way across the yard, slowing some as I neared the house. The windows were low enough to peer in, but curtains or blinds covered all of them. The first window I came to was dark. I paused beneath it, listening, but there was no sound. Moving to the next window, also dark, I did the same thing with the same results. Oh for two. I skirted the front porch and hesitated before approaching the big picture window right beside it. This window was lighted and probably the most likely place to spy someone. It was also the most likely place to get caught. Easing up next to the edge of the window, I tried to hear what was going on inside. Muted sounds, probably coming from a television or radio, were all I heard. As hard as I tried to get a good angle, nothing was visible in the tiny cracks between the curtains and the window. Even if someone was standing just inside, the condensation would have made it impossible to see more than a vague shadow.

Another clap of thunder caused me to jump and I moved quickly away from the window and around the corner, stopping short when I saw another window right there. A flash of lightning startled me again, illuminating the lakeshore only a few yards away down a slope in the yard. By now the shivering and chattering were non-stop and I was drenched from head to toe. Some job. Where was Byron? I felt a twinge of fear remembering the last time I'd lost him in the dark. Keeping close to the house, I moved toward the rear and peeked around the corner.

Black as night, I could see nothing and had to stifle a scream as I stepped into the darkness and felt a hand clamp around my forearm.

"Shhhh, come here and listen," Byron whispered almost inaudibly in my ear and pulled me further into the dark.

As my eyes adjusted, the faint outline of a window slowly came into focus, the center barely lighter than the edges. Leaning close, I wondered what it was he wanted me to hear. All I heard was the rain.

"What…" I started but he shushed me with a finger on my lips. I leaned closer, resting my ear on the glass. There it was – the low murmur of voices. I tried to look up at him but couldn't make out his face in the dark. An instant later I got a chill of a different kind. There was a faint sound of a child crying followed immediately by the soothing tones that only come from a mother.

Byron nudged me back in the direction he'd come and I held his arm and followed him blindly back around the house. Skirting the trees, we sludged our way back to the road and headed for the car.

"They're in there!" I said as soon as I dared.

"We don't know it's them," he answered, leading me across the road to the car.

I stared at him in disbelief as he unlocked the doors. He couldn't be serious. I sank wearily into the seat, closing the door hard and enjoying the warmth for a moment before I turned to face him. "You know it's them."

"It probably is," he nodded, "but we've got to think." He started the car and cranked up the heater but didn't move to put it in gear or turn on the lights.

"Why don't we just go in and get them?" I asked. "Brant's not here."

"No, but he's probably on the way. Something doesn't feel right."

I thought about it for a moment but my brain was as numb as my hands. What possible reason could Brant have for keeping his wife and daughter here with Emily Marshall, assuming that's who she was? I began to see his point. There was too much we still didn't know.

"So what do we do?" I asked, peeling the wet gloves from my hands and wiggling my fingers in front of the heater vent.

"I wish I knew," he said, rubbing his face wearily with his hands.

"What's going on in there?"

"Your guess is as good as mine," he mused again. I was getting tired of hearing it. "We can't make a move until we know for sure who's in there."

CHAPTER TWENTY-FIVE

I let my head fall back against the headrest and wondered if I'd get warm faster by opening my coat. The cold went all the way to my bones and my bed was calling me from afar. "Okay," I lifted my head for fear I'd doze off, "I'll go. I'll go to the door and tell her my car broke down or something and I need to use the phone."

"No," he shook his head. "If it is Emily Marshall, she's probably seen a picture of you. Too risky."

"All right then, I'll go to the door and shoot whoever opens it." Desperate times and all that.

He didn't bother to answer that. "I'll go."

"And leave me out here alone? I don't think so. How about we both go?"

"And have Brant and his hired help come and find us in there?" He shook his head again.

"If you think I'm spending the night in this car in all these wet clothes you're crazier than I am."

"We know there's a child in there now. If we leave she might not be there when we come back."

That thought was sobering. "Then call Barker. We'll make a report of child endangerment or something."

"Out of his jurisdiction," he argued. "It's a different town, different county."

"Well what then?" I was running out of options. "We've got to do something!"

Byron rested his forehead against the steering wheel and sighed loudly so I let my head roll back against the seat and closed my eyes again. He was the pro, not I. No one could get in or out of there without coming past our car first, not unless they went by boat which was not likely in this weather.

It seemed a lot later than nine something, though, and I knew we were in no condition to wait out the night.

"Why don't you catch a nap while I try to figure this out?" Byron's voice penetrated the fog around my brain.

"Mmmhmmm."

But, drowsy as I was, sleep didn't come. Instead, a kaleidoscope of pictures played through my head. Geneva's pleasant, public face at Greaves' funeral with her adorable daughter by her side followed immediately by the look of stark fear when I asked about the child. An instant replay of her red-rimmed eyes, swollen from intense crying and near panic at her daughter's disappearance. The vacant look of lost hope when she met me, bruised and battered, at the park that day. My head popped up and I looked over at Byron.

"I'm going in," I told him, pulling my gloves back on.

"Jesse…"

"I mean it. I'm sure Geneva has her flaws like everyone else, but she doesn't deserve this, Byron. She came to me for help and I'm going in. I'll go get her and the girl and bring them back here and we'll take them somewhere safe." It was all I could think of. Whatever the possibilities or the dangers, I couldn't just sit there knowing they were inside and needed help. "We'll be in and out in no time."

"Jesse, wait a minute. We've got to think this through…"

"Byron," I turned to him with my hand on the door handle, "how hard can it be? Brant's not here, we didn't hear any other voices. I'm done with this. Are you going to help me or not?" I stepped out of the car, holding my breath against the surge of cold air, and stooped over so I could see his face. "Well?"

He didn't look happy but he didn't try to stop me either. When he didn't answer, I slammed the door and started across the road, pulling my Glock out of my pocket and taking the safety off before I wedged it firmly in my hand. He caught up with me halfway across the road.

"Jesse," he tugged at my sleeve.

"Byron!" I turned and snapped. "Why do you want to wait? You must have done this hundreds of times. I don't get it."

The look on his face scared me a little, but I was wet and cold and tired and just wanted it all to be over.

"Yeah I've done this. And a million things can go wrong. I didn't always wait for backup, but I usually had a partner who went in with me."

That was like a cold slap. "Well what am I?"

His jaw clenched and started to flex. "You're a civilian and an unpredictable one at that. You've also been a prime target since all this started. I'd rather not see you wind up dead!"

Electricity sparked in his eyes and shot through me like lightning. "You don't trust me."

He looked at me for an eternity. "Trust is something you earn. I never know what you're going to do next."

"That's a good one, coming from you! Watch close," I frowned. "You'll find out." I started on toward the house.

When I reached the porch, he stopped me again. "I'll be right here."

I looked over at him. Whatever our differences, that was comforting news. Slowly, I climbed the steps and held my gun at my side, knocking with my left hand. To my thinking, there was only one way to find out who or what was inside. I braced myself and knocked again when there was no answer.

"Who is it?" a muffled voice called through the door. No peephole, that was good. I looked over at Byron who was on the ground right beside the porch.

"Electric company," he whispered to me.

"Electric company," I called. "We're checking a problem from the storm. Could I talk to you for a minute?"

"There's no problem here," the voice called, a little louder.

"Ma'am, we need to check the lines," I replied. "It will only take a minute."

I heard shuffling, then silence. I reached to knock again but the door opened just enough for me to see the face peering out through the crack.

"Geneva!" I'm not sure what I expected, but that wasn't it. "I've been so worried about you!" All pretense was gone and my guard crashed to the ground with a thud. "Are you all right?"

Instead of a welcoming smile, her face was a mask of annoyance and consternation. "I'm fine. What are you doing here?"

That blew me away. "Are you going to let me in? It's freezing out here." Maybe everything was all right now, but she could at least give me some answers. She did hire me, after all. Turning slightly to the side, I slid my gun back in my pocket as discreetly as I could.

Geneva wavered a moment, then opened the door wider and motioned for me to come inside. I glanced at Byron who put a finger to his lips and waved me on. Guess I was on my own. The bright light assaulted my eyes and I blinked a few times, trying to adjust. The living room was casual but elegant and a fire roared in the stone fireplace opposite an overstuffed couch. Geneva's face still wore the fading yellow and purple streaks of a painful bruise around her left eye but the swelling was gone.

"My husband will be here soon, you can't stay," she said in clipped tones, leading me to the couch.

"What the hell is going on?"

She perched on the edge of an armchair beside the couch and I did the same on the nearest seat, looking at her steadily through narrowed eyes.

"I'm sorry I got you involved in this," she offered. "Everything is fine now. My daughter is asleep in the other room. I should have trusted my husband."

I let that sink in for a moment. "Can I see her?"

Annoyance flickered in Geneva's eyes again. "My husband will be furious if he finds you here."

A million questions paraded through my mind at such a rapid pace it was hard to even catch one. What happened to Emily? Where was she? Why did Brant insist his wife and daughter were with relatives when they were here? Why did Geneva hire me to find her daughter, then not call me to tell me she was all right?

"I want to see that she's okay," I insisted.

Reluctantly, she got to her feet. "Just a quick peek, then you've got to go." I followed her down a short hall and saw a shadow pass from the open doorway beyond the room where she stopped. Emily. I suddenly wished Byron had come inside with me and wondered why he chose not to.

"See?" She opened the door and motioned toward a sleeping form in the bed along the far wall. "She's just fine."

Sliding my hand in my pocket for reassurance, I took a few steps into the room so I could see the sleeping child's face. I had a deep sense of something terribly wrong but couldn't put my finger on what it was. She looked like an angel without a care in the world, soft, baby hair framing her sleeping face and one fist curled lightly around a teddy bear's floppy ear. I turned back to Geneva, glaring at me from the doorway.

"Why don't you get the girl and come with me?" I asked, joining her in the hall as she closed the door behind me.

"What?"

"You heard me," I looked at her steadily. "My car's right outside. We can be gone before he gets back."

"Why the hell would I do something like that? I told you everything's fine. I think it's time for you to go." Was that a flicker of fear in her eyes?

"Geneva, something is very wrong here. Lying to me won't help anything."

I saw her eyes dart quickly to the open door at the end of the hall and realized someone was listening. I moved back toward the living room, hopefully out of earshot.

As I expected, she followed me nervously but stayed near the hall where she could keep an eye on things. Maybe Emily and Brant were holding them hostage, threatening them both. What I didn't understand was why they were all still here. Not that I'd wish her dead, just that I suspected her husband did.

"Geneva," I spoke softly, "your husband has been lying through his teeth. Your parents are concerned about you and I know about Emily Marshall. I know she's here. Why won't you let me help you and end this whole thing?"

Once again, fear flickered in her eyes, but was immediately replaced by something else I wasn't quite sure about. Anger, maybe? Byron was right, things weren't always as they seemed. The trouble was – I didn't have a clue about what was really going on there. We stood for a moment, staring at one another with indecision in the upper hand on both our parts apparently.

"I suggest you go. Now. Before it's too late," she said finally through gritted teeth.

"Or what, Geneva? What will happen if I don't go?" I stood my ground. Even as I said it, I questioned myself. What was I doing here? Obviously Geneva wasn't dead and the child was sleeping soundly in another room. Wasn't that all I needed to know? Common sense told me to go back to Byron and sort out details later. I certainly had no legal right to be there and I went in with the intent of helping Geneva who no longer seemed to want or need my help.

"This will happen," a plump, heavily painted blonde stepped out of the hallway with a shotgun pointed squarely at my midsection. My heart jumped up into my throat, nearly gagging me and Geneva moved aside to let her get a better aim.

"Emily Marshall, I presume," I said, sounding a lot less nervous than I felt.

Emily's nostrils flared. "You're a real pain in the ass, you know that?"

Yep. It was the voice from the phone. Beverly Gafford reborn. I smiled. "The same could be said for you. Now what are you going to do? Shoot me?"

"Get some tape," Emily told Geneva who hurried to do as she was told. I wished there was a pause button to give me time to sort things out. Nothing was making any sense.

"Geneva, you don't want to do this," I warned as she approached with a roll of duct tape. Where the hell was Byron anyway?

"Don't think I won't shoot," Emily waved the gun at me. The look on her face was deadly. "Put your hands behind your back," she barked.

I considered the gun in my pocket, but she was too close. Not close enough to get her gun out of the way, but close enough to blast right through the Kevlar I was wearing. I put my hands behind my back and Geneva proceeded to tape my wrists tightly together, then, for good measure, added a strip across my mouth. Any time now, Byron.

When Geneva backed off, Emily stepped up and knocked me down on the couch. The last thing I remember was the butt of the shotgun connecting with the side of my head and a burst of stars that faded to black.

You know that strange, fuzzy place between asleep and awake? When dreams merge with reality but the lines are blurred and you finally wake up not knowing what was real? I knew I was dreaming because Joey was there, but I didn't want to wake up. I really, really missed him. No matter what happened, I was always safe if Joey was there. Safe. What was it about that word?

I was lying on the floor but nothing looked familiar and Joey was gone. Where was I? I blinked to be sure my eyes were open. They were but they burned. And there was a flickering light off to the side. When I tried to turn toward it, my head throbbed like I'd been hit with a brick. Oh shit! The gun. I held absolutely still and tried to focus. The blonde woman hit me with a gun and Geneva... Damn! Gritting my teeth together, I tried to roll over on my side but my hands were still fastened behind me. Checking further, I found my feet taped together too. This was not good.

A persistent crackling sound came into focus and seemed to be coming from the flickering light. Doing my best to ignore the throbbing in my head, I wiggled and scooted around until I saw something I recognized. Fire! Think, Jesse! No wonder my eyes burned. She taped me up and set me on fire! I kept scooting until I ran into the couch, then used it to try to prop myself up with my elbow. Indescribable pain started in my head and radiated to points I didn't even know I had. Willing myself to take it slow and steady and praying I wouldn't pass out again, I finally finagled my feet around and got into a sitting position where I could see. It didn't offer much comfort.

The entire south wall was flickering with flames slowly creeping toward the door. As much as I hated the thought, if Byron was able, he'd have been here by now. I couldn't see my hands so I had no idea how long I'd been out but I was grateful I woke when I did. I might have slept all the way to death. Damn! All I could think to do was try to get to my feet and hop over to a window that wasn't covered with flames. But already, I was starting to cough from the smoke. It would only get worse if I made it to a standing position. But I couldn't crawl very well with my hands behind me. Maybe on my back.

Sensing it was the only chance I had, I let myself slump to the side and tried to prop myself up on my hands and scoot along backwards on my butt. The process was incredibly slow and painful, but it was progress. The kitchen seemed darker than the other areas I could see so I headed that way. By the time I made the tile floor, I was gasping and choking from the smoke that filled the room. My head seemed to be moving in a downward spiral and I began to fear that I'd be too dizzy to stand even if I was able. Hoping like hell one of the windows Byron and I tried to see in last night was in the kitchen, I persisted until I came up against a cabinet. After a few free falls, I managed to get my feet under me and leaned heavily on the counter, looking around for anything that might help.

Spying a toaster on the counter that looked within reach, I wriggled over to it and managed to get it in my hands. Toasters are heavier than you think. I dropped it twice trying to make my way to the window. Squatting to pick it up wasn't too hard, but seeing where it was when it was behind my back in the dark was a challenge. By the time I'd inched my way down the counter and past the refrigerator to the window with the toaster in tow, I wasn't sure I'd have the strength or the ability to hurl it through the window. Mom would be glad to know that stubbornness isn't always an undesirable character trait.

Shoving as hard as I could, the toaster ricocheted off the windowsill and landed on the floor. Unfortunately, the window was still intact. Wouldn't you know Brant would go for the heavy duty storm panes? Wearily, I squatted again and retrieved the toaster. This time, I positioned it on the sill then closed my eyes tightly and rammed it with my shoulder. It worked! Well, kind of.

The glass broke, but there was a screen and it didn't even make a big enough hole to reach through and force the screen off. At my house, all you have to do is look hard and the screen will fly off. This one appeared to be nailed on. I hopped back to the refrigerator and ripped the towel that was hanging from the handle off in my hands. Wrapping my hands as tightly as I could, I hit the broken glass and tried to break through to the screen. Glass cuts through terrycloth without much effort. Maybe I was in shock or just in so much pain from my head that I couldn't feel much in my hands, but the first clue I had was the warm, sticky feeling inside the towel. I finally let it fall to the floor.

Suddenly, what I wanted more than anything was to go to sleep. Maybe I'd just lean beside the window and rest for a minute. The smoke burned so bad, the only relief came when my eyes were closed, and that relief was minimal. The persistent crackling sound in the other room was rapidly becoming a dull roar and it was getting lighter, even in the kitchen. It's hard to cough with your mouth covered with duct tape. My eyes were wet, but I couldn't tell if it was the smoke or the sweat or just the hopeless, sleepy feeling that was overruling my stubborn desire to get the hell out of there. I was trying to ignore the smeared blood on the windowsill and convince myself to give it one more try when I thought I heard someone call my name. It was a familiar voice. Joey? Oh God, maybe I was already dead and didn't know it. There it was again. Byron!

I tried to call but it's hard to do that with tape on your mouth too. Still, it gave me the incentive I needed to squat and retrieve the toaster one more time and bang the hell out of the window.

"Jesse!" Much clearer and closer this time.

I kept banging.

"Jesse, thank God!"

I turned and saw the most beautiful face in the world. Byron, dripping wet and beat to shit standing outside the window. In a matter of seconds, he did what I'd been trying to do for years. He ripped the screen right off the window and used a stick to knock out the rest of the glass. I didn't wait for him to tell me what to do. I sat my butt in the windowsill and launched myself out, not really caring if he caught me or not. He did.

At least I think he did. We both wound up on the grass.

"Jesse, my God! I thought you were done."

"Mmmph!"

"It'll hurt," he warned. He was right. I think he took part of my lip when he ripped the tape off.

"Bout damn time you got here," I grumbled, not resisting at all as he cradled me in his lap.

"Sorry," he muttered, stroking my hair. "I got detained."

Something in his voice made me look up, then I sat up and scooted off his lap. "Could you get this tape off my hands?"

"Sorry again," he halfway smiled and I turned so he could reach them. The sun was just starting to come up behind the trees around the lake. I must have been out awhile. The wind blew a gust of smoke our way and a huge crashing noise reminded me we might be a little too close to the house.

Once I got the tape loose from my feet, I tried to stand up, using Byron as a leaning post. He looked like hell warmed over. At least it wasn't raining anymore. "What happened to you, anyway?"

"Long story," he said as we limped toward the water.

"Shouldn't we head for the car?"

He shook his head. "Tires are all flat."

"Phone?"

"Smashed to hell."

Shit. I followed him to a dock I hadn't seen in the dark, figuring he planned to use the little motorboat that was tied up there. Instead, he sank to a heap on the dock and motioned for me to sit down. From that vantage point, I saw what looked like a body laid out on the front lawn. "Who's that?"

"Marcus Brant," he groaned.

"I guess he's dead."

"Yep."

Wearily, I lay back on the planks looking up at the sky. My head still pounded like a sledgehammer on an anvil and my vision was in a constant state of blur. "Are you going to tell me what the hell happened here or are we playing twenty questions?"

"I don't even know where to start," he sighed. "Except I should never have let you go in there."

I would have chuckled if I could have. As if he could have stopped me. "Hindsight. What happened to you? I know what happened inside, not that any of it makes sense to me at all."

"I waited outside under the window. It sounded like everything was all right, although I was very curious about what Geneva Brant was doing answering the door. You didn't seem to be in any trouble and I heard a car down the road so I doubled back to get a look. There was no sign of a car, but when I got there, mine had tires slashed and the front window broken. The phone was smashed too. I hotfooted it back to the house, knowing that someone else was stalking the place and they still got the drop on me. Whoever they were. When I came to, I headed for the house, found Brant in the yard and the place on fire."

"Then you really don't know, do you?"

He shook his head. "What happened inside?"

"Geneva wasn't glad to see me. I made her take me to see the girl and tried to get her to leave with me, then Emily Marshall came out of the back room with a shotgun and had her tie me up. The last thing I remember was Marshall cold-cocking me in the side of the head with the gun. What the hell was that about?"

"You think the two women were in it together?"

"I don't know what to think. At first, I thought maybe Marshall was holding Geneva and the girl hostage somehow, but in the end I just don't know." Suddenly, I sat up straight and looked in horror at the house, now engulfed in flames. "You don't think anyone was still in there, do you?"

Byron shook his head. "I started at the other end, breaking out windows and checking the rooms. I didn't see anyone."

I heaved a sigh of relief that ended with a cough and leaned back on my hands. The sound of a faraway siren was like music.

"Guess someone finally reported the smoke," he said.

"It's not supposed to end like this," I closed my eyes and laid back down.

"What makes you think it's over?"

When I peeked at him, he was smiling.

"What the hell am I going to do with you two?" Barker was probably only half kidding, sitting across from me and Byron at the Outback Steakhouse. "Everywhere you go, something terrible happens!"

"Geez, Barker, you're so touchy," I teased.

"You might have called me sooner," he rebuked me.

"I might have but Byron wouldn't let me," I joked.

"My bad," Byron raised his hands in mock surrender. "Weirdest damn case I've ever seen."

"Man, you got that right," Barker shook his head.

I just smiled. It was really the only damn case I'd ever seen. Up close, anyway.

"How you gonna top this one?" Barker asked.

"Shit, all I have to do is let Jesse answer the phone," Byron said.

"Smugass."

"Well, you got the job done," Barker said, "that's what counts when the dust settles. Here's to you!" he raised his beer mug and we toasted what had to be one of the most bizarre partnerships formed in a while. "Next time – call me sooner," Barker laughed as he got up to go.

"Later Barker," I smiled at him. He was a good friend.

"You beat everything, you know that?" Byron looked at me with a twinkle in his eye.

I shrugged. "I don't know how else to be. Besides, I didn't catch anyone."

"No, but you're the one who remembered about the cabin and figured out about Marshall."

"Yeah," I laughed, "but I thought she was Brant's mistress and the two of them were in it together!"

He shrugged back at me. "But you're the one who decided to go in after them."

"Oh, yeah, good for me! I went in because I thought the lady was in trouble. Instead, she was the one behind the whole damn thing!" I could still remember the feeling in the pit of my stomach when Barker told us that they'd picked up Geneva and Melinda at the Mexican border. Marshall's body was recovered from the back of the Expedition when Geneva got stopped.

"She was a good actress, I'll give her that," he agreed. "But the main thing is, the girl is safe with her grandparents and Geneva is locked up tight."

"I still don't get it," I shook my head. "Of all people, Geneva didn't need the money. What was she thinking?"

Byron offered a familiar shrug. "Who knows? Maybe she's just crazy. They said something snapped when she lost that first baby, but maybe she was already in a precarious state when that happened. Or maybe she just got tired of Brant hitting her. If she found out about Emily, she could have taken him to the cleaners."

"That's my point," I said. "She had grounds for divorce and the money to get a PI to follow him around until he got caught in the act. She'd walk away with a huge chunk of his money and custody of the little girl. Why go to so much trouble?"

"Remember, this whole case seems complicated to us, but we were getting it from three sides. We had Gafford trying to get his daughter back and collect his insurance money. He's the one that sent Greaves to help track her down. Then we had Emily trying to do the same to get at Gafford. Weasel worked for her, by the way, not Gafford. When he spotted Greaves, he took him out. Meanwhile, Emily was playing footsies with Brant so she could get to the kid, and we had Geneva trying to get back at her husband. Barker said when they picked her up she kept babbling about how one baby can't replace another and how Brant was going to pay for that. Bottom line, sooner or later, they all saw you as a threat. None of them did it all, but when you put it all together, it made one hell of a party for us, didn't it?"

I snorted. "Some party. But how did Emily and Geneva get together? I don't get that."

"I don't know. My guess is that Geneva figured out that Emily wanted more than quality time with Brant and bought her off. Course, then she killed her."

I shivered. Scary thought. "I can't believe Geneva sucked me in like that," I told him. "She had me totally convinced. Some detective I am."

Byron chuckled. "Don't lose sleep over it. She really does have mental problems. The really bad ones are always convincing because they convince themselves they're telling the truth before they ever try to convince anyone else. She's nuts."

I shivered again. "Yikes! It still creeps me out. But in the end, we wanted to find the little girl and we found her. Guess our case is closed, huh?" I smiled at him.

"Yes, ma'am," he smiled back. "But there is another case I've been meaning to talk to you about."

I frowned at him. "Must you?"

"The case of the fickle partner," he said.

I frowned more. "You really want to go there tonight?"

"I do," he watched me intently. I silently cursed Barker for leaving.

"Tell me why things seemed so good between us and then you turned on me," he insisted, reaching over to rub a finger lightly along my shoulder.

I have what some might consider a fatal flaw. When I'm cornered, I'm a terrible liar. Probably not the best characteristic for a private investigator, but there you go.

"I saw you kissing a slinky brunette downtown in broad daylight."

He looked stunned. You know, the deer in the headlight kind of look. I wasn't surprised, at least not until he laughed out loud.

"You're shittin' me! That's what that was all about?" You'd think he'd just heard the funniest joke in the world.

I didn't think it was so funny. I glared at him.

"Jesse," he leaned forward like he was telling me a secret. "That woman was my sister. I had her stop by downtown so she could meet you but you never showed up. That's why I told you 12:30, she had to be in court at 1:00."

I'm sure there was a good answer to that, but at the time it escaped me. "She was staying with you?" I remembered the voice on the phone later that night.

He nodded. "She's an attorney in San Antonio and she had to testify in a case up here."

I nodded back at him. Figured. Did I have egg on my face or what? It was time to apologize and eat some crow but I had trouble saying the words. I just kept nodding, waiting for inspiration to strike. Ever notice how it never does when you need it?

"I guess I should have told you instead of trying to surprise you, huh?" he offered when I just kept nodding without talking.

God, did he have to be so nice about it? I'd heard that love means you never have to say you're sorry. I figured love means you better say it twice. But then, who said anything about love? This was my partner. My friend. My future? Who knows?

"Byron, I'm sorry." There. I said it.

A slow smile tugged at the corners of his mouth. Damn, the man was hot.

"I mean it, I'm sorry," I said again. Anything to make him stop staring and smiling. It didn't work. "Byron!" I got up, rolling my eyes. "Can we go now?"

"Case closed," he kept smiling, tugging my hair on the way to the car. What have I gotten myself into this time?

ABOUT THE AUTHOR

As with most things, PJ Nunn's career started out as something else entirely. She started out in retail then moved to property management. That led to teaching high school, then serving as a counselor and liaison to the local police youth services division. She also spent five years as chairperson of the Coryell County Child Welfare Board and spent years counseling abuse victims and serving law enforcement as a trauma counselor and consultant (something she still does today). When she moved to Dallas, a family illness caused her to leave a job teaching psychology at Dallas County Community College District to become a freelance writer, but found that a few favors she was doing for friends—writing press releases and setting up book signings—was better suited to her talents and her drives.

In 1998, she founded BreakThrough Promotions, now a national public relations firm helping authors, mostly of mystery novels, publicize themselves and their work. The business is thriving and PJ is excited about the release of her first novel, *Angel Killer*. PJ lives with her husband some of their five children near Dallas, TX. You can find out more about her books and upcoming releases at www.pjnunn.com.